BLACK WIDOW

A SPELLBOUND REGENCY BOOK TWO

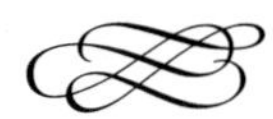

LUCY LEROUX

http://www.authorlucyleroux.com
ISBN: 978-1-942336-18-1

First Edition.

Created with Vellum

TITLES BY LUCY LEROUX

Making Her His, A Singular Obsession, Book One
Available Now
Confiscating Charlie, A Free Singular Obsession Novelette
Book 1.5
Available Now
Calen's Captive, A Singular Obsession, Book Two
Available Now
Stolen Angel, A Singular Obsession, Book Three
Available Now
The Roman's Woman, A Singular Obsession,
Book Four
Available Now
Save Me, A Singular Obsession Novella, Book 4.5
Coming Soon
Take Me, A Singular Obsession Prequel Novella
Available Now
Trick's Trap, A Singular Obsession,
Book Five
Available Now

Peyton's Price, A Singular Obsession,
Book Six
Available Now

The Hex, A Free Spellbound Regency Short
Available Now
Cursed, A Spellbound Regency Novel
Available Now
Black Widow, A Spellbound Regency Novel, Book Two
Available Now
Haunted, A Spellbound Regency Novel, Book Three
Coming Soon

Codename Romeo, Rogues and Rescuers, Book One
Available Now
The Mercenary Next Door, Rogues and Rescuers, Book Two
Coming Soon

Writing As L.B. Gilbert

Discordia, A Free Elementals Story,
Available Now
Fire: The Elementals Book One
Available Now
Air: The Elementals Book Two
Available Now
Water: The Elementals Book Three
Available Now
Earth: The Elementals Book Four
Available Now

Kin Selection, Shifter's Claim, Book One
Available now
Eat You Up, A Shifter's Claim, Book Two
Available now

Tooth and Nail, A Shifter's Claim, Book Three
Coming Soon

Forsaken, Cursed Angel Collection
Available now

DISCLAIMER

CREDITS

Cover Design:
Robin Harper
http://www.wickedbydesigncovers.com

Editor:
Cynthia Shepp
http://www.cynthiashepp.com/

Thank you to all of my readers especially to Jennifer Bergans for her editorial comments. And thanks to my husband for all of his support even though he won't read my sex scenes!

PROLOGUE

The blood spread out like a ruby halo. It was a startling contrast to the white marble floor. It darkened the pink of her skirts, the white lace fringe soaked in a red so dark it was almost black.

We should never have come home.

"This is all my fault," Amelia whispered. "What have I done?" She pulled her husband's broken body closer until he was cradled in her arms.

She hadn't moved from that spot at the foot of the stairs since returning from her round of afternoon calls. That was when she had found him—a nightmare in full daylight.

It was night now. Dusk had come and gone without her awareness. That was as it should be. Her world would be dark now. Her memory of other locations was faulty. Only this spot was solid earth, this and the grand staircase in front of her—the one she had so admired when they first let this house to be near Viscount Worthing.

How many stairs were there? She hadn't counted them before. How could she not know how many stairs were in her home? And did everybody have this much blood? It covered the stones all around her in an endless pool. She was an island in a sea of blood.

She and Martin should have stayed on the continent, in Italy where they had both been happy. She should have never let him convince her to come home. England was a cursed land, its society full of hypocrites and liars. It had taken her family and her home. And now it had taken Martin, her only solace in a life bereft of love and affection.

She had nothing now.

All around her, chaos reigned, but she barely took note of it. Servants ran to and fro, shouting, some weeping openly. Or was that her? She couldn't tell. Her face was wet and her throat ached, so perhaps she was also crying. The only sensation in her numb body was in her hands, the ones clutching Martin's shirt.

Amelia ignored the footman trying to make her let go of his body. Shrugging him off, she tightened her grip on her husband's thin shoulders.

If she let go, they would take him away and he'd be gone forever.

So, she held on. She was still cradling Martin to her when the great shadow passed over them. Blinking, she looked up into the darkness over the stairs and saw the glowing yellow eyes staring back at her. The next second, they were gone. The darkness was empty.

CHAPTER 1

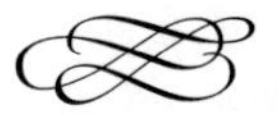

A YEAR LATER

"She's here."

Gideon Wells, Earl of Flint, schooled his expression until it had been wiped clean of all emotion. His stomach roiled, but there was no trace of the anger or disdain he felt knowing Amelia Montgomery had re-entered society, her year of mourning at an end.

It was an event he'd been waiting months for, ever since he had been recalled from the continent.

Gideon craned his neck, searching for Amelia's dark curls, but the ballroom was crowded and he hadn't seen her in years. He wasn't sure what she looked like now. The last time he'd seen her she had been little more than a child.

"Lord Worthing is with her," Clarke whispered.

In a flash, Gideon's composure was gone. He fisted his large hands and inhaled sharply.

"Steady, man," Clarke said, raising a fine red eyebrow before casually looking away with a placid expression.

"I'm fine," Gideon lied, nearly choking on the words.

He was as good as he was going to get knowing the woman who'd murdered his cousin was in this ballroom on the arm of her lover—the bastard who no doubt had helped her kill Martin.

His heart ached at the injustice. His cousin had only been three and twenty when he died. Gideon remembered Martin as a slight and sweetly spoken young man.

Though he had visited the Montgomery estate in Northumberland as a youth, their difference in age had kept them at arm's length until Martin had gotten older. They had grown close when his younger cousin had attended the Abingdon School, near Gideon's family home in Oxfordshire. Martin had often come for weekend visits. When he had, he'd spoken warmly of Amelia, his father's ward. Gideon had liked her on principal. He'd been pleased Martin had a friend at home. Sir Clarence, his uncle, was a dour and cold man, overly concerned with his position in society, the kind who looked down on those beneath him.

Once upon a time that had included Gideon himself. Sir Clarence hadn't approved of the match his younger sister Anne had made. But things were different now. A series of accidental and premature deaths on his father's side of the family had resulted in Gideon inheriting an earldom along with several prize estates. Sir Clarence had been forced to eat his words about his father. In fact, the last time Gideon had seen him, Sir Clarence had even hinted he would like to visit Tarryhall, the Earl of Flint's family seat in Derbyshire.

Martin had never seen his new estate. He had married Amelia when Gideon was still abroad in France. By the time Gideon returned, his cousin had already departed for the continent with his bride—something Sir Clarence still spoke of with bitterness.

Gideon thought the couple's return would settle some of his uncle's ruffled feathers, but the old man was still bitter. Clarence complained they had settled too far from home, choosing to divide their time between London and Kent.

He knew why now of course. Viscount Worthing's principal estate was in Kent. Somehow, Amelia had manipulated Martin into settling a stone's throw from her lover's home. And no doubt his amiable cousin had seen nothing wrong with indulging her.

Now he was dead.

His friend shifted his weight, lifting a glass to hide his lips. "She's there in that cluster straight ahead, in the cerulean gown. Worthing is the tall blond man on her right."

Gideon narrowed his eyes, turning to behold his quarry.

The sight of her hit him like a physical blow. He shouldn't have been surprised—a peacock like Worthing wouldn't be involved with a homely woman. Nevertheless, he hadn't expected this singularly beautiful creature.

Though passably pretty as a child, Amelia had grown into a diamond of the first water, one who easily eclipsed every other woman in the room. Amelia's complexion was pure, with rose-tinted cheeks. Her lips were a darker shade of pink, lush and full. A dark crown of jet curls gleamed in the candlelight. He was too far to see the color of her eyes, but her lashes were a thick fringe against her ivory and rose skin.

Though her birth was low, Amelia Montgomery was captivating, a true siren whose looks and grace could lead a man to his doom. That fact, combined with her immense fortune, and he no longer wondered at the interest society had taken in the young widow.

"Are you sure you want to do this?" Clarke muttered in an aside. "I know you feel you need a purpose now that your title prevents you from helping the war office, but is this how you want to spend your time? Chasing after a notorious widow? She's been barred from the best houses. It's only Lady Anderson's interest in salacious gossip that won them entry here tonight."

Gideon scowled at his friend. Clarke was exaggerating, and he knew it. A few houses might be snubbing Worthing and his "friend," but society loved a scandal. Having the season's most disreputable couple attend one's ball or soirée would be a feather in the cap of most of the ton's hostesses.

"I won't let this go. Martin was an innocent, too trusting. He deserved better than this."

Clarke frowned. "Sending a young woman to the gallows is not the same thing as disarming an enemy agent or intercepting a spy's intelligence. I know you are restless now, but I don't believe this will satisfy your craving to serve your country."

Gideon took exception at the implication that he was trading one mission for another. "This has nothing to do with being recalled home," he muttered, his eyes following Amelia's movement across the room. "My new lands and tenants are my chief concern, which is why I spent the last few months buried with estate agents and stewards, untangling the messes my predecessors have made. But I also have a duty to my family—what's left of it. I will have justice for my cousin."

Clarke sighed. "I just don't think this is what Phineus had in mind when he asked you to come home."

Gideon snorted. "Phineus didn't *ask*. It was an order—one I couldn't disregard."

He'd tried to reason with his superior at the war office, but Phineus had been adamant. The Earl of Flint's holdings were in chaos. Contradictory efforts at improving the lands, combined with the sheer number of times the title had changed hands in so few years, had rendered the old but valuable estates unproductive. Despite how much Phineus valued Gideon's efforts on behalf of the crown, he had recalled him home to care for his unexpected inheritance. His reasoning had been that a strong economy at home was just as important as one spy's efforts abroad, even when the country was on the brink of war.

Deep down, Gideon knew the decision had been the right one, but...Clarke may have been right about the reality of coming home. Gideon now had wealth and position, but also responsibilities he had never expected. Though his work for the war office had played a small but pivotal role in ensuring the safety of the nation, being a landholder meant people depended on him far more directly. His obligation had been transformed from a strong but formless concept of duty to king and country to a tangible demand in the form of his tenants. His burden now had a face, or rather, many faces.

In some ways, it was true he was chafing under the restraints of his new position, but proving Martin was murdered wasn't a distraction. He'd worked himself ragged the last few months to get his properties and other holdings back on sound financial footing. Though he hadn't had time to implement all the agricultural improvements he wanted, he'd at least ensured his tenants wouldn't starve this winter.

Now that Amelia was out in society, he had a much better chance of getting close to her than when she was cloistered in the requisite year of mourning society demanded of widows.

And I'm not the only one who wants to get closer.

A fop named Binton was bending over Amelia's hand, presumably asking for a dance. With a charming tilt of her head, she agreed, pairing with him for a Scottish reel while Lord Worthing observed with approving, but watchful, eyes.

Viscount Worthing's view of the dance floor must have been obscured momentarily by some other guests. Without appearing too obvious, he stepped a few paces to one side, drawing the woman he was speaking to with him. From his new vantage point, he could see Binton and his partner once more, never breaking off his conversation.

"He rarely allows her out of his sight," Clarke observed.

"So it would seem," Gideon muttered in agreement.

"It may be difficult to speak to her alone under these circumstances."

Gideon narrowed his eyes at the dancing couple, dismissing Worthing entirely. "Her lover won't be a problem."

"And just how do you plan on speaking to her alone?"

"The same way I got the French officer's wife to follow me into the garden that night in Rouen," he said, signaling for a waiter to bring him some wine.

Clarke smiled sardonically and appeared ready to say something else, but Gideon forestalled him with a heavy glance. He recognized the last strains of the reel. Moving into position, he got ready to intercept Amelia at the end of the dance before Worthing could reclaim her.

His plan was to sweep her into the next dance without missing a beat. It was a maneuver that had worked very well with the French officer's wife, but, in this case, the musicians didn't oblige him by launching into the next song.

The music ceased just as Amelia saw him. Her lips parted in surprise as she recognized him. Gideon smiled and inclined his head in her direction. Her answering smile was hesitant. She stepped toward him, pausing as Worthing hurried toward her.

But Gideon reached her first. With a warm welcoming expression, he took her hand and bowed.

"Hello, cousin," he said in a soft tone, turning her slightly so their backs were to Worthing.

"Gideon," she breathed.

Her eyes, a deep blue, caught the candlelight and seemed to shine brighter as she looked up at him. If he didn't know any better, he would have guessed she was pleased to see him. Something told him that wasn't going to last.

CHAPTER 2

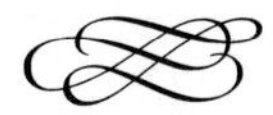

Amelia's heart was racing as she stared into Gideon's dark eyes. Pulse pounding in her ears, she bit her lip before taking the arm he offered.

He was bigger than she remembered. It was strange because he was a giant as a child, an unusually tall youth who dwarfed even her guardian, Sir Clarence. But now, Gideon had the body of a man. He'd filled out, adding layers of muscles to his once-lanky frame. Combined with his height, it made him an imposing figure, even in a ballroom full of blue-blooded nobility.

His hair was also darker than she remembered. The vivid streaks of gold he had from spending so much time in the sun were gone now. His boyish handsomeness had matured into something harder and darker.

He almost looked dangerous, but, if anything, his appeal was only heightened.

Every woman in the room is staring at him—including myself. Her face heated and she started to pull away, but Gideon forestalled her. He pressed his hand over hers, making sure she didn't let go of his arm. The muscle underneath the fine cloth of his fitted waistcoat was like steel, and she wondered what sport he indulged in to become so fit.

The hair on the back of her neck lifted. Amelia didn't know if it was because of the number of eyes trained their way, or because she was with Gideon again, the small touch of her hand on his arm a burning brand.

Seemingly aware that most of the guests were watching, he led Amelia to the relative privacy of the balcony on the far side of the ballroom. Once on the other side of the doors, she let out a pent-up breath, one she hadn't even been aware she'd been holding. She laughed self-consciously, about to thank him for rescuing her, when she checked herself.

How much did he know? Did he blame her for Martin's death as well? If he did, why was he being so solicitous?

"I heard you were back in town," Gideon said, not acknowledging her obvious relief at being away from the crowded ballroom. "I'm sorry I didn't come to see you before. I was still traveling on the grand tour when Martin…"

He coughed, his face tightening. For a moment, she imagined some of the weight of her grief had been transferred to him, pressing them both down into the earth.

Amelia ducked her head, her throat tight. "I know. He—he used to read me your letters."

The words were hoarse, revealing the effort she'd made to get them out. She cleared her throat. "It sounded exciting…so much that he decided he wanted to travel himself. Nothing as extensive as your explorations, of course, but we ended up spending most of our marriage abroad. I half expected to stumble upon you one day."

Gideon cocked his head to the side. "I did as well, but I was always on the move, trying to make the most of the opportunity before my cousin Matteo changed his mind and decided to stop funding me."

He smiled, but his face was still too hard for it to be a happy expression.

"Oh, I see," she said. Martin hadn't mentioned that detail to her. "I like your cousin Matteo very much. We spent some time with him and Isobel our last few months abroad—right after their twin sons were born."

Gideon leaned against the terrace balustrade and crossed his arms. “She was your governess, I believe?”

She nodded, warming to the subject. “Only for a short while. Then Matteo visited. Before you could blink, they were married. But she wrote every month.”

Those letters had been one of the few bright spots in her bleak childhood. She had treasured every one of them. Isobel was one of her few confidantes, but there were some things Amelia hadn’t told her…not yet.

Perhaps I need to change that.

“Amelia?”

She jerked her gaze up to find Gideon watching her expectantly.

“Woolgathering?”

Her shoulders dropped, but she was suddenly too tired to be embarrassed. It wasn’t like she was in the company of some stranger. There was no need to fabricate a delicate excuse. “I’m sorry. I haven’t been sleeping much of late. I have trouble focusing on even simple tasks, conversations included. Please excuse my distraction.”

His face softened. “There’s no need to apologize. Not on your part anyway. I am the one who needs to make amends. I should have come to see you after I returned from the continent.”

“I was traveling myself then,” she said, gripping her hands tightly together. After Martin’s death, she couldn’t stay in that house. “I decided the Lake District was more to my liking.”

Amelia glanced at the ornate glass doors of the terrace. In her imagination, the well-dressed horde was staring at her with their faces pressed against the glass. The reality was not far off. She turned back to Gideon. “I don’t expect I’ll stay in town very long.”

“That’s disappointing…I had hoped we could renew our acquaintance. I’d like to hear about Martin and your travels.” He uncrossed his arms and put one of them on the railing behind him to brace himself. “I let too much time pass since seeing him last. Tell me, was he happy those last few months?”

“He was the happiest I’d ever seen him,” she said, not thinking, and then wanted to bite her tongue. She hoped he wouldn't ask her for more details.

"*Really*? Was there something in particular, some change that was responsible for such a state?"

Her lips parted. *Oh, dear.*

Amelia belatedly realized the conversation had ventured into troubling territory. She had been too unguarded with him. But Gideon interpreted her hesitation as embarrassment.

"I'm sorry if I overstepped. I didn't mean to imply the marital state alone was not sufficient to achieve bliss. I'm sure he was very happy married to you."

"He was," she assured him with a blush. "But you're right; there was more. The return home to England for one. I don't think he realized how much he had missed home until we returned."

"But you didn't return to Northumberland. You settled in Kent."

"Err, yes," she said, looking out the corner of her eye for Crispin.

He warned you about situations like this.

"I did not think you had any connections there," Gideon continued, his relentless questioning as inexorable as the Flood.

"No family connections to speak of. Only friends. Martin was my only family," she said, a shaft of lonely longing spearing her.

"And Uncle Clarence," he pointed out.

"Yes, of course. There's Sir Clarence," she replied weakly.

"Have you spoken to him recently? I heard he's also in town this season, but I've not had the occasion to visit with him yet."

"Well…"

As if on cue, Crispin, Lord Worthing, stepped outside at that moment, displaying his impeccable sense of timing. Her relief was short-lived, however, dwindling to nothing when she saw who was on his arm.

"Amelia, darling, where have you been hiding?" The graceful woman at Crispin's side was dressed in a fashionable cerise gown paired with a modest string of pearls. Amelia recognized the dress as the work of her own modiste, an exclusive dressmaker whom Crispin had recommended.

"Mrs. Spencer," she said, feigning enthusiasm to see her former guardian's mistress. "How nice to see you again. I wasn't aware you were here tonight or I would have come to pay my respects."

Ellie Spencer laughed, a light tinkling sound. "No need to be so formal, my dear," she said with a charmingly dismissive wave. "I saw the viscount here and imposed upon him to find you. I wanted to make sure you were attending my little garden party next week. You will attend, won't you?"

The look in Mrs. Spencer's eyes and the surreptitious glance she gave Gideon told Amelia all she needed to know. She had been neatly trapped. Somehow, Ellie Spencer guessed Amelia did not want to appear ill-mannered in front of Gideon.

"Of course I will attend."

"But, my dear, you've already agreed to attend the Marston's country party next week," Crispin interjected smoothly. "I don't believe I've had the pleasure," he said, extending a hand to Gideon. "I'm Worthing."

Gideon hesitated so long Amelia was afraid he was about to deliver the cut direct, but he eventually accepted the hand and shook it. She suspected his grip was painful because Crispin winced, but her erstwhile protector managed to smile and murmur something polite about being members of the same club.

"Congratulations on the title, by the way," Crispin added after a moment. "I have some property near one of your new estates in Cornwall. We are neighbors in fact."

"Is that so? Is yours the old Cavendish estate or do you own the bit of land to the east?"

"It's the latter. I'm eyeing just the right spot for a snug cottage or country house. It's a pretty little piece."

"That it is," Gideon agreed, turning back to her. He raised an eyebrow when he saw she had a hand to her mouth.

Amelia was mortified. "Oh dear, I forgot you're an earl now!" He must think her a perfect ninny. "At the very least, I should have congratulated you as well."

"Think nothing of it." In a swift economical move, he leaned over.

"I remember your father's views on the nobility—don't worry. I haven't let it go to my head."

She blushed and ducked her head, hoping that was true. Hazy memories of certain conversations trickled back to her. Her father had choice words about the peerage. Words she had repeated, uncensored, to Gideon as a girl.

At the time, he had been highly entertained by her knowledge of certain colorful, vulgar expressions. *And now he's an earl.*

"Oh, what a shame you can't attend," Mrs. Spencer interjected during the awkward pause, accepting defeat with her trademark good grace. "But perhaps I can impose on the earl to come instead. I know Sir Clarence would love to see him."

Gideon turned to Mrs. Spencer as if he'd forgotten she was there. He belatedly introduced himself, bowing over her hand. "Pardon me, how do you know my uncle?"

The older woman smiled, waving a graceful hand over her bosom. "Oh, Sir Clarence and I are good friends. I often act as hostess for him on those rare occasions when he chooses to entertain."

Understanding lit Gideon's eyes. "Oh, you're *that* Mrs. Spencer." He nodded. "A pleasure. If I'm in town, I will be sure to attend, although I plan on catching up with Sir Clarence at the club this week."

"He'll be delighted to hear it," Mrs. Spencer said before nudging Crispin. "Darling, I'm parched."

"One champagne on the way." He stepped away to flag down a waiter, asking for two flutes. Then he returned with a regretful expression. "I'm afraid we can't stay to partake ourselves. Amelia and I are expected at the Turner soiree."

With barely time for a civil parting, Crispin ushered her away.

"That was hardly subtle," Amelia chided once they were safely ensconced in the dark interior of the viscount's carriage.

"Neither was using your uncle's mistress as a distraction, but you had spent long enough in the earl's company."

"Crispin, he's a friend. He's also Martin's cousin."

"And he's also a dangerous man from what I've heard," Crispin said, inclining his head with a dark expression. "You must take care what you say to him."

"Don't you think you're exaggerating? I've known Gideon since I was a child." She paused to smooth her skirts. "I admit I was anxious when I first saw him. I didn't know if he believed the rumors about me."

"You mean the rumors about *us* and whether we were involved in Martin's death," Crispin said with his trademark bluntness.

She shook her head. "If Gideon thought I killed my husband, he would have confronted me or publicly cut me. He's always been direct. Even as a youth. I don't think he would have spoken to me at all if he blamed me."

Crispin threw her a pitying glance. "Amelia, you must listen to me. That is not the young man you knew. Gideon Wells has changed—and I'm not talking about his new title. There are some disturbing rumors about him and what he was really doing on the continent a few months ago. If what I've heard is correct, then there is no chance he's overlooking the gossip."

She frowned at her companion. "What sort of things did he do?"

He sniffed. "Well, as to that I'm not precisely certain. A well-informed friend with connections to the war office mentioned something but wouldn't elaborate. Suffice to say it was a warning of sorts. Don't tangle with the earl. He is to be avoided at all costs."

She clasped her hands together, the omnipresent weight on her shoulders growing heavier. "That's going to be difficult. He's a family connection. And he wants to hear more about Martin, about our time together."

Crispin straightened in his seat. "Even more reason to avoid him."

Amelia sighed. "Fine. I will do as you ask, but it will be difficult unless..."

"Unless what?"

"I've been thinking I should leave town. Go back abroad."

Crispin passed a hand over his face. "I was afraid you were going to say that. But it's not safe to leave England at the moment. The rumors say we are on the brink of war with France. Travel is growing more hazardous. Soon, it won't be possible at all."

"Which is why I should leave now."

He argued, naturally, and she countered his assertions, but her effort was half-hearted at best. In truth, she suddenly had a reason to stay.

Leaving would mean not seeing Gideon again.

And despite her promise to Crispin, she wouldn't—couldn't—stay away from Gideon. That had always been beyond her abilities.

Hours later, finally done with the night's round of parties, Crispin delivered her home. She had told her butler not to wait up, so she let herself in with her key.

Amelia had just closed the door behind her, preparing to go upstairs to her bedroom, when she saw it.

Lying in the middle of a pool of moonlight was a small object. Bending, she took a closer look. It was a dead rose. Puzzled, she bent to pick it up, and it crumbled in her hand. Even the stem fell to pieces.

She spent a few minutes picking up the fragments. Had one of the maids dropped it when cleaning? She didn't remember having any fresh-cut roses placed in any of the rooms. Perhaps one of the staff had cut it in the garden and forgotten about it.

"Damn." A particularly sharp thorn had pierced her finger. A drop of blood fell to the floor.

A rushing sound filled her ears. She straightened abruptly, her ears filled with whispers. Turning in circles, she searched the shadows for their source. It was as if she was surrounded by an unseen crowd of people, but there was no one there.

She tried to calm herself, but her skin broke out into a cold sweat. Covering her ears, she turned on her heel and ran up the stairs, dropping the fragments of the rose in the process. Once she'd reached the second floor, the noise stopped as suddenly as it had started.

Wiping her hands on her skirt, Amelia hurried to her bedroom, locking the door behind her.

CHAPTER 3

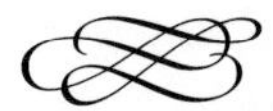

Gideon impatiently pushed away his plate and sank deeper into the fine leather chair.

"Will that be all, Lord Flint?" Ames, the Standard club's steward bent over him solicitously.

"Yes, Ames. Just show Mr. Clarke to my table when he comes in."

"Of course, my lord."

"Thank you," he murmured, picking up his paper again, turning back to an article about flooding down south as Ames took away his plate.

Gideon tried to focus on the news sheet, but in his mind, a pair of bright blue eyes burned brightly. Eventually, he threw the sheet aside. Passing a hand over his face, he sighed and examined the minute changes in the familiar surroundings.

Despite the number of years that had passed, little had altered at the old Standard. Just a few new touches here and there. A new leather chair in the corner, a vase on the table next to it. Though other clubs had invited him to join their rolls—some of which he had—loyalty compelled him to spend most of his time here, despite his membership in other more fashionable and exclusive establishments.

The Standard had granted him membership when he was a mere

mister. Old Ames had even given him extensions when he hadn't been able to pay his dues on time. As a young man, Gideon had privately teased Ames about his preference for him having more to do with his dislike of his uncle, who was also a member. Old Ames steadfastly denied it, insisting he felt the same way about all their patrons.

Many members of the Standard were either very young men or part of the old guard. During his time with the war office, he had found both types useful. The younger military types were happy to talk as long as the liquor flowed freely. Something similar could be said for the older set, although in that case, the vintages he'd been required to buy to encourage loose tongues had been substantially more expensive.

That reminds me. He ordered a fine bottle of port and displayed it prominently on his table. When his quarry appeared, it would be useful. A few minutes later, his uncle walked into the room.

"Sir Clarence," he hailed.

Across the room, his uncle looked up. His face stiffened before breaking into something resembling a grin.

Close, but not quite right.

"Gideon, my boy, hello." He sat down across from him, making sure the others in the room noted his easy familiarity with the wealthy earl. "How are you doing?"

"I'm well, Uncle, and very glad to see you," he said, pouring himself a few fingers of port. "Would you like some?"

"Don't mind if I do," his uncle murmured, accepting the glass Gideon offered. He relaxed in his seat, chatting for a few minutes before asking. "So…when did you arrive in town?"

The unspoken implication that Gideon should have notified him hung in the air.

"I arrived yesterday. I was planning on calling on you tomorrow if I didn't find you here."

His uncle waved that away. "Don't be silly. You're an earl now. It's my place to call on you," he said generously, though his tone was a trifle flat.

"There is no need for us to observe such formalities as rank. We are family," Gideon assured him smoothly before segueing into a discussion of mutual acquaintances. After his uncle had helped himself to a few more glasses of port, Gideon guided the conversation toward his true aim.

"I met a friend of yours last night."

"Which one?" His uncle wasn't slurring yet, but his speech was deliberate and careful, a sure sign he had imbibed too much before his arrival at the club.

"Mrs. Spencer."

"Ah yes, Ellie. Met her a few years ago." Sir Clarence coughed, his florid round face growing a touch redder. He hesitated. "She's a fine woman…and after a certain age, a man needs companionship."

Gideon leaned in. "There's no need to explain. Aunt Carol has been gone for a long time now. Your new friend is quite charming. Very bright and vivacious."

"Yes, she is, isn't she?" Sir Clarence didn't smile, however. "She mentioned meeting you…and Amelia."

Gideon murmured noncommittally. Instinct told him to keep quiet.

"That girl never listens," Sir Clarence hissed before taking a long sip. "Running all around town with that fop Worthing. What an embarrassment." He polished off his glass in one swallow. "No matter. She won't be a problem much longer."

That last was said without much heat, but it didn't seem to matter. Gideon's whole body reacted as if he'd heard a trumpet's call to arms. He stifled the inexplicable impulse to leap out of his chair and beat his uncle senseless, forcing himself to remain passive and distantly amused. The only thing that betrayed his true feelings was a twitching muscle in his cheek, the side effect of clenching his teeth too hard.

"Soon, she'll be someone else's problem." Sir Clarence sighed and rolled his eyes.

Gideon took a deep breath and forced himself to relax. *Interesting*. "Why do you say that?"

His uncle poured himself another, substantially fuller glass. "She'll remarry. I doubt her new husband will allow her to fritter and waste her time about town as she is doing now."

Gideon frowned. "Do you mean Lord Worthing? From all accounts, he seems to enjoy town."

Clarence laughed shortly. "No, not that sod."

"Then who do you mean?"

His uncle squinted at him, his hand lifted halfway to his mouth. "Never mind, boy, never mind." He looked around and spotted a pair of his cronies in the corner. "Oh, there they are."

Sir Clarence rose, putting down his glass. "Fine vintage, my boy, thank you. I must run along. Promised Southeby and old Tremaine I would luncheon with them."

"Of course, Uncle. And please send my regards to your friend Mrs. Spencer. I enjoyed meeting her last night."

"Hmm. Oh good, good." Sir Clarence wandered away without another word, weaving slightly.

Kyle Clarke slipped into his vacated chair, watching Sir Clarence stumble before joining his party in the corner.

"Potent stuff, isn't it?" he said quietly, lifting the bottle of port and examining the label.

"It's his favorite," Gideon muttered, weighing the distance to the nearest men in the room and deciding they were too far to be overheard provided they didn't shout like his uncle had.

"Learn anything new?"

"One or two useful things. For one, he doesn't share society's impression of his former daughter-in-law. There's more, but I believe that's the most significant because Clarence has always been excessively conscious of popular opinion. He follows the crowds in that regard, but not this time."

"Do you suspect he knows more about Martin's death than he's saying?"

Gideon considered that. "If he did, I think he'd be angrier. He was never one to prevaricate or hide his feelings. I suspect he believes it was an accident. He wrote as much in the letters we've exchanged since."

No, whatever Clarence was hiding had to do with Amelia...

If Amelia were to remarry, Worthing was the only possible candidate. Her name hadn't been attached to anyone else—not publicly anyway. Gideon would have to get closer to her to be sure.

Gideon was still mulling mystery suitors when Clarke waved a hand in his face. "Sorry. I was thinking."

Clarke huffed. "That much was obvious." He paused and tilted his head to one side. "I don't suppose you've reconsidered this quest now that you've met and spoken with the girl."

Gideon narrowed his eyes at his old friend. "And just why would I do that?"

"I was watching the two of you last night, in case you've forgotten. You two and Worthing. I thought you were going to interrogate her, but from my vantage point, you were...gentle with her."

"In case you've forgotten the finer points of espionage, making your target feel comfortable is often key to winning their trust."

"And you forget I've seen you work—often enough to know when you're dissembling. This was different."

Gideon glowered. "Of course it was different. I've been acquainted with her since she was in the schoolroom."

Clarke raised a brow.

Gideon set down his glass with a thump. "Fine," he muttered. "There is a chance—a small one, mind you—she wasn't directly involved."

Clarke looked triumphant, but Gideon forestalled him. "I still think she killed him. All the evidence points toward it...but I'm willing to entertain the idea she brought his death about unintentionally. Perhaps Worthing acted alone. It's too soon to be sure."

"Hmm. You never explained what evidence you had, aside from all the rumors and conjecture."

Gideon glanced around to confirm no one was close enough to hear them. "It's something I got from one of the maids who was there that night. Several of the servants overheard what Amelia said when she found Martin's body. She blamed herself."

"You spoke to her servants? When was this? Weren't you buried in Derbyshire with your estate managers the past few months?"

"I was. Did I introduce you to my new footman Jessup?"

"*Ah*. I take it this man came to you from your cousin's household."

Gideon nodded in confirmation.

"And has this new servant proved useful?"

"Up to a point. He admits to being there in the aftermath, but claims there was at least one man, an old retainer named Willie, who witnessed the deed. Jessup also confirmed Amelia arrived home *after* Martin had died. It was Willie and one of the maids who found his body and alerted the other servants. Amelia came home from her afternoon calls in the carriage soon after."

"So at least you know she didn't push him down the stairs. Any chance of tracking this Willie down, or at least the maid?"

"The maid stayed on with Amelia. Most of the servants did. The bulk of them had been hired when they lived abroad, and Amelia didn't downsize the household. Only the ones hired after their return to England left, Willie included. I have people looking, but they haven't heard a hint of him yet. According to Jessup, the old man was spooked by the death but wouldn't say why."

"Well, let's hope he has something useful to add," Clarke said with a contemplative sip of port. "Is there anything you want me to do?"

"As a matter of fact, I think it's time you dug up your cosmetics case from your attic storage."

His friend wrinkled his nose. "I take it you want me to resurrect my servant disguise?"

"Don't worry. I don't expect you to take a position in Amelia's household."

"Of course you do."

Gideon's lip curled. "All right, if I thought there was a chance she would hire you—but she's got too much staff as it is. Her townhouse requires a much smaller number than the home she kept in the country, but she didn't let anyone go. By all accounts, they have to invent tasks to keep busy. Amelia either doesn't care or hasn't noticed they're bleeding her dry."

"From what I hear, it would take a legion of servants to make a dent in her fortune. Precisely what is it you wish me to do?"

"I would like you to befriend the maid, an Italian woman named Carlotta. Charm her with your dismal pronunciation of her native tongue. I'd also like to take a closer look at Worthing's staff, but the only one who travels with him is his valet, and he's a loyal man."

Clarke's lip quirked. "How inconvenient. But even the most loyal men need something. I'll just have to find out what it is."

"Make sure your disguise is a good one when you do in case his employer happens to get a look at you."

"If I could fool Napoleon..."

Gideon laughed aloud, the booming sound filling the room. Several heads turned in their direction. "I told you it was not Napoleon, just a short officer," he said, lowering his voice.

"You don't know that. It gets very dark in the French countryside at night."

"The dark is the same everywhere."

Clarke's mouth compressed. "Well, considering what we're investigating—murder in your own family—I wouldn't bet on that."

CHAPTER 4

Amelia hurried down the sun-dappled corridor formed by the high green walls with little thought to her surroundings. Crispin had told her the hedge maze on this Mayfair estate was famous. Lovely statues and fountains could be found tucked into all sorts of blind corners and dead ends. She wasn't interested in any of them, however, nor was she concerned about getting lost. In addition to the note Gideon had sent, he also provided a little map.

Truthfully, she had little need for the map now. A few minutes of study and she had memorized the path she had to take. She had always been adept at that sort of thing. Puzzles and riddles were one of the few diversions in her life, in addition to her passion for novels.

It was far easier to ignore the tedious loneliness of her life when she had her nose buried in a book.

Of course, the last thing she was feeling at this moment was bored. No, ever since she had received Gideon's request to meet her in the maze, her heart had been working double time.

She had no idea what an earl was doing at this dreadful lawn party Viscount Worthing insisted she attend. But since Crispin had decided against joining her, he couldn't prevent her from meeting Gideon now.

I just have to be cautious. As long as she kept her guard up and didn't reveal too much, everything would be well. Crispin had overreacted to the earl's overture of friendship. It was only natural that Martin's relation wanted to know more about him and their marriage. The two cousins had been quite close at one time.

In a few more turns, she would be at the center of the maze. Amelia smiled and took a few moments to repair her coiffure and straighten her skirts. Martin would have teased her mercilessly for her mad dash to get to Gideon.

"You would knock me over like a ninepin if he crooked his finger at you," Martin had teased her once during one of Gideon's visits. It had been true then. Unfortunately, it appeared it was true now. But she couldn't help her reaction.

She could almost hear Martin laughing at her now. How she missed his laugh.

Sighing, Amelia turned the last corner, expecting to see Gideon's tall golden form in front of her. Her blood ran cold when she saw who was lying in wait.

"It's about time you appeared," Sir Clarence said crossly. "You've kept me waiting long enough."

She stood frozen, a few steps from the refuge of the hedge. Her impulse was to turn and run back into the safety of the maze, but her mind threw up an image of her father, so she gathered herself and stood ramrod straight.

She was not a little girl anymore. This man had no power over her. It was time she made that clear.

"Well, quit dallying, girl. Ellie should have brought you round a full ten minutes ago."

I should have known. That duplicitous schemer was behind the note. And to think, Amelia had once wanted her former guardian to marry the woman so he would have something else to occupy his time.

Feeling like a French queen walking to her execution, Amelia marched forward. At the center of the maze were two semicircular benches situated under a trellis of ivy to shade them from the sun. It would have been a lovely spot to converse with a confidante.

"Hello, sir," she said dutifully, sitting across from her former guardian.

Sir Clarence sneered. "Don't hello me, you undisciplined chit. I know you've been avoiding me. I have summoned you several times in the last few weeks."

She inclined her head. "I was not at liberty to visit when you directed, but I did call on you twice last month when I arrived in town."

He toyed with his cane. "Yes, and I was conveniently out both times."

Amelia hoped her shrug was as unaffected and casual as she intended. "I completely understand. You're a very busy man," she said generously.

"Don't try to fob me off with flattery, girl," he said, narrowing his eyes at her. "I know you didn't *accidentally* miss me. But the time for your little games is over. We're going to decide once and for all what to do with you."

Her spine stiffened, heat creeping up her neck. "*We*? Don't you mean you?"

Sir Clarence glared at her. "Obviously, I mean *me*. In the short time you have been in town, you have demonstrated you can't be trusted to run your own affairs, so I have to do it for you."

"And just what do you mean by that?" she asked, fully aware of the answer.

"You disgrace yourself and me by running around with that fop Worthing. You will cut all ties to him immediately."

Amelia was incensed. "I will do no such thing. Lord Worthing is my closest friend. He was Martin's closest confidante. I consider him family."

Sir Clarence flushed a deep purplish-red behind his beard. "*I* am your only family. As I am your only male relation, you will do as I say!" He took several deep breaths until he was no longer near apoplexy. "I don't care what that bastard Worthing is to you. You will stop associating with him now…and in a few months' time, we will announce your engagement to Lord Cannonburry."

"*Cannonburry?*" Amelia couldn't have been more shocked if he'd declared an interest in taking religious orders. "But Elmer Cannonburry is one step away from being bedridden. The man is practically decrepit!"

Without signaling his intention, Sir Clarence calmly reached over and slapped her in the face.

Compared to some of the times he'd struck her as a child, the blow was not that powerful. No, there had been slaps that had made her ears ring, leaving red impressions on her face for days. By comparison, this was mild, but it had been years since anyone had raised a hand to her...

Amelia could feel her resolve to deal with him as an equal waver. Her spirit was shrinking down, leaving a frightened, child-sized soul rattling around in her adult body.

I am not that child anymore, she reminded herself desperately. Fisting her hands, she blinked rapidly until she had fought back the tears and won.

"We'll wait until the wedding before bringing you back to town," Sir Clarence continued as if nothing had happened. "In the meantime, you will accompany me back to Northumberland until the banns are read."

"*No.*"

"You don't get to say no."

"Yes, I do." Her heart was threatening to stop, but there was no way she'd allow this farce to continue another second.

"You have no say in my life anymore. I came of age over three years ago. I control my life *and* my fortune." Amelia cocked her head to one side. "Did you make some sort of arrangement with Cannonburry? Is he under the impression that as my husband, he would control my fortune? You know it's not true. The man I marry receives my dowry and nothing more. And since Martin already gave it all to you, there is nothing left for Cannonburry if I make a second marriage—or for you."

Sir Clarence leaned back on the bench and watched her through slitted eyes. "Martin told you?"

"Of course he told me," she said from between gritted teeth. "It was my idea. You see I hoped—in vain—that my dowry would be enough to satisfy your greed."

He reached out to slap her again, but Amelia shot to her feet and dodged the blow. He followed suit, his finger pointed at her accusingly.

"How dare you accuse me of greed? I gave you a home, fed and clothed you when you had no one."

Amelia shook her head. This was an old argument, but she'd never had a chance or the will to rebut it. She would do so now. "Even an orphan has options when they possess a fortune as large as mine. I know full well this was the reason you took me in. I also remember how angry you were when you learned my guardian did not have the right to touch my funds beyond the stipend provided to educate and clothe me."

She folded her hands in front of her. "My father thought of everything when he realized your claim to be my guardian would be strongest. He didn't trust you an inch."

Sir Clarence's glare was hot enough to blister her skin, but he said nothing.

"I told Martin to give you the entire sum of my dowry in the hopes you would leave us alone," she said. "Did you already spend all ten thousand pounds?"

Her eyes swept over him, taking in the fine cut of his coat. Even if he'd purchased a hundred like it, he couldn't have spent the entire sum. "Was the money lost in some wild scheme? Poor investments? Or is ten thousand simply not enough for you? Did Cannonburry agree to turn some portion of my funds to you? Or do your solicitors believe they've figured out some sort of legal trickery to break the terms of my father's trust? Is this why you are pushing for this farce of a marriage?"

Sir Clarence's hands shot out, taking her arms above the elbow in a tight painful grip. "You owe me more than money. You owe me your very life."

"No, not you," she said. Her throat was so tight she could barely get the words out. “My debt was to Martin. And I paid him back by being a loving and devoted wife—a wife who kept his secrets.”

She pulled away so abruptly his nails marked the delicate muslin cloth of her sleeve. “As his widow, I will continue to keep those secrets, but this is the last time I will meet you in private. In public, I will acknowledge you as my father-in-law with all the respect and courtesy that tie demands. But you no longer have any rights over my person or my fortune. Accept this now or...”

“Or what?” Sir Clarence spat. “Do you expect me to believe you would really desecrate his memory?”

Amelia suppressed a shudder. “He’s gone. Through some twist of fate, my reputation went with him. I have nothing left to lose.”

She turned, forcing herself to walk away at a normal pace.

“You’re wrong Amelia,” Sir Clarence spat after her. “You still have quite a bit to lose.”

She ignored him, refusing to turn around to look at him. It took every ounce of willpower she had but managed to keep walking until she was past the first corner, beyond his sight.

Then she ran.

CHAPTER 5

"You should have told me about this confrontation sooner!" Crispin grimaced as he examined the bruises on her arm.

"I'm fine," Amelia assured him, pushing his hand away and readjusting the sleeve of her gown so the marks would not be visible.

"Amelia, the bastard threatened you."

"And I threatened him." She sniffed, trying to pass herself off as unaffected by her recent encounter with her former guardian, but Crispin saw right through her.

He tsked. "Darling, you couldn't deliver a threat if your life depended on it." She scowled at him, and his mouth compressed. "I'm sorry, that was a poor choice of words. But you know I'm right. Sir Clarence won't stop pushing you into another marriage. Not if it can benefit him in some way."

She knew where this conversation was leading. It took Crispin another few minutes of hedging before he finally came to the point.

"Amelia, you know Martin wanted me to watch over you in case anything happened to him. I think we should revisit our discussion about that. Sir Clarence can't force you to marry anyone if you are already wed to another."

She sighed and shook her head. "Crispin, I can't marry you."

"Why not? It's the most reasonable solution. We're close friends, and we understand each other's needs."

"I'm aware of all this. But…I don't want to live in England."

He snorted softly. "And yet, you're still here."

"What does that mean?" she asked in annoyance.

"Just last week I was actively dissuading you from traveling abroad. But now you seem ensconced in town. And something tells me it has little do with my scintillating company or the perils of travel abroad."

He appeared about to say something else when the coach stopped. In another moment, the coachman had opened the door. "We'll finish this discussion later. We're here."

Here was the Ashton's bash. Though smaller gatherings often proceeded it, this annual event was considered the official start of the ton's social season.

"Are you sure I should even be here?" Amelia asked. "I wasn't invited."

The Duke of Ashton was part of the old guard, a paragon of propriety and social decorum. His party was attended by everyone and, to date, Amelia had avoided large crowds, particularly when she was unsure of her reception.

"Well, I was invited. By now, everyone knows I am your escort to all the ton's functions. Everyone expects you to be on my arm, so have no fear. Just stay close to me. No more private conferences with dashing earls or despotic former guardians," he said exiting the carriage and turning to hand her down. "By the way, you never mentioned how Sir Clarence lured you to the maze, only that he used some form of trickery."

She took his arm and leaned into him. "He had Mrs. Spencer write me a note. Sir Clarence caught me by surprise. I did not expect him to attend such a function," she replied, omitting one salient detail.

Come to think of it, I really should not have expected Gideon there either. She had been foolish.

Crispin hummed, continuing to eye her suspiciously before

resuming his assurances that all would be well. In the same breath, he warned her against straying from his sight. "Don't worry. We're making a fashionable entrance—the receiving line should be long over. We will simply slip inside and blend in with the crush."

Amelia took his warnings to heart once they were circulating through the crowd inside. She had no desire to leave the shelter of his side.

La belle monde was gathered in all their finery, their sly glances and little barbs as polished as any weapon. Amelia smiled stiffly and tried to ignore the attention they were garnering, but the whispering started almost immediately. A few of the less discreet women of the ton pointed at her from behind the safety of their fans. Men looked down their noses at her. A few stared at her so lasciviously she felt exposed even though her gown's neckline was far more modest than most others in the room.

Feigning gaiety as best she could, she ate, drank champagne, and conversed with those polite enough to give her and her champion a civil greeting. Eventually, she forgot the crowd as the novelty of her appearance wore off, allowing her to feel the tedium of such events.

Despite Crispin's enthusiasm for them, Amelia detested balls. The conversations were all superficial, pointless discussions on fashion or the weather.

At one point, Crispin was compelled to dance by a particularly aggressive young miss in her second season, Cecily Chisholm, the daughter of an impoverished baron, who nevertheless had impeccable family connections.

"Go," she ordered, accepting the glass of punch he had just fetched her. She rather liked Cecily, who was refreshingly forthright. "I will not stir from this spot, I promise."

"Very well," he relented, offering his arm to Cecily with a charming, if somewhat forced, smile.

Amelia hovered at the edge of the dance floor, her eyes fixed on the whirling figures. Looking neither right nor left, she studiously avoided making eye contact with anyone. However, her refusal to engage only prodded her detractors to action. A figure swathed in lilac satin barreled into her.

"Oh, I'm so sorry!" the smug-looking matron who had spilled the contents of her wine glass on her exclaimed loudly. Several heads turned in their direction.

Amelia's lips parted as she stared down at the stain spreading across the front of her dark blue skirts. Clamping her teeth together, she schooled her expression into one of bored serenity. She racked her brain for the woman's name.

"Think nothing of it, Lady Everly. I have hundreds of gowns like it," she exaggerated.

The flash of annoyance that crossed Lady Everly's face was the only satisfaction Amelia was likely to get. Normally she did not flaunt her wealth, but reminding the ton she possessed it might help to shield her. At the least, it might silence some of the tongues whispering she killed her husband for his money, as he had none outside of what she had provided him.

Before Lady Everly could think of a reply, Amelia moved away. She retreated to the ladies' withdrawing room, repairing her appearance as best she could.

Lingering, she took advantage of the relative emptiness of the inner chamber to shore up her emotional defenses. Amelia had been aware that these parties would be a trial of endurance. She'd thought herself prepared, but, in truth, she was barely coping. At times like these, she wondered why she was subjecting herself to the slights and slurs of society, despite Crispin's opinion.

The viscount was adamant Martin would not want her to lock herself away. He faulted her for her solitary nature. Crispin insisted she needed to mix with others, assuring her once the ton grew accustomed to her presence they would stop entertaining such dark suspicions. She merely needed to brazen it out.

There was a logic to his advice, but given Crispin's repeated offers of marriage, she wondered at his motive. She knew he did not love her...but he did need to marry and produce an heir. Under the circumstances, it was quite natural he would want to marry her.

In this light, forcing her social rehabilitation served a dual purpose. His was not a large estate, but his title was old and venerable. His future wife could not be a social pariah.

"Did you see her?" A loud nasal voice interrupted her thoughts.

"I saw what Lady Everly did. I could not believe it!"

"I can, and wonder she did not do worse. She is Mapleton's cousin, after all."

Amelia turned, pressing herself against the wall next to the door-frame. Who was Mapleton and why was Lady Everly tormenting her on his behalf?

Peeking through the opening, she spotted two females in white muslin. Both appeared very young. She would have pegged them as green girls in the midst of their first season if not for the venom spewing from their lips.

The taller hawk-nosed girl leaned down to her shorter rosy-cheeked companion. "Mapleton is planning on confronting her. He thinks it's shameful she's invited to all the functions. I can't wait to see the look on her face!" A nasty giggle followed.

So Lady Everly's attack would not be all she had to endure this night. *And to think, the season is just beginning.* How much of this would she be subjected to? Hadn't losing Martin been bad enough?

Ignoring the tremor that ran through her, Amelia inhaled deeply and picked up her skirts. She counted to a beat of three and then glided past the two debutantes, nodding at them coolly as she passed. Their mouths dropped open and the shorter one gasped, but she didn't stop to speak to them.

Amelia hoped Crispin had finished his dance with Miss Chisholm. They needed to leave. She was officially at the end of her tether.

The crowd prevented her from reaching the dance floor with any speed. By the time she reached the spot where Lady Everly had accosted her, sweat was trickling down her spine. She felt as if she had pushed her way through a hostile mob. The stares and sneers had followed her across the entire ballroom. Any minute now, they would start throwing their champagne glasses in lieu of stones.

Her composure hanging from a thread, Amelia scanned the dance floor for Crispin's blond head. There were several men of that description, and she was having trouble identifying him. Her small stature worked against her there. Pivoting on her heel, she was turning to head toward the balcony when a hand grabbed her arm—the part bruised by Sir Clarence.

The unfamiliar black-haired man seemed to take satisfaction in her wince, although he had to be aware his hold was not tight enough to be painful.

"Madame, allow me to introduce myself. My name is Mapleton," he said coldly.

Smiling sweetly, she jerked her arm out his grip. "I would say it's a pleasure, but you are a stranger to me, sir."

The corner of his mouth curled up. "I was acquainted with your husband at Abingdon."

Amelia hummed, her temper flaring. "Really? He spoke warmly of his schoolmates, but he never mentioned you."

The skin above Mapleton's snowy-white cravat began to redden. "We were friends."

"Is that so? How odd. Your name is completely unfamiliar to me, and he spoke often of his friends from school."

It was the truth. Martin had never mentioned anyone of that name or this man's description.

The man shuffled his feet. "Yes, well, the fact remains I did attend school with him. I was in the year ahead," he said, the self-righteous tone losing a little steam.

Mapleton was clearly annoyed at having his public set-down interrupted by little details, like having to explain who the hell he was.

"But you were not close friends," Amelia asserted, cocking her head. "Or I would have received a note from you when he passed," she added.

The skin above Mapleton's cravat was a dull shade of purple now.

"Why would I write to a—"

"Nor did you write earlier to congratulate us on our marriage or I would have seen the letter," she interrupted, snapping her fan open. "You see, I took care of all my husband's correspondence and I never forget a name, so no, you were not very good friends at all, were you?"

Mapleton's entire face was purple now. Around them, heads turned. Everyone seemed to be holding their breath as the man raised a finger and waved it in her face.

He opened his mouth to speak—or shout—but he snapped it shut when someone collided with him.

"Amelia, here is the punch you asked for. Oh, sorry Mapleton. Didn't see you there," Crispin said hurriedly as he upended a glass of fruit punch all over the man's bright yellow waistcoat.

Apparently, Crispin had decided to take a page out of Lady Everly's book. Mapleton sputtered, his hands going to the damage. The viscount took advantage of his distraction to whisk her away. However, their escape was blocked by the crush of people who'd gathered close to witness her humiliation firsthand.

The strains of a waltz almost drowned out Mapleton's vicious swear. Crispin continued to smile as if nothing was amiss. He bent and loudly asked her to partner him on the dance floor.

"No," a deep voice interrupted. "This dance is mine."

Amelia whirled and looked up. Her heart leapt at the sight of Gideon, his golden-brown head haloed by the candlelight.

She blinked and smiled, finding it necessary to remind herself Gideon was not an avenging angel coming to her rescue.

Although he resembles one. Compared to the other men in the room, his clothing was cut plainly and severely. His black coat and pants set off a crisp white shirt. A single pin adorned his breast, but with his height and the breadth of his shoulders, bright colors or more jewelry would have been overwhelming.

Gideon stood a full head taller than Mapleton, but he didn't need to use his superior size or strength to intervene. One cold glare was sufficient to stop Mapleton in his tracks.

Cutting in front of Crispin, Gideon swept her onto the dance floor before either man could react.

The people blocking the floor were forced to move in the face of the earl's authority. He guided her through the throng until enough space was cleared for them to dance. After a few turns, other couples joined them.

It no longer mattered that everyone was staring at them. She was in Gideon's arms. She held on tight, the familiar lines of his face blurring with her tears.

He tsked. "Here now, we'll have none of that," he murmured, his thumb caressing her waist in a small show of comfort.

"Thank you," she whispered.

"For what?" He seemed amused. "From what I could see, you were doing a credible job of defending yourself." He whirled her through a tight turn before continuing. "But I'm sorry you were subjected to that scene with Mapleton and his busybody of a cousin, Lady Everly, in the first place. Had I been closer, I wouldn't have allowed it."

He trailed off, suddenly distracted. "Or this..."

Amelia glanced down. Somehow during one of the turns, her sleeve had shifted, revealing the dark line of bruises Sir Clarence's grip had left on her white skin.

For an instant, rage burned in Gideon's deep brown eyes, but it was gone the next second.

Amelia blinked, confused. If she hadn't been studying him so closely, she would have missed the flash of emotion. Now his face was a mask, one so perfectly controlled most others wouldn't have noticed anything amiss.

However, she was not most others. "*Gideon?*" she asked, suddenly apprehensive.

It was not fear she was feeling. She could not possibly be afraid of him, but she was suddenly unsure. The youth she had known was open, guileless. Gideon *had* changed.

"Who did that to you?" he asked softly, his head tilted to indicate her bruises.

Amelia racked her mind. Though Gideon and Sir Clarence did not precisely enjoy an amicable relationship there was no sense in borrowing trouble. "Mapleton took my arm just now."

"*No.*"

Gideon's tone was low and his face remained impassive, but she sensed his frustration with her answer. "Those marks are old. Several days at least."

When she didn't reply, he increased the pressure of his hold on her, not enough to hurt her but to hold her more securely. Already giddy and emotionally exhausted, it took active restraint to keep from collapsing into his arms.

"It's nothing. Old business." Amelia's smile was careless, masking her misgiving and discomfort at having to dissemble with him—the one person she wanted most to confide in.

Instead, she let her pleasure in his company warm her expression, leaning closer to him. "Gideon, I really must thank you for dancing with me again."

"Again?" He frowned.

She beamed at him. "Don't you remember? We danced a few times that summer Martin was studying with Fontaine, the French dancing master."

The memory must have surfaced because his expression lightened. "Oh, yes."

His eyes narrowed, a devilish twinkle in his eye. "Although I seem to recall you hid when the man would come around."

"Well...you and Martin were taking turns crushing my toes. I hid to preserve my ability to walk. I'm pleased to see your skill has considerably improved since then."

His lips twitched. "Hmm, yes. I forget exactly when it was, but there came a point when I decided dancing was a useful skill to have."

Amelia laughed. "It was probably when you realized all those village girls expected you to partner with them at those local assemblies..."

Though he smiled in response, his expression was distant. "Actually, I believe it was much later."

"In any case, I am grateful," she rasped, looking down to avoid his too-perceptive gaze.

"It's just a waltz, cousin."

It was much more...and he knew it. By coming to her rescue and sharing a dance with her, he was publicly declaring his belief in her innocence. As one of Martin's closest relations, the gesture could not be disregarded or ignored.

Though Gideon was new to his title, he was a powerful man. Not only was he a major landholder, but if what Crispin said was true, Gideon also possessed a dangerous reputation. Few in the ton would dare cross him. From what she'd just witnessed, the anger so quickly and efficiently hidden—it was starting to dawn on her he might have earned that reputation.

"Amelia, you know you can tell me anything. I will keep your confidence."

Her lips parted, the temptation to do that overwhelming. But the weight of all her secrets was too much. She closed her mouth.

Gideon reluctantly released her as the song ended. "Perhaps in time," he murmured, surprising her with a surfeit of patience he hadn't possessed as a youth.

He bowed and offered his arm, walking her off the dance floor. "Incidentally, Martin did mention Mapleton to me once. It was while he was still at school."

She looked at him, raising an eyebrow.

He bent to whisper conspiratorially. "Martin said he was a self-satisfied prig that secretly picked his nose when he thought no one was looking."

Her levity returning, Amelia giggled, watching Crispin out of the corner of her eye as he rushed to join them.

"Regrettably, we must leave," the viscount announced breathlessly as he reached their side. "I promised to make an appearance at the Duquesne ball," he added with a reasonable facsimile of regret and a charming grin.

"Of course." Gideon inclined his head, his inflection as correct and unconcerned as Crispin's. "Don't let me keep you."

Still marveling over Gideon's new air of self-mastery, Amelia waved goodbye, allowing herself to be ushered away. But once they were inside Crispin's carriage, she pleaded exhaustion and asked to be taken home instead.

"It has been an eventful night," Crispin agreed with bright eyes, directing his driver to change course.

For the remainder of the drive, he marveled at Gideon's chivalrous behavior, prattling on about how she now had the upper hand in the ton thanks to the earl. His gratitude was not enough, however, to stop the admonishments about taking the man into her confidence.

"Don't worry. I haven't forsaken all caution, my friend," she assured him before bidding him good night.

Amelia walked to her door slowly, feigning fatigue. In truth, she felt energized, her heart and mind fully occupied. She opened her door and dismissed her butler.

"Will you want the fire in your room, ma'am?" he asked before retiring.

"No, thank you, Adolfo. Go on to bed," she said, sending him on his way.

He bowed and headed for the servants' quarters.

Too restless to retire to her room, she made her way to her private parlor. She crossed the room to open the windows, still humming the tune of tonight's waltz.

That's odd.

Amelia straightened, examining the glass panes of the open casement. She traced her finger over the surface. Though the house was relatively new, the glass in the panes looked different from when she'd seen them last. Now it had waves and ripples in it, the kind found in the windows of much older manor houses.

It was as if the glass had melted somehow. Amelia frowned. In her father's old texts, she'd read that glass was melted sand, and though it appeared solid, it still had some of the attributes of a liquid. Over prolonged periods of time, glass revealed its liquid nature, by warping and running…except this morning, the glass had been clear. This house was only about a decade old. Nor had the window glass been exposed to a fire.

Perhaps she had drunk too much champagne at the ball. Rubbing her head, she debated on ringing for tea, but the hour was late and the staff had all gone to sleep. Instead, she pulled a favorite novel off a nearby shelf and settled on her settee to read.

It was all a pretense, however. Amelia could not even be honest with herself. All she wanted was to close her eyes and pretend she was still dancing with Gideon. Perhaps if she relived that moment in her mind she could create an imprint of the sensation, a treasured memory she could take out and examine when she was in her dotage.

Absently, she reached out to set the book on the adjoining table, laughing over her own clumsiness when the book tumbled to the floor. She bent and picked it up, frowning as she set it on the wooden surface.

Someone had moved the table. *No*. Someone had moved her settee. It was no longer in the same alignment with the fireplace.

Amelia stood and examined the furniture. There were no marks in the rug showing the settee had been moved. Which meant the rug had been moved as well. The Aubusson carpet was quite large, extending more than half the length of the room. It would have taken several servants to shift it.

She pivoted on her heel, taking in the whole room. It wasn't just the settee or the carpet. Her desk, the sofa, and all the end tables had also been moved. Even the smaller objects had shifted. Vases, books, pens. Their locations were the same in most cases, but they were now off by less than an inch.

Either the maids had been overzealous with their dusting, or...The door. The door was also in a different place.

Apprehension prickled her skin. How was this possible?

It had to be her imagination. A doorway couldn't move. But she knew the dimensions of this room like the lines of her own hand. The entrance had been several inches to the left, slightly off center from the decorative flower in the molding above. Now the edge of the doorjamb was aligned with that flower.

Wait. The heavy shelf in the corner could not have moved. It was built *into* the wall. But her eyes did not deceive her. It, too, had been repositioned. She could see the gap next to it—and it was growing before her eyes.

Amelia inhaled sharply, trying desperately to get enough air into her lungs. The room was no longer static. It appeared to swell, the walls ballooning out, furniture scraping the floor as it expanded.

She tried to scream, but no sound came out. There was no air in her lungs. Her fear was literally choking her.

The last thing Amelia remembered was the pattern of the carpet as it rose to meet her face.

CHAPTER 6

"What do you mean she's not here?" Gideon was beyond the point of irritation. "You told me yesterday that she is always back from her afternoon calls at this hour."

"I am very sorry, Lord Flint," the butler said, clutching Gideon's card. "I'm sure if Mrs. Montgomery had known you were the one who called yesterday she would have made a point of staying home."

Gideon suppressed a snort. What the man meant was if he'd known Gideon was an earl, then he would have actually passed on his message.

"Do you know when she'll return?" he asked, running his hand roughly through his hair.

"Um, I'm not certain." The butler coughed. "I believe she's supposed to be taking a turn in the park right now, but madam has been keeping unpredictable hours of late."

Well, if that wasn't an understatement.

"I'll be sure to give her your card as soon as she comes home," the butler said helpfully.

Gideon slammed his beaver hat back on his head and turned up his collar against the drizzling rain. Was the bloody woman riding in this weather? Or was Amelia lying about her whereabouts to her own staff?

True the rain had only just started, but the dark clouds had been threatening to burst since before breakfast. And from what he remembered, he didn't think Amelia was devoted enough a rider to voluntarily be out in this weather. No, if memory served him, she would rather be curled up with a book on a day like this.

And to think Gideon had started to give her the benefit of the doubt.

After that night he'd waltzed with her, he'd begun to think her innocent. With those bruises on her arm, he'd cast her as a victim. He'd even suspected Lord Worthing was hurting her, forcing her to do as he instructed.

But since that night, Amelia had been out riding in the park or paying afternoon calls *every* day. Every night, she attended at least two or three functions. He lost count of the number of balls and soirees he'd attended in the last week trying to run her to ground. And half the time, she hadn't bothered to take Lord Worthing with her.

Clarke may have been right. Now that Amelia Montgomery had the Earl of Flint's social approbation, she was throwing herself into the whirl and glitter of the ton.

"She's glorying in her newfound social acceptance," his friend had said at the club last night after Gideon had missed Amelia at the opera. "She married very young, didn't she? And before that, old spendthrift Clarence never gave the chit a season. I wouldn't judge her too harshly. It can be overpowering to experience freedom for the first time. It's only natural she would want to partake in society's little pleasures and peccadillos now that she's able to."

Those words rang in Gideon's ears as he turned up his collar against the damp air, but he rejected them. It was true Amelia had spent most of her life buried in Northumberland and had only socialized among foreigners, but he didn't agree with the assertion that Amelia wanted to be embraced by the ton.

She doesn't consider them her people, he thought as he cut through the park on the way to his townhouse.

Amelia's father had taught her to detest the artificiality and pretense of the British upper class. Gideon knew that because whenever Sir Clarence would make his snide comments about his and Amelia's parentage, she would repeat her father's words.

A man's worth is defined by his actions, not his birth.

Though Gideon had never been cut as deeply by Sir Clarence's constant barbs, he had found comfort in the earnestly delivered words at the time. He still did despite his unexpected inheritance.

However, Amelia had been little more than a child when she'd said them. What if she'd only been spouting her father's ideas with no understanding of what they truly meant?

He hadn't believed that at the time. Or did Amelia simply not hold to them now?

What if she'd changed? It wouldn't be the first time a young sheltered woman was seduced by the glitter and pomp of high society. Gideon would never have guessed that Amelia could be one of them; however, recent events were making him re-evaluate what he knew about her.

Could she be a murderer? He snorted. Just because Amelia suddenly enjoyed balls did not mean she had committed such a heinous act. He needed to adhere to the facts at hand. The problem was that he had precious few of them, despite his best efforts.

Clarke had successfully befriended Amelia's maid, Carlotta. He'd managed to meet the Italian woman on one of her half-days off in the market, but little had been learned from that source. The language barrier notwithstanding, all Clarke had managed to get out of her was that the maid was lonely.

As for Willie, the servant who'd witnessed Martin's death, he was being as elusive as Amelia.

The buzz of questions in Gideon's mind stopped when he spotted a woman in a navy riding habit in the distance. By rights, she was too far away to be sure of her identity, but he knew it was her. He would recognize the graceful lines of her figure anywhere.

There were other women in the ton with similar coloring and figures just as fine, yet for some reason, he could always spot Amelia in a crowd—even when her back was turned or his view was partly obscured. *Funny that.*

Gideon studied her impatiently as she and her companions approached. Amelia appeared more comfortable in the saddle than when he'd last seen her riding. She'd been an accomplished rider as a child, but lack of opportunity to continue practicing had made her more hesitant as a young girl. It had been his teasing that had gotten her back on a horse—but only when Sir Clarence had been away on business.

Amelia must have ridden often since then. Her back was straight and she held the reins with grace, but even from this distance, he could see the strain in her form.

She was between two men riding on matching chestnut mares, both eager young pups he recognized as belonging to the dandy set. Ignoring them, he raised his hand in greeting as she approached. The involuntary scowl that darkened his face went unnoticed as the trio passed him.

Amelia hadn't acknowledged his wave. Indeed, she never even glanced his way. And her companions were too engrossed in their conversation to notice him. He caught enough of what they were saying to know they were gossiping, sharing the latest amusing on-dits as if they were competing for her attention.

But she wasn't paying them any mind. Amelia looked distracted and...miserable.

She was hiding it, but he recognized that resigned blankness of expression. It was one she wore whenever Sir Clarence had started disparaging her father. He'd seen it multiple times on the faces of others during his time with the war office.

The wind picked up, its icy tendrils working their way under the collar of his greatcoat. He pulled it closer around him, debating if he should follow the riders. Hesitating, he swore and decided to head home. Tonight was the Duke of Marlboro's ball—one of the largest and most lavish events of the season. If socializing was now a priority, there was no way Amelia would miss it.

Gideon took great care with his attire that evening. He didn't go in for the brightly colored waistcoats and jackets that were all the rage at the moment. He chose a dark blue waistcoat, white shirt, and a simply tied cravat.

He was meeting Clarke at ten, a few hours after the ball officially started. Clarke was already there. If Amelia arrived early, his friend would follow her and send word of her movements. So far, no messages had arrived, meaning she hadn't yet made an appearance.

By the time he arrived, the event was officially a crush. As expected, everyone in the Beau Monde had decided to attend the Marlboro's ball tonight. He greeted the duke and duchess, spending the better part of a half-hour talking to the old duke about the possibility of a war with France.

Not normally one for socializing, Gideon was nevertheless having a fine time disparaging Napoleon's prospects with the old hawk when the duchess interrupted.

"That's enough war talk, my dear," she scolded good-naturedly. "Don't monopolize the earl."

She took Gideon's arm and led him away to the refreshments table, chatting politely on the decorations and the many preparations she had made for the evening. All too soon, however, the conversation veered into dangerous territory.

"You simply must dance with Lord Harrow's daughter," the duchess instructed, tapping him on the sleeve with her fan. "She's a lovely girl fresh out of the schoolroom. Then there's Clarissa Scott, the Earl of Quinnay's niece. She does the most beautiful watercolors."

Unsure why he was getting that advice, he nodded. "Err, thank you, Your Grace. I will be sure to ask her about them should I be fortunate enough to dance with her tonight," he said, looking out of the corner of his eye for Clarke.

His instincts belatedly began to prick him, and they were telling him to retreat.

The fan tapped him again, harder this time. When he looked back at the duchess, her expression was a trifle pinched. "I am only trying to help you, young man," she chided.

"Thank you," he said automatically before wondering why she had taken an interest in him. She didn't keep him in suspense for long.

"Yes, well, one would hate to see such a fine young man making a mistake and tying himself to a woman with…shall we say…a questionable reputation."

Gideon stiffened. "If you're referring to Mrs. Montgomery, I should explain she is a family connection."

He could tell the duchess was trying not to roll her eyes. "No need to take umbrage, my boy. I know Amelia Montgomery is your kin by marriage, and she is charming and well-mannered enough. Truly, I have no issue with her. But I thought you should know your interest in her has been remarked on these last weeks. And I knew the former Earl of Flint for many years. He was a good friend."

The duchess broke off and sighed. Her mind was no doubt deep in the past. After a beat, she continued. "Yours is an old and venerated title. Make sure you keep that in mind when you are selecting a countess to stand at your side."

His smile was taut when he nodded. "Thank you for your concern, but I'm not pursuing a bride at the moment."

"That does not mean they are not pursuing you." The duchess laughed. "You're at the very top of every matchmaking mother's list this season."

"*Oh*." Well, it was not news that he was a target on the marriage mart; nevertheless, it was disconcerting to hear that he was considered the main prize—and from a duchess no less.

A mental image of his head mounted like a deer in a hunting lodge flashed before his eyes as he caught Clarke's eye from across the room.

"Well, I see I've given you something to think about," the duchess said when he turned back to her. "I shall leave you to it. Lord Harrow's daughter is over near the window, by the way, in the white muslin."

With that less than-subtle-hint, the grande dame departed in a cloud of scent.

Behind him, Clarke sniggered. "Never understood why they call them the weaker sex."

Feeling wrung-out, Gideon spun around to face him, accepting the glass of champagne he held out with alacrity.

"Trust me, I've never made that mistake," he muttered. "I don't suppose there's any chance of getting our hands on something stronger?"

"I bribed a waiter to raid the old duke's liquor cabinet. I'm not sure what we'll be getting, but it should do the job."

"That is why you're my closest friend," Gideon said gratefully.

He drank the champagne in one gulp, looking around. The Harrow chit was making calf eyes at him. He nodded politely, trying to summon the enthusiasm to ask the girl to dance.

"Best get it out of the way now," Clarke said when the musicians began to play a cotillion. "You don't want to have that hanging over your head when Amelia arrives."

An excellent point. He nodded at Clarke. "Save me that glass of purloined liquor when it comes. Something tells me I'm going to need it."

The next quarter hour dragged as he did his duty and danced with Lucy Harlow. She was as advertised—a lovely girl, but painfully green. He knew it was the usual practice for a man of his age and station to marry a girl as young as sixteen or seventeen, but he personally couldn't stomach the idea. Miss Harlow and all the debutantes of her age were little more than children in his eyes.

Amelia had only been two years older when she married Martin, he reminded himself. Perhaps she resented being forced to wed at such an early age despite her affection for his cousin. And she had some—that much he remembered.

With an effort of will, he forced himself to stop thinking about Amelia and applied himself to the task at hand. He chatted and danced with several girls in their first or second season. He also paid court to the matrons and singled out one or two wallflowers, careful not pay too much attention to any single female. While he couldn't stop the ton from speculating on his marriage prospects, at least he wouldn't fuel the rumors that he had someone particular in mind.

After doing the rounds, he found Clarke again. The contraband French brandy he'd procured wasn't a good year, but by then, he didn't care.

"She's been here for twenty minutes. The reception from the duchess was a little frosty, however, Amelia didn't appear to notice. Actually, she looks a bit fatigued."

Trying not to be too obvious, Gideon and Clarke moved in the crowd on the edge of the ballroom until they were in sight of Amelia. She was with Worthing again.

Gideon stood much closer to her than he'd been in the park, near enough for him to know that "fatigued" was an understatement.

"She looks bloody exhausted."

Though Amelia was striking in a muted violet bombazine gown, there were dark circles under her clear blue eyes. She was also paler than he'd ever seen.

"What the hell was she doing out riding in the park this afternoon? The woman should have been abed."

Clarke made a rough sound of agreement in his throat. "Something is bothering her. That much is clear. I believe it's time you forced the issue—provided you can run her to ground this time."

"I'll break into her house if I have to," Gideon vowed, his eyes tracking Amelia's every movement.

He let her dance a few more times, comfortably aware that her partners weren't anything special to her. There wasn't even a spark of interest in her expression when she looked at any of them.

Taking advantage of a break in the music—and the fact Worthing had departed to the card room—he stepped forward to greet Amelia with a benign nod. She closed the short distance between them.

"Good evening, my lord." The skirts of her violet gown stopped swinging as she stopped in front of him.

"Good evening, cousin." He waved a hand to a passing waiter and asked for two glasses of champagne. "I would ask you to dance if I did not think you would topple over like a ninepin."

Amelia's head drew back, and she blinked a few times. Much-needed color flooded her white cheeks. He was being quite rude, but that did not seem to signify. She didn't chastise him.

"I..."

"Yes?"

Her shoulders lifted and dropped and she looked away. "I've been having some trouble sleeping again, I'm afraid."

"Then I prescribe an early night and bed," he said.

He did not have to feign the concern in his tone. Face to face, Amelia appeared fragile and wan. A stiff breeze could have knocked her over.

Without looking directly at him, she answered in a whisper. "I don't want to go home."

Was there a problem with her townhouse? "Why not?"

"Oh, no reason really. It's just...so empty there."

"Has something happened? You seem unsettled."

Amelia's head shot up. "Well...I suppose I am. Nothing out of the ordinary has occurred." She laughed brittlely. "On occasion, one's imagination gets the best of you, I suppose. I've been told that sort of thing is commonplace when one lives alone."

Except you live with a horde of servants. Gideon nodded in understanding anyway. "It's understandable after spending so much time in one person's company. You must miss Martin terribly."

"I do," she breathed, looking down as tears flooded her eyes.

Guilt swamped him when she surreptitiously dabbed at her eyes behind her fan. A brave smile lit her face. "Never mind that. Tell me more about you. How are things at your estate?"

"Which one?" he asked with a grin before launching into a detailed description of his new holdings.

Despite his desire to interrogate her, Amelia's gentle and insightful questions had him lowering his guard. Before he knew it, they were discussing the improvements he was implementing to improve agricultural yields—debating benefits of crop rotation and drainage.

After a few minutes, he caught himself and apologized. "I must be boring you to tears. Really, you should have stopped me at least ten minutes ago."

Amelia shook her head. "On the contrary, I was about to suggest you read Mr. Shipman's article in the latest Agricultural Review. It's called *Innovations and Improvements in planting and harvesting of cereal crops.*"

Gideon blinked. Yes, her questions had seemed informed, but he'd had no idea of the extent of her knowledge…

"I had no idea you were so well-versed in farming techniques."

One corner of her mouth turned up. "My father always said an investor had to be informed about all the commodities they trade."

He should have expected such an answer. *No, she hasn't changed as much as you think.* "So you are investing in crop futures?"

"Among various other things. I also dabble in manufacturing, shipping, and the like. Variety is the key to a sound investment strategy."

Gideon didn't bother to hide his surprise. "That much? I know your father was an expert investor, but I wasn't aware you had followed in his footsteps."

Her father had left her a fortune. Naturally, he assumed she was living off that money. He had underestimated her. But had she grown the fortune or lost some of it?

"I find a little gambling on the 'Change keeps things interesting."

The stock exchange? Even he didn't invest there. The market could be capricious, and he was still unused to possessing a fortune. True, he'd spent some time in the hells in the last few years, but only when he needed to fleece certain gentlemen for information. Hells, or rather the men who ran them, were excellent sources of gossip.

"Can I ask how you managed that?" he asked after a moment. Most traders wouldn't take bids from a woman.

She knew exactly what he meant. "My father's solicitor, Callaghan, makes most of my bids for me. We meet once a week. I enjoy it for the most part. It keeps my mind occupied."

This was unexpected news. "Would that be Tolbert Callaghan?"

Amelia brightened, no longer appearing so tired. "Yes. He was a close associate of Papa, as well as his attorney. Do you know him?"

"Only by reputation."

Tolbert Callaghan was one of the nation's top solicitors—one often consulted on legal matters by the crown. He was wealthy in his own right. The fact such a renowned man spent an hour every week with Amelia gave Gideon an excellent idea of just how skilled she was at choosing investments.

Or they were having an affair, his cynical side said. Except Callaghan was in his sixties and happily married by all accounts. Gideon needed to stop assuming the worst and gather actual evidence.

"I take it you do well in these endeavors?"

"Quite well, thank you," Amelia said, adorably smug.

The brilliance of her smile shot warmth through him. "What—"

His next words were drowned out as multiple reports sounded behind him. A sudden howling wind swept the ballroom. More than half of the tapers were extinguished in the blast, plunging his portion of the room into darkness.

In a split second, he had shoved Amelia behind him before turning to face the enemy. The sound had come from the left. Despite the darkness, he could see every door to the garden patio had been thrown open.

But the doorways were empty. There were a few guests near them but none close enough to have opened them. Napkins fluttered wildly and the sound of broken glass could be heard as people stumbled and stepped over champagne glasses they had dropped.

The startled screams of the women didn't even register until one long shrill cry filled his ears, nearly stopping his heart.

"Amelia!" He turned around, groping for her in the darkness. She wasn't behind him anymore.

Adrenaline flooded him as he shouted her name once more. The panic in his voice did nothing to quell the pandemonium breaking out around them. Cursing under his breath, he tried to calm himself so he wouldn't feed the hysteria.

Amelia was only a few feet away. He could not see her features, but her arm was clear enough. She pointed up behind him at the darkened balcony that overlooked the ballroom. That part of the room was pitch black. He couldn't see anything up there.

He'd only taken his eyes off Amelia for a second, but when he turned back to her, she was on the floor.

"Bloody hell!" He ran to her side, swinging her into his arms.

"Did you see them?" she whispered, her head lolling against his chest.

"See what?"

"The eyes that killed him." Amelia swooned, going lax in his arms. He shook her, but she didn't move.

"Give her to me," someone called. Gideon looked up to Worthing struggling toward him. The viscount stepped over a fallen man a few feet away and held out his arms.

"Not on your life," Gideon growled, pulling Amelia's unconscious form closer to his chest.

Worthing scowled at him. "I don't know how to help them," he yelled, gesturing to the people in disarray behind them.

Footmen were rushing in with lit candlesticks, illuminating the scene.

People had fallen over each other. Those on their feet milled aimlessly. Others were on the floor, hurt. If the darkness had lasted even a few moments more, the duke's guests might have trampled each other to death.

Just to the right of him, there was a young girl in white holding up a bloody hand. She had fallen on a champagne flute and cut herself.

Gideon swore again and reluctantly handed Amelia's still form over to his rival. "Don't you dare leave until I come back to escort her home," he ordered.

Worthing's lips compressed, but he didn't argue with him. Gideon turned his back to him, going to the young girl's aid first, belatedly recognizing her as one of the Turney chits.

He took her hand, examining her palm. He tsked. "It's a paltry cut. You're going to be fine."

The girl's wide eyes didn't shift from her hand. "It's bleeding. There's b-blood," she stuttered.

"Yes, but not too much of it," he assured her, trying not to sound impatient as he untied his cravat and pressed it to the wound. Unceremoniously, he hauled the girl to her feet, happy to give her to a concerned gentleman hurrying toward them—one of her brothers judging from the family resemblance.

There were a few other injuries equal to Miss Turney's, but luckily none more serious. Gideon helped a few more people, most of whom appeared merely overset. Servants hurried to relight the extinguished tapers, and the duke called for more champagne be passed around to the guests that remained.

The strains of a determined country reel began before Gideon could look for Amelia and Worthing. They were nowhere in sight. He searched the ballroom for a full twenty minutes before the footman at the door confirmed their departure.

Gideon swore a blue streak and left the ball. He tried her townhouse first, but they weren't there.

"Not again," he fumed, staring daggers at her butler.

"Um, madam was here," the man said, fingering his collar nervously. "But she asked that her trunks be loaded to her traveling coach immediately. She departed a few minutes ago. Madam suddenly decided to accept an invitation to visit the country."

Adolfo pointed to one end of the busy street, but Gideon didn't see the brown and cream equipage he knew to be Amelia's. "I don't understand. I just saw her. How did she get packed so quickly?"

It should have taken a lady of the ton most of the day to pack all the gowns and other necessities required for a weekend country visit.

Adolfo appeared relieved to have an answer for him. "Madam's trunk was packed," he volunteered. "She's had one at the ready for the last few months, apparently for such an occasion."

Damn and blast. "Did Worthing go with her?"

"I believe so, my lord," the butler added a bit more reluctantly, cautiously starting to close the door in anticipation of his displeasure. When Gideon glowered and nodded, Adolfo bid a hasty adieu and shut the door, making good his escape.

"*Bloody hell,*" he muttered, heading back to the Marlboro's ball.

He was going to collect Clarke and then, come hell or high water, he *would* find Amelia—and nail her skirts to the floor.

CHAPTER 7

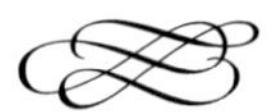

Lord Westcliff's country party was in full swing. Their host and hostess had organized all the usual country amusements as well as a few others unique to their household. For the women, archery had been followed by croquet and then a trip to the local village. The men had been indulging in endless rounds of billiards interspersed with the occasional grouse hunt. That afternoon, there was a contest to see who could make it through the immense garden maze first.

Having had more than enough of hedge mazes, Amelia pleaded a headache and excused herself to rest in the ladies' salon. The well-trained staff had left a tea tray at her disposal, and she selected a novel from the library before sitting down.

Crispin had gone fishing with the men. His family had been connected to Westcliff's for generations. Despite their eleventh-hour arrival, they had been welcomed to the country party with ready grace and good humor. They waved away the fact Crispin had already sent his regrets.

If their hosts were reluctant to have Amelia under their roof along with Crispin, they showed no sign. Indeed, the Westcliff's were all that was gracious, a rarity among the ton. It was the first time Amelia had felt accepted at one of these affairs. But her host's opinion of her was the least of her concerns at the moment.

I am either being pursued by a monster or I am going mad.

Either prospect was terrifying. She set her book aside and picked up the fine china cup set in front of her. Ignoring the rattling of the saucer on the bed, she drank until her hands steadied.

It was a terrible situation when madness was the best prospect she faced, but Amelia could not afford to deny reality any longer. But how did one know when they were going mad?

Well, imagining monsters was probably an excellent indication of mental derangement. She shuddered involuntarily, the image of those unnatural eyes watching her from the balcony of the Marlborough's ballroom burning in her mind.

It hadn't been the first time. They had watched her from the upper story of their house in Kent the day she had found Martin's body.

You are not mad.

In the year since her husband's death, Amelia had convinced herself she'd imagined that ghastly vision.

Self-delusion had been easy. Nothing out of the ordinary had happened while she had been in mourning. It was only now that she was reentering society at Crispin's behest that strange and unnerving events had begun to occur.

But those eyes belonged to no man or animal she recognized. Their glow was not the reflective sheen of any night beast. It was the light of hellfire. And it had been as real as the floor under her feet.

She hadn't known what to tell Crispin after she collapsed at the ball. He'd been so concerned about her this past week. He hadn't understood her frenetic need to socialize the last few days—she who had avoided and criticized the shallow frivolity of the ton at every turn. Crispin had been confused and a little hurt by her behavior and the silence she had maintained about it.

Amelia hadn't wanted to come to the Westcliff's. She had been determined to quit England altogether that night, to flee to Italy and travel to her former governess' home. Isobel would take her in.

This had been Amelia's plan for some time, although she hadn't admitted that to herself. But she'd had her maid pack her trunks in preparation to depart since the morning she woke up on the floor of her private parlor.

That troubling episode had merely been the first. In the time since, Amelia had begun to see things out of the corner of her eye. She would get to her feet to chase the flicker of movement around a corner or into another room only to find there was nothing there. And sometimes, late at night, she would hear whispers in rooms that were empty save for herself.

Yes, she should have left England. However, at the last minute, she had been too shaken to think clearly. All she had told Crispin was that she wanted to leave town. He had tried to convince her to travel back to his estate in Kent, but Amelia would not set foot anywhere near the place.

Crispin's estate was only a stone's throw from the house where Martin had died. That was where this nightmare had started. She was determined it wouldn't end there as well.

When Amelia had rejected traveling to his home, Crispin had remembered his invitation to this country party. He had taken charge, bringing her here. And in her weakness, she had let him.

Would the beast follow them all the way here? Was she putting these innocent people in danger? What if the creature decided to harm Crispin?

I should have gone to Italy. The shadows and darkness plaguing her couldn't survive under the hot Italian sun, could they? She honestly didn't know. What if she made it all the way to Isobel and Matteo's home only to find she was still being pursued? She could not bear it if Isobel and her family were harmed because of her.

Every move she made felt like the wrong one.

"Amelia?"

She started, her eyes flying to the doorway. Crispin frowned at her response.

"Oh, I didn't hear you come in. Is the fishing outing over?"

Crispin came and sat next to her on the couch. "No, I found myself falling asleep and decided to come back early for a few fortifying cups of tea. Did you sleep well last night?"

"Better than I have in ages," she confessed.

Crispin's light blue eyes flicked to her face before he turned to the tea tray to pour himself a cup. He drank deep before turning to her. "Amelia, I know what's going on."

Her eyes widened. "You do?"

"Of course. You told me about the confrontation with Sir Clarence yourself and his desire to wed you off to that pile of dust Cannonburry. It's obvious he's made more threats, and you've been afraid to confide in me."

Her mouth dropped open. She was unsure what to say, but Crispin didn't require an answer. He held up a hand.

"I'm no fool, Am," he said, using Martin's pet name for her. "You can save your denials. I've put it all together—that confrontation in the maze, your sudden need to be out in public. Even your sudden preference for other men's company. I know you haven't been avoiding me completely, but you've certainly cut down on the amount of time you have spent with me—before this sojourn to the country that is. You're afraid to be with me, but you're more afraid to be alone. Obviously, Sir Clarence has made some manner of threat against me, something you've taken to heart. Well, I'm not afraid of him, and I won't let the bastard get away with intimidating you!"

She sat gaping at him while he took her hand. "You don't have to worry anymore. I have the solution. We will announce our engagement. In a few months' time, we can be married and Sir Clarence will have no choice but to leave you alone."

Amelia tried unsuccessfully to retrieve her hand. "Crispin, you are my dearest friend—indeed you are my only friend—but you know that is quite impossible."

His chin lifted. "I know marriage to me is not what you would wish, but you weren't meant to spend your life alone. Martin wouldn't have wanted that. You deserve more, a family. Children. You can't tell me you've never desired a child of your own. I know of your plans with Martin."

Her mouth tightened. Forcibly, she withdrew her hand from his.

Crispin winced. "I'm sorry. I'm only trying to say I understand what you've lost because I've lost it, too."

Amelia picked at her skirts and sighed. "I know. But a marriage between the two of us will not restore those dead dreams."

He nodded but did not give up. "It won't be the same. Everything will be different. But that doesn't mean you won't find a measure of happiness with me. Our relationship is not unlike yours and Martin's."

He broke off and patted her knee. "We did not grow up together, but I know you better than you think."

Crispin leaned closer. "You see, Martin confided certain things to me. Things about you."

She was tempted to roll her eyes. "I'm aware of my husband's proclivity to be indiscreet."

"But you loved him anyway." Crispin's smile was as devilishly charming as Martin's could be.

"Of course I did. So what exactly did he tell you?"

He looked around before answering. There was no one else in the room, but he lowered his voice anyway. "About Gideon and the way you felt about him."

Heat crept up her cheeks. "Good God, Crispin. I was little more than a girl back then. I'm a grown woman now. Those sorts of childish feelings fade."

He looked skeptical. "Do they? In my experience, the strong emotions of youth tend to stay with you into adulthood. It might be different if the man in question had a receded hairline and a paunch, but the Earl of Flint cuts a dashing figure. The ton adores him. All the men want to be his friend and the women want to marry him. Just last night, I heard a grey-haired dowager waxing poetic on the breadth of his shoulders and the way he fills out his breeches."

She huffed an unwilling laugh, but Crispin's face was sober. "He'll marry soon enough and when he does, it will be to one of the young innocents making their debut. It's what men in his position do. The future Countess of Flint will be some chit fresh out of the schoolroom with an unstained reputation and significant property as her dowry."

Amelia blinked, waiting for the sudden lump in her throat to subside before she answered. "I know all that."

He continued relentlessly as if he had not heard her. "Martin said he was your girlhood hero. And now he's a man, an attractive and commanding one at that. You can't tell me you haven't wished for something more. I've seen the way you look at him. And…there have been more unpleasant rumors since he danced with you."

Amelia could feel her patience wearing thin. Would she never be free from spiteful tongues? "What sort of rumors?"

Crispin had the grace to blush. "People are starting to whisper. They say you are his mistress. I caught the first hints of that last night."

"What rubbish," she snapped, her blood heating. "As if the earl would engage in such a liaison with his own cousin's widow. Society has nothing better to do than invent vicious stories for their own amusement. If they spent half the energy trying to do something productive like helping the poor not a single person would go hungry in town. But they only do and say things for their own selfish ends. I can't believe you would listen to such drivel."

Crispin gave her a chiding glance "Am, it's time to stop being naive. We must stay informed about what people are saying about you. And you need to be realistic about your prospects with the earl."

"For the last time, I have no designs on Lord Flint. He is a family connection, nothing more."

Crispin did not look convinced. "I don't mean to depress your spirits. I only wish to help. Regardless of your decision on whether to take me up on my offer, we will find a way to deal with Sir Clarence. And perhaps in time, you might meet a man willing to overlook the rumors, someone you can love. Although, I would like to add that being married to me would not be an impediment to such a future. It's one of the small blessings of our society. A girl can't dance too many times with the same gentlemen before she is a bride, but once she is married and gives her husband an heir, she is free to do as she wishes."

"A widow has a certain amount of freedom as well," she pointed out. "And I'm not prepared to give it up because of…an uncomfortable situation."

Like going mad or being hounded by a demon.

Crispin reached for her hand again, squeezing it before rising from the settee. "At least think about what I've said."

"I will," she promised, but she didn't meet his eyes.

"I'm going to find our hosts. They should be stationed outside the entrance to the maze. Once all the women are through it, the staff will serve refreshments on the south lawn. I hope you will join us."

"I will—later. I think I shall go for a walk first," she said as she rose. "I have a lot to think about."

"That sounds like a fine idea," he said, gesturing for her to precede him out of the room.

A maid fetched her bonnet, and she and Crispin parted in the garden. She skirted around the massive hedge maze, heading toward the nearby path to the fruit orchard.

Amelia wandered, lost in thought, heedless of the time, until the small noise of a twig snapping jolted her out of her reverie.

She spun in a circle, startled to see she'd wandered much farther than she'd intended. She had meant to stay in sight of the house, but now all she could see were trees and unkempt shrubbery. Pinpricks of apprehension assailed her before she took a deep breath and forced herself to get her bearings. The house couldn't be that far away. She would start back now and meet everyone on the south lawn a little late.

It wasn't until she heard leaves being crushed behind her that Amelia realized how foolish she had been. Not bothering to turn she ran, blood pounding in her ears.

She'd not gotten more than a few steps when large hands seized her, pulling her into an unbreakable embrace.

CHAPTER 8

Gideon caught Amelia easily, stopping her with a firm grip on her upper arms. Then he remembered the bruises he'd seen on her. Forcing himself to relax his hold, he held her a little away from him. But he didn't let go of her. He didn't want to.

"Gideon!" Amelia stared at him in openmouthed surprise. "I mean, my lord, what are you doing here?"

He tried to come up with a civil answer, but his temper was hanging by a thread. He'd been up all night trying to find out where Amelia had gone with no luck. Even Clarke's impressive social contacts and network of household spies had run dry. It wasn't until they had found a footman in Viscount Worthing's household willing to take a bribe that they'd learned he and Amelia had departed for Lord Westcliff's estate a few hours outside of London.

Gideon had arrived just in time to hear Worthing propose to Amelia. His sudden thundering heartbeat had been louder than the words that followed—although he had heard Sir Clarence's name mentioned. He had no idea what her reply had been, and he hadn't stayed to confront them because Lady Westcliff had come down the hallway just then.

He'd hoped coming outside would calm his overheated blood.

Instead, it had afforded him the opportunity he had long sought—to have Amelia alone. But he couldn't proceed with his plan to charm the truth out of her. All his eloquence and restraint had been burned away.

"Are you going to do it?" he asked, unable to keep the bite from his voice.

"Am I going to do what?" she asked, looking up at him with a dazed expression.

"Are you going to *marry* Worthing?" he ground out from behind clenched teeth.

Amelia's lovely lips parted, but she didn't say anything in reply.

"Damn it to hell," he swore, crushing her to him.

Her scent of clean soap and jasmine had been driving him crazy since that first ball. It enveloped him, teasing his senses until it seemed as if his skin was marked with traces of it. Every hair on his body stood on end. He was too hot, but he had a solution now. His mouth descended on hers with a hunger so ravenous it blinded him.

He moved his hands to cradle her face, deepening the kiss. Gideon poured every ounce of his pent-up energy and heat into her. He licked her soft lips, probing and parting them with his tongue until they opened enough for him to slip inside.

Her taste was indescribable. It was sweet and intoxicating, more potent than any wine.

The little sound Amelia made as she melted against him vibrated deep within him. This was what he'd wanted from the moment he'd seen her. He knew that now. Part of him hated himself for it, but it was easy to ignore when he was holding her in his arms.

His arousal was almost painful. It was pressed against her, but he couldn't feel her heat through the volume of her skirts and petticoats.

Just a little bit more. He reached down, ready to pull the layers of fabric up so he could reach for the wet heat he knew was waiting for him. Having her was all that mattered.

Gideon was trying to justify taking her down to the ground when the sound of something crashing through the undergrowth only a few yards away interrupted them.

He swore, snapping his head up and pushing Amelia behind him.

"What is it?" she whispered, her hand reaching around his waist to press against the front of his greatcoat.

"Some sort of animal," he said in a murmur, keeping his voice soft in case he startled it.

Given the noise it made, the creature was very large, possibly a boar. Keeping his eyes trained on the source of the noise, he bent to pick up a fallen branch. Walking with soundless steps, he moved toward it, ready to swing his makeshift weapon in case the animal charged. He rounded the trunk of the thick oak only to hear rapidly retreating footsteps and the sound of more shrubbery being crushed and broken.

As the sound retreated, he turned back to Amelia, walking back to her quickly and taking her by the arm. Her face was no longer flushed with passion. She was pale and her eyes were wide.

"We need to head back to the house in case it comes back."

"What do you think it was?" she asked, quickening her steps to match his brisk pace.

"Most likely a boar. They're common enough in these parts and can be quite dangerous." He scowled at her suddenly. "You shouldn't have been walking so far from the house on your own."

"I was just…thinking."

"About marrying Worthing?"

"No, of course not," she said, quickening her step to keep up with him. "Crispin is my friend, nothing more."

"Do all your friends propose marriage on a regular basis?" he asked, still annoyed.

"No. I mean, yes. Crispin does, but only from a sense of obligation. He wants to protect me."

He snorted derisively. "I'm sure that's all he wants," he said, before a flash of guilt passed through him. He was the one who'd been about to ravage Amelia here in the woods where anyone could have come upon them, not just an animal.

Swallowing his frustration, he slowed down so she wouldn't be obliged to run beside him. "I need to apologize for what just happened. I'm not myself..."

It was the lamest excuse he'd ever given a woman, but he couldn't think of better one. And it was his fault. Amelia *did* something to him. Every time she was near, his mind turned to soup, laying waste to his carefully detailed plans and questions.

I'm becoming a bloody milksop, he thought as the house appeared ahead.

"You never told me what you were doing here," she said tremulously, peeking at him with a sideways glance that did nothing to cool the ardor still burning under the surface of his skin.

"I have recently begun to do business with Westcliff. I came to discuss some issues I have with a recent joint venture," he said, using the excuse he had foisted on his surprised host when he'd shown up unexpectedly on his doorstep this morning.

Westcliff had been caught off guard when he arrived, but when Gideon launched into a detailed list of questions and concerns regarding their most recent enterprise, the questions in the other man's eyes faded. He assumed, as Gideon wanted him to, that the new Earl of Flint was poorly versed in business affairs and had come to be reassured by a more knowledgeable investor. Meanwhile, Gideon pretended surprise at finding himself at a country party.

"Lady Westcliff invited me to join in the festivities," he added, searching her face for a reaction to their kiss, but Amelia's face was carefully blank.

"Is Sir Clarence the threat Worthing is trying to protect you from?'

"Did you hear that?" Amelia sounded alarmed by the prospect he had eavesdropped on her conversation.

"I just caught his name," he assured her. "Lady Westcliff came down the hallway haranguing a maid. I decided not to interrupt you or embarrass our kind hostess by letting her know I witnessed her reprimanding a member of her staff...so is it true? Has Sir Clarence been harassing you in some way?"

She looked down, her face was troubled.

"Amelia, it's time to tell me what is going on."

She paused, but his patience was rewarded. "He wants me to remarry."

"Sir Clarence?" he clarified.

"Yes, that is why Crispin proposed just now. He promised Martin he would take care of me, and he believes that is the most effective way to do it."

"Who does Sir Clarence want you to marry?"

"Lord Cannonburry."

"*Elmer Cannonburry*?" he asked in disbelief. "The man is older than Methuselah. And he suffers from chronically poor health. Cannonburry may not live another year, two at the most. Why in the world would Clarence want you to marry a man with one foot in the grave?"

Not to mention the rumors of impotence.

"That's a slight exaggeration," she chided. "And I'm not certain why. My guess is Sir Clarence believes he's found some legal maneuver to transfer some of my inheritance to himself."

"Your dowry?"

"No, he has that already. I'm talking about my personal fortune—the one only I control."

"Hmm…I suppose that makes sense. Sir Clarence let slip something about the arrangements your father made long ago. He was… irritated," he said, softening the amount of ire his uncle had displayed. "And now my uncle has found an ally who is willing to turn over some of those funds to him."

Gideon should have been surprised that his nearest relation was trying some underhanded trickery to manipulate Amelia, but he wasn't. Money and position had always been the most important things to his uncle. Sir Clarence had never believed in a woman's right to direct her own fortune.

Marriage should have transferred control of those funds to her husband, but Amelia's canny parent had been prepared for such a possibility.

"Your father must have loved you very much," he said suddenly.

She stopped short and blinked. "Yes, he did."

She was still staring at him when Worthing hurried up. "Amelia, dear, we were starting to worry. You were supposed to join us half an hour ago." He nodded in the direction of the other guests, who were enjoying a picnic near the entrance of the estate's famous hedge maze.

"I was lost in thought and didn't realize how far I wandered in the woods. Lord Flint found me and kindly offered to escort me back."

"And prevented you from encountering a boar or something equally dangerous. You should have stayed in the house," Gideon couldn't help adding waspishly.

"On that, we are in total agreement! A boar. Dear lord, what a narrow escape. So what brings you out to this corner of England, Lord Flint?" Worthing asked with a poor imitation of welcoming joviality.

"Business with our host," he said shortly, walking along with the pair until they reached the other guests.

A waiter hurried over with a glass of champagne. He took it, wishing it were something stronger.

"Well, I'm pleased you were able to join us," Amelia said with a soft smile as Worthing helped her settle on the blankets stretched onto the lawn. She spread out her skirts and accepted a plate from her neighbor.

With easy grace, Gideon settled down across from her, noting with satisfaction the flicker of irritation cross Worthing's face. He ignored the man, focusing all his attention on Amelia.

The soft rosy flush on her cheeks extended all the way down to her décolletage. It was an unholy temptation, mocking him with the irresistible urge to find out how far down that blush went.

CHAPTER 9

By the time the picnic ended, Gideon had gotten ahold of his rampant lust. He berated himself for falling for Amelia's charms like some lovestruck dandy.

What is wrong with me?

It wasn't like him to fall under the spell of a woman. In the past, he was always the one who ended romantic liaisons, usually when it became clear that the woman involved desired more than he was willing to offer.

His desire for Amelia was nothing like what he'd felt for his former lovers. The almost violent nature of his passions cast the entirety of his previous relationships in the shade. He found the fact that the focus of all this maelstrom of emotions was a woman of dubious character distinctly unsettling.

He had yet to establish if Amelia was involved in his cousin's death. Until he knew what had happened that day, he couldn't allow himself to give in to his baser desires. *And if she's not guilty of any wrongdoing, I still have to stay away.*

She was Martin's widow, for Pete's sake. He had no business kissing her, let alone contemplating an affair.

At least she was starting to trust him. Today he had learned one of her secrets—hers and Sir Clarence.

Elmer Cannonburry. What the devil was his uncle thinking? The idea of a young and vibrant woman like Amelia in the arms of that old fossil was disturbing on several levels.

Gideon didn't stop to ask himself why it bothered him so much. Very old men frequently married girls fresh out of the schoolroom. He didn't approve of the practice, but such marriages were common in the ton. Only it was clear Amelia didn't want this one.

As a young girl, Amelia hadn't had much of a choice who she married, but as a widow, she had the right to decide the course of her life. Whatever machinations his uncle had planned couldn't possibly work now.

At least he had an explanation for her most recent behavior. Worthing was right. Amelia was throwing herself into the social whirl to avoid Sir Clarence's ill-conceived matchmaking. The poor girl had grown up criticized and belittled by his nearest relation. The fact she still lived in fear of him stirred his pity.

Rolling his shoulders, he slipped away from the other guests to confer with Manning, his valet. The former cockney errand boy had originally begun as his father's valet when he was a young man. Though he was now getting on in years, his loyalty and discretion ensured Gideon kept him on despite his recent elevation to the earldom.

Manning had arrived late this afternoon with his travel carriage and a trunk packed for a week's stay. Gideon had been grateful for the change of clothes, as well as the other invaluable services Manning provided. The grey-haired manservant had proven quite adept at gleaning information from other servants during his time on the continent. It was a skill he hoped had proved useful now.

"Did you learn anything?" he asked as soon as he reached the privacy of his room to change.

Manning's long face grew impossibly longer. "I'm afraid Viscount Worthing's man, Simpson, proved to be a difficult nut to crack. He wasn't in a particularly talkative mood earlier. Didn't take kindly to the offer to gossip about his employer. Man's a bit high in the instep for a servant."

"Did he rebuff you?" Gideon frowned. Manning was usually subtle when it came to this sort of thing.

"I let one of the new housemaids do the questioning," Tom replied. "The staff was quite eager to gossip about Mrs. Montgomery, but her maid pretended not to speak English so they turned to his lordship's valet without success."

Gideon scowled as Manning helped him with his waistcoat. "Blast. Loyalty is commendable in your own servants but decidedly inconvenient in anyone else's."

Manning nodded. "Don't lose heart yet. I haven't given up. I brought a bit of your least expensive brandy to share with the other servants and housekeeper this evening. I'm hoping it will loosen Simpson's tongue."

"You're welcome to the most expensive bottle I have if you can get the man to talk about his master's reaction to Martin's death. I would also like to know his exact whereabouts at the time of the accident."

"I thought you established Lord Worthing was out visiting his tenants when it happened."

"That's what I was told by those servants who left Amelia's household just after the accident, but I would like corroboration from someone in Worthing's employ. Anything you learn about his relationship with my cousin would be of note. Amelia insists they were good friends, which I find hard to believe."

"It could be the truth, but it doesn't mean there wasn't an affair. Your cousin might simply have been ignorant of it."

Gideon nodded, acknowledging the possibility. "Martin always was a bit naive when it came to the darker side of men's natures. He tended to believe the best of people," he muttered, adjusting his cravat. "One last thing. Find out if Amelia is warming Worthing's bed now if you can."

Something in his voice must have alerted Manning. "Err…I thought you were convinced she was."

"So goes the gossip, but I'm no longer certain," he admitted as Manning straightened his coat.

"I will do my best to learn whatever I can."

"Good." Gideon nodded at him. After a few more minutes of conversation and adjustments to his attire, he headed back downstairs for dinner.

Despite the upheaval of his emotions, it wasn't too difficult to pretend he was like all the other male guests—a privileged and jaded nobleman seeking to relieve his boredom with country entertainments. Interminable cases of ennui were a popular affectation among his class, and for a former spy of his experience, easy to emulate.

At dinner, he was seated directly across from his hostess—too far from Amelia and Worthing to even consider conversing with them. Normally being situated so far from the subject of an investigation would have been enough to annoy him, but in this case, he used the opportunity to shore up his resistance to Amelia's charms.

If only there weren't so many damned charms. His quarry was looking especially lovely tonight. She wore a lovely silk damask dress the color of deep violet. The creamy silk of her skin seemed to glow in the candlelight. It was a challenge not to stare at her—one other men did not seem to mind failing. One man, a young and gangly baron name Bruxton, was practically drooling.

Amelia pretended not to notice the attention. She conversed with Worthing and her neighbors, only occasionally peeking toward the head of the table to look at him and their hosts.

After dinner, the women retired so the men could enjoy their port. After, the two groups met again for cards and subdued conversation in the main salon. Gideon thought he'd acquitted himself quite well until later that night after Amelia and most of the other women had retired.

The men drifted into the billiards room. Gossip and spirits flowed freely. At first, Gideon was hopeful Worthing would soon be in his cups. Unfortunately, his nemesis decided to focus on the game instead of his drink.

"I was surprised to see you here," Worthing confided as he leaned over the table to align his shot.

Gideon stood near the other end, cue in hand. "I wanted to speak to our host," he said.

"Mmm-hmm." Westcliff gulped the brandy he was drinking. He made an approving sound in the back of his throat. "Yes, we are partners in a new consortium. Flint here had a few questions about it. Came to me to clear them up," he said, managing to sound more paternal than boastful.

"Your expertise in the matter was enormously helpful," Gideon assured him, bending to align his cue when Worthing's ball bounced on the bumper, missing the pocket.

Gideon sank his ball effortlessly and walked around for the next shot while their host preened.

"How fortunate that your business with Westcliff coincided with his seasonal house party," Worthing said, not bothering to inject any enthusiasm in his voice.

"It was lucky, wasn't it?" Gideon said blandly, sinking the next ball neatly. With a vindictive little flourish, he proceeded to clear the table.

"Congratulations," Worthing said with a courtly bow better suited to a drawing room—and directed at a female matriarch.

Gideon acknowledged that with a nod. The glitter of something gold on Worthing's breast caught his eye.

It can't be. He narrowed his eyes, staring at the small ornament in the shape of a key on Worthing's waistcoat.

"That's an interesting pin," he said, a hollow feeling growing in the pit of his stomach. "Where did you get it?"

Worthing stiffened. His hand went to his waistcoat, covering the key in an abrupt instinctive move. "My father gave it to me."

He was lying, and they both knew it. "Did he? Was he very good at maths?"

"Maths?"

Gideon could see the small flicker of panic that crossed Worthing's face.

"Why yes, he was quite good at them. This is a school prize."

Except that pin is given as the classics prize at Abingdon—not mathematics. Martin had been inordinately proud of it. Literature was the one field he excelled in. He'd been a miserable mathematics student.

The realization that Amelia had given Worthing one of Martin's most prized possessions settled in his gut like a lead weight.

"Would you all excuse me? I seem to have developed the headache." He exited the room abruptly, heedless of the reaction of his host and the other assembled gentlemen.

Once he was alone he took a deep breath, but it did little to calm him. The slow burn kindling in his breast was building into a towering rage. He stalked off, intent on getting as far away from the other guests as possible. It was a move that guaranteed he meet the last person he should be near.

"Gideon."

He spun on his heel to find Amelia standing alone in the dimly lit hallway.

Unable to form a civil greeting, he stared down at her. She hesitated, her lips forming words she did not let fall.

"Yes?" he asked coldly.

"I…err…Lord Westcliff has a fine conservatory. I thought you might enjoy taking a turn with me."

His stomach was roiling. He swallowed heavily before straightening his spine. "I don't think that would be appropriate."

Amelia drew back, visibly stung by the coldness in his voice.

"Oh, I see."

Gideon fought to keep an even tone, but it was difficult with his composure in threads. "No, I don't think you do. I regret I gave you the wrong impression today in the woods, but I don't intend to share your bed tonight or any other night. It's a little too crowded for my taste."

Amelia's mouth parted, a shocked look on her face. She blinked rapidly before spinning on her heel and running away.

Muscles tensing, Gideon forced himself not to run after her. *Would a cold-blooded killer be so sensitive?*

CHAPTER 10

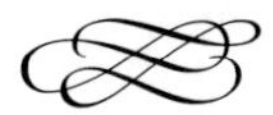

Amelia flew up the stairs. It felt like she had been struck, a body blow that was threatening to knock her to the floor.

Reaching her room, she dismissed her maid. As soon as the door closed behind Carlotta, Amelia flung herself down on the bed. Hugging a pillow to her stomach, she let the violent storm of tears overtake her.

How could Gideon say those things? What had happened between now and this afternoon to change his opinion of her so radically?

He had kissed her. Though she wasn't overly familiar with it, she thought she had glimpsed sincere desire in his eyes. His embrace had been more fervent than that Italian count in Modena who had tried to lure her into an illicit liaison during her honeymoon.

Amelia had told herself not to dream, but despite her stern lecture, she had managed to build an entire future around that one kiss. For one glittering moment, anything had seemed possible. The impossible fantasy she had spun since childhood, one of a future with Gideon, almost seemed within her grasp.

But now her dream was a pile of glass shards at her feet.

It's your own fault. She had let herself hope, and despite her great wealth, that had been a luxury she had never been able to afford.

Amelia wiped away the tears with a rough hand. There were always plenty of members of society ready to spread lies and innuendo about her, but she had thought Gideon was above listening to them. Clearly some viper had been whispering in his ear tonight. It was only to be expected. She was deeply unpopular among the ton. There were several ladies present who would love to fix the earl's attentions on themselves. The fact Gideon had believed whatever lie they had told meant she had overestimated both his intelligence and noble nature.

A little shudder passed through her, but she ignored it. Taking a deep breath, she sat up. She no longer had Martin, but she still had her pride. Gideon could choose to believe the lies about her, but he wasn't going to get away with belittling her. In the morning, she would take him aside and give him a dressing down he would never forget.

Hardened by her resolution, she began to undress and prepare for sleep. It was still early. With luck, none of the other guests had returned to their rooms in time to hear her cry. Whatever spiteful creature had been gossiping about her would only be too happy to spread the tale of her tears. *From notorious to pitiful in one evening.*

It was unlikely anyone was about. Everyone was still downstairs playing cards and drinking. They would not have come back upstairs yet—not unless they had pre-arranged a tryst in their bedroom.

The convenient access to bedrooms explained why country parties were so popular despite the largely insipid entertainments. Affairs and illicit rendezvous were much easier to conduct away from the watchful eyes in town.

Amelia put down the pillow she was holding on the empty bed with a snort. The only crowded thing about it was the abundance of cushions. Their hostess was very fond of tiny embroidered pillows and velvet bolsters. She felt the irony of her situation bite deep.

With a little more energy than was strictly necessary, she tossed the many pillows aside and climbed into bed. She lay there staring at the canopy for some minutes. After a few more moments of feeling sorry for herself, she fell back on the trick her father had taught her to quiet her mind.

The yearly compound interest of fifty thousand pounds is two thousand. The interest on sixty thousand pounds is twenty-four hundred pounds.

Amelia continued calculating interest until she was numb, the pain of her confrontation with Gideon receding into the background. Hollowed out and empty, she fell asleep.

Several hours later, a noise startled her awake. She opened her eyes, expecting to hear one of the other guests in the hallway, but the crashing sound that followed was not some drunk reveler stumbling to their room.

Someone was pounding on her door. The force was enough to make the wood vibrate in the jamb.

Bang! Bang!

Amelia gasped as the wood shuddered in the bright moonlight illuminating that part of the room.

Good Lord, the house must be on fire. Scrambling out of bed, she threw on her pelisse over her bed jacket and hurried to the door.

"I'm coming," she called out.

The door shook once more. It was so violent that Amelia hesitated for a moment. Whoever was on the other side was massive and agitated. Fear tightened her chest, but she shook off her apprehension and went to open the door.

She threw it open, expecting to see a footman or Lord Westcliff on the other side. There was no one there. Confused, she peeked out, scanning the empty hallway.

Rushing footsteps signaled the approach of a pair. Mrs. Kimball, another widow, rushed up with a man she recognized as Lord Windmere. The much younger man was adjusting his waistcoat and trousers.

"What was that noise?" Mrs. Kimball asked.

"I don't know. Is the house on fire?"

"No. We just heard the pounding and…er…we ran upstairs to see what the matter was."

Comprehending that the pair had exited one of the bedrooms farther down the hall, she nodded nonetheless. She pulled the pelisse closed tight wondering who had been knocking at her door.

The murmur of conversation grew in volume as more and more guests gathered. "What was that racket?" a newcomer asked.

"Someone was pounding on Mrs. Montgomery's door. I think they were trying to break it down," young Lord Windmere said, the excitement in his voice growing with the promise of scandal.

"I'm sure that's not the case. Perhaps there's an emergency," she said, looking around for Gideon.

He wasn't there, but Crispin was running up the hallway with Lord Westcliff at his heels.

"Amelia! What's going on? Who attacked you?"

"No one, there's been a mistake. Someone was knocking on my door is all."

Amelia wasn't sure he could even hear her. The volume of the conversation around them had grown precipitously. She continued to assure him everything was fine, but Crispin did not pay her any mind.

"Excuse me, my dear." Lord Westcliff was frowning. He stepped around her, pulling the door closed.

A little wave of dizziness blurred her vision. She forced herself to focus, a familiar dread creeping up her spine.

Whoever had struck the thick oak door had done so with enough force to splinter it in the center—someone *very* strong.

CHAPTER 11

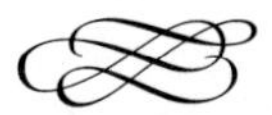

"What are you saying?"

Gideon's head was aching. He could not make out what his valet was telling him.

After he'd confronted Amelia, he had gone into Westcliff's library. He then proceeded to consume most of a bottle of brandy he had found there. Sometime near dawn, he had finally made it upstairs and collapsed in bed without talking to anyone. Now the aftereffects of his long night of drinking were making themselves felt.

Manning looked at him with a frown. "You missed all the excitement. Someone tried to break into Mrs. Montgomery's room last night."

Gideon sat bolt upright. "*What?*"

"According to the household servants, Lord Westcliff is beside himself. A man broke into the house last night. No one saw the intruder, but the villain somehow made his way up to the guest hallway. He must have been trying to find one of the ladies alone up there. Mrs. Montgomery had locked her door, so he was not able to ravish her. The door was badly damaged so determined was the villain, but he ran away when the racket attracted an audience."

"Good God." The pounding in his head retreated to the background. He swallowed heavily. "Is she all right?"

"I believe so. Lord Westcliff was most apologetic. He put her in another room with a footman stationed outside to guard all night. Her maid was roused to share her room as well. In fact, most of the women elected to have a maid in their room last night."

His mind was reeling. "I can't believe I didn't hear a thing."

"Well, the library is in another part of the house," Manning said with a little grimace. "Mrs. Montgomery was understandably unsettled. Lord Worthing escorted her and another lady back to town early this morning."

A knock sounded at the door.

"That should be the breakfast tray I ordered. I assumed you wouldn't want to go down to breakfast this morning."

"Thank you. Start packing; we will be leaving within the hour," he said as Manning let the maid inside with the tray.

"Are you sure that is wise?" Manning asked once the girl had left. "Riding with a sore head will be most uncomfortable."

"My own fault," Gideon muttered in between bites of toast. He had let his temper get the best of him last night. In a fit of self-indulgence, he had incapacitated himself during an actual crime.

"I'm going to have a look at the door that was damaged. Then we're leaving."

"Yes, my lord. I'll have everything ready."

A few minutes later, Gideon was standing in the guest hallway.

"What the devil happened here?" He hadn't been expecting an answer, but Westcliff came up behind him.

"I was hoping you would tell me."

Gideon swung around to face his host. "What the hell does that mean?"

"Err…well, one of the servants mentioned that you and Mrs. Montgomery had a small disagreement last night. Perhaps you went to go see her last night after overindulging in some of the fine brandy I keep in the library?

"This wasn't me." Gideon traced the splintered wood. A reddish dust lined the fissure. He felt the texture of it between his fingers, a considering frown on his face.

Westcliff cleared his throat. "Are you sure you recall all last evening? Someone almost broke this door down and then tore through the garden." He sounded almost hopeful.

Gideon held up his gloveless hands. "I admit I owe you a new bottle of brandy, but I don't owe you a new door. You still have a housebreaker to find."

His knuckles didn't have a single mark on them. If he'd been the one in the hallway last night, his hands would bear some bruises or cuts, so great was the violence done to the door.

"Oh, I see." Westcliff's face clouded. "Well...your boots did look a bit small for the prints we found."

Gideon paused. "You found prints? Are they inside the house?"

"No. They're in the garden."

"*Show me.*"

The marks in the muddy garden were massive. He and Westcliff were leaning over them, marveling at their size.

"The servants are in an uproar," his host confided in a murmur. "They are whispering about giants."

"I can see why." Gideon shook his head. "But these prints are too large for any man."

Westcliff straightened. "You think these are manufactured? Someone fabricated them?"

Gideon rose, scrutinizing the marks in the mud with a critical eye. Even the tallest man he had met did not have feet on this scale. "I believe so. The scale is impossible. If a man this size was wandering the countryside, you would have heard of him. There is no way such a person could've escaped the locals notice."

"I suppose you are correct. But who would do such a thing?"

Gideon shrugged. "Some miscreant youths having a lark. I wouldn't be surprised if a wager was involved."

"A wager and a considerable amount of alcohol, I suspect," Westcliff scoffed. "They must have guessed that with so many guests, they could slip in and out and stage this scene with little chance of getting caught. It was a crime of opportunity. In a way, it's a relief. I would hate to think someone was intentionally targeting a female guest."

Though it was his suggestion, Gideon couldn't let Westcliff blindly accept that this was the act of young men bent on mischief. "I wouldn't let my guard down if I were you. Post men around the house for the next few weeks. Whether a bet was involved or not—breaking into the house was a step too far."

"Agreed. What are young people coming to?" Westcliff shook his head and thanked him for his advice. With an air of exhausted resignation, he went back inside the house.

Gideon bent down once more, measuring the length of the boot print with his hands before dismissing them once more. The miscreant who created these had miscalculated when he made them unrealistically large.

His conscience pricked him at the thought of leaving. By rights, he should have stayed behind to help Westcliff find the fools responsible for this business. But the women they had almost victimized was no longer here.

Amelia could have been hurt, or worse. Regardless of what he'd learned last night, she didn't deserve to be terrorized.

Yet she deserves to hang?

Stop it. He hadn't proved her guilty one way or the other. And he wasn't going to discover the answer here in the country.

Gideon was on the road a few minutes later.

AMELIA THREW a pair of shoes in a trunk with a thump, silently cursing Gideon's name. Not only had he insulted her character, but he had tried to terrify her at Westcliff manor.

Except it hadn't achieved his desired result. Amelia wasn't afraid or ashamed. She was furious.

Strangely enough, Crispin had defended him when he had dropped her at her townhouse.

"He must have been intoxicated," he said. "Luckily for everyone involved, the earl must have regained his senses and taken himself off before anyone spotted him knocking at your door."

Crispin had gone on to imply that Gideon had experienced some sort of upset at the billiards game, but wouldn't elaborate on what it was.

She had nodded in agreement, but Amelia no longer cared about what Gideon was thinking or even the threat of scandal. The incident at Westcliff's had given her the final push she needed. She was leaving London and the hypocrisy of the ton behind.

The war with Napoleon made travel to Italy impossible, but that didn't mean she had to subject herself to the scorn of society any longer—and Gideon could hang.

Amelia was going home.

She was still supervising the packing of her trunk when a great commotion sounded below stairs.

"Carlotta, go see what is happening," she said, rising from her settee.

Her maid returned less than a minute later.

"The Earl of Flint is downstairs. He insists on seeing you immediately," Carlotta said in Italian.

Of all the… How dare that man show his face here!

Amelia had had enough. It was bad enough she was forced to endure the slings and barbs of society. She would not endure that sort of treatment from Gideon. *Or worse,* she thought, remembering he had tried to knock her door down in a drunken fit.

You have nothing to fear, she told herself bracingly. *It was only the drink.*

She had seen firsthand how spirits could affect an otherwise gentle and reasonable man. Gideon may have shown his true colors at the Westcliff estate, but he would never harm her when he was sober. She knew him well enough to believe that at least.

Carlotta shifted uncertainly. "Shall I send him away, signora?"

"No." Amelia's decision was made. "I will see him. Put him in the parlor."

"You do not want help dressing?"

"No," she said, putting on a thick robe over her nightshift. If Gideon was going to be offended at seeing her in her nightclothes, then he shouldn't have come calling at this hour.

Ignoring the lingering sense of betrayal she felt at the accusation he'd flung at her last night, Amelia swept down the stairs in high dudgeon, preparing herself for battle.

The door was standing open, so he didn't hear her approach. For a moment, she watched him. Gideon was pacing, making the parlor appear much smaller than it really was. He filled the room, seeming to take up all the space and most the air with little effort.

He was like the caged tiger she had seen on the estate of an Italian duke. Like that beast, he prowled restlessly, giving the impression that iron bars would be no barrier to being pounced on and mauled.

Trepidation made her hesitate. Crispin was right. Gideon was no longer the young man she knew. She didn't know him at all. There was too much masculine strength and fury trapped in his powerful form. It had only been a matter of time before that power lashed out at her.

It was the way of most men. She had let herself forget that.

A shudder passed through her when he turned and saw her. The intensity in his expression took her breath away. It was one thing to imagine all the clever insults she would use against him. It was another to say them to his face.

She was silent too long.

"Are you well?" he asked.

That wasn't what she had been expecting, but his tone was not one of concern. It was charged with too many emotions for her to define a single one.

Martin is no longer here to slay your dragons. She had to do this herself.

Amelia swallowed hard, but when she finally found her tongue, it was sufficiently sharp. "Am I to believe you burst into my home at this hour of the night to ask after my health?"

"*No.*"

He faced her, standing straighter. It made him seem even larger. "I came here to learn the truth about the day Martin died. No more lies. No more secrets."

She had known the question was coming, but her skin prickled and grew colder anyway.

"You're no different from all those societal parasites who whisper their lies about me behind my back. You think I killed him."

Gideon's mouth tightened. "I didn't say that."

"You didn't have to! Your actions speak for you."

His brow creased. "My actions?"

Amelia took a steadying breath, but her hand trembled as she pointed at him. "You have a lot of nerve to confront me like this after what you did last night," she accused.

Gideon stopped short, confusion flickering on his face—and sympathy. "I realize you had a fright at Westcliff's, but you don't honestly believe I was the one knocking on your door?"

"You deny it?"

"Of course I bloody deny it! I admit I was angry with you, but I would never behave in such a disgraceful manner no matter how deep I was in my cups." His words rang with self-righteous indignation.

Amelia ran her eyes over his face, trying to decide if he was telling the truth.

"Do you doubt my word?" he asked.

She wanted to say yes. Somehow, she knew that it would hurt him. But she couldn't bring herself to lie, so she said nothing.

His eyes widened. "It was not me. I swear it on Martin's life."

Tears flooded her eyes, and she wrapped her hands tightly around herself. "I hate you for what you said."

"Then tell me how Martin died. I promise you will never have to see me again."

She ignored the stabbing pain somewhere near her heart. "He fell down the stairs."

His breath was ragged. "Did someone help him down the stairs? Worthing, perhaps?"

She shook her head violently. "How can you say such a terrible thing? Crispin adored him, and the feeling was mutual."

He stepped up to her. "You know, the latter may be true to the best of your knowledge. Martin was an innocent and naive young man. He did not see the truth of people until it was too late. Worthing would not have had to expend much effort to fool him."

His face was like stone as he towered over her. "On the day Martin died, you came home from your morning calls. You found him at the bottom of the stairs—and you said *This is all my fault*."

How did he know that? Had he been making inquiries about her? Spying on her?

"I don't remember saying that," she said, pressing her hands together.

It was the truth, although those words were familiar. They had become an almost daily refrain in her thoughts for the past year.

"Are you and Worthing lovers?" Gideon's voice was ragged, as if the question had been ripped from his very core.

"No!"

His hands opened and closed as if he was contemplating strangling her. "I know you are lying because I saw the pin myself," he said, his jaw so stiff she thought it would break.

"What pin?"

"The one awarded for the Classics prize at Abingdon. It was one of Martin's most-treasured possessions. He was inordinately proud of it and always wore it. I know because I nicked it once as a lark when I visited his rooms at the school. I felt terrible when he tore his room apart afterward. He was frantic to find it."

Gideon took her by the arm, his grip biting into her forearm. "The only person Martin would have given it to is you, his wife. And you gave it to your lover."

"*I did not.*"

"So I'm supposed to believe Martin gave it to Worthing?"

"*Yes, you fool*. They were close!"

"Don't try to fob me off with that Banbury tale. The prize meant everything to Martin—more so because Sir Clarence derided it. Martin would never have given it away to a mere friend. And now Worthing wears it like some sort of blasted souvenir of his conquest."

Amelia clenched her fists and leaned forward. "Martin gave that pin to Crispin. I saw him do it. I was there!"

Gideon stared down at her furiously, raising his hand. She flinched and took a quick step back.

He hesitated, his eyes flaring with an intense heat. Reaching out, he took hold of her hair. His grip was not painful as he pulled her inexorably toward him.

His mouth came down on hers. Shocked, she froze, but his kiss was as relentless as the rest of him. As potent as any drug, it demanded a response. She tried to give him the one her conscience demanded. She beat on his chest with her fists and tried to claw his face before he caught her hands in his.

Amelia expected his grip to tighten so he could lord his superior strength over her, but to her surprise, he let her hands go. Instead, he stroked down her back, coaxing her against him. A flash of awareness came and went. She had melted against him, her token resistance burned away by the heat of his passion. His mouth was robbing her good sense, plundering and claiming with a skill she had never dreamed existed, let alone experienced.

Gideon raised his head. He moved his hands up to the sides of her face. There was a visible tremor in his fingers.

"Do you want me?"

Amelia was shaking from head to foot, but her "*Yes,*" was clear enough. Her trembling hands rested briefly on Gideon's shoulders before she snatched them back like they had scalded her.

Her assent had freed Gideon from whatever gentlemanly restraint had been holding him back. He carried her to the floor, covering her body with his. His mouth flamed over her mouth, his tongue teasing until she parted her lips.

She whimpered as his taste filled her mouth. His response to the small sound was telling. He rocked against her, his hands shifting clothing and exposing her.

She should have been chilled by the cool night air, but all she felt was heat. He caressed her with rough hands, but she could not have borne gentleness from him. Not then.

Somehow, Amelia had developed a second heartbeat. To her shame, it was between her legs. The flesh there had grown moist. As Gideon's fingers moved over her, tracing patterns in the moisture he found there, she could feel herself pulsing under his touch.

There was a rustle of fabric as Gideon unfastened his trousers. In the next moment, he had fitted himself between her legs with a husky groan.

"Gideon, what are you doing?" Why wasn't he moving down her body?

Amelia thought they were going to make love, but he was pressing his heated member against her where his mouth should have been.

At first, the delicious weight of him felt good, but something was wrong. The blunt pressure of his staff was starting to hurt. "Gideon, I don't mean to tell you your business, but I think you are going about this the wrong way," she said in a thin voice.

He stopped, holding himself in check with a supreme effort of will. "Have you changed your mind?"

A shudder racked his body. She couldn't begin to guess what those words had cost him. "*No.* It's just..."

"Then this is all right—Martin will forgive us. I can feel your need. You're so hot and wet for me. I'm going to take care of you—I'll make you forget the viscount," he vowed.

"Forget him?" Surely he still didn't believe she would ever let Crispin touch her so intimately?

Gideon didn't answer. Instead, he pushed his hips against her, thrusting deep inside her body in a single stroke.

All the heated pleasure incited by his touch vanished abruptly. The sharp pain overwhelmed her senses and made her body arch violently.

"Amelia?" Gideon sounded bewildered. His dark burning gaze was boring a hole into her. It was as if he could see directly into her soul. "What's wrong? Did I hurt you?"

The pain made her eyes tear. She pushed at his shoulders. "Get off me!"

He swore heavily, trying to soothe her ineffectually by stroking her shoulders. But she was having none of it.

"I said get off me."

For a second, he didn't respond. He seemed utterly bewildered by her response. Another shove and he finally moved. The strangled gasp she gave as his body lifted from hers seemed to hit him like a blow. He flinched, his shoulders drawing down.

Ever so slowly, he stood. His clothes were in disarray, but he made no move to right them. Gideon just stared at her, his face waxen. From some unseen pocket, he produced a handkerchief. Surreptitiously wiping himself clean, he looked down at the blood staining the pristine white cloth.

This was too much. She loved him so much, but all he felt for her was contempt.

"You did it on purpose, to punish me," Amelia flung at him, the pain and confusion evident in her voice.

She got to her feet, shakily covering her legs with the skirt of her gown. "I thought you wanted to make love."

Gideon stared at her as if she was some apparition from beyond the grave.

"Amelia," he whispered. "We *were* making love."

He looked back down at the blood staining the handkerchief, and his eyes widened.

"I don't understand. You were married to Martin for years. How could you possibly still be a virgin?"

Amelia could feel the blood draining from her face. She swayed on her feet.

Gideon's arms reached out, but she steadied herself and ran toward the door.

"Amelia!"

"Never come back here. I never want to see you again." She flew up the stairs, locking herself in her chambers.

CHAPTER 12

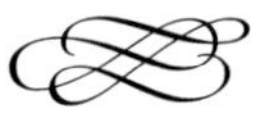

What have I done? Gideon fastened his trousers, his mind reeling.

He stared down at the bloody handkerchief before shoving it into his pocket. Though he didn't fully understand what happened, he had managed to hurt Amelia very badly tonight.

And last night as well. He sucked in a deep breath as the suffocating twin weights of grief and confusion crashed down on him.

Amelia had been married to his cousin when they were both eighteen. Martin had died *years* later. All his letters had been full of affection and praise for his clever and kind bride. Theirs had been an affectionate and loving marriage.

His cousin would have told him if she had denied him his marital rights. *Wouldn't he*? Had Amelia somehow convinced Martin that theirs should be a chaste union?

No, that made no sense. Like all young ladies of the middle and upper classes, Amelia would have been raised with the expectation that it was her duty to give her husband an heir. The idea would have been drummed into her while she was still in the schoolroom—especially in Sir Clarence's house.

Whatever the truth was, his cousin must have accepted the state of his marriage. To all appearances, he had been content. But clearly, there were many things Martin hadn't confided in him. Only one thing was certain.

Amelia had *never* been Worthing's lover.

Suddenly, he could breathe again. Gideon needed to speak to Amelia right now.

Someone cleared their throat. Adolfo, the butler, was in the doorway. A burly footman was standing next to him.

"My deepest apologies, my lord, but we must ask you to leave." Adolfo's voice was high and thin, betraying the anxiety he felt at having to eject an earl out of the townhouse.

A muscle in Gideon's cheek twitched. "Is that so?"

"I regret to say yes," Adolfo squeaked. He gestured to the hallway.

Gideon stalked toward them. The butler hurriedly got out of his way, but when Gideon pivoted on his heel and headed for the stairs, the oversized footman scrambled to block his path.

Though the servant was the same height, he was thinner and less muscular than Gideon. Confident he could deal with the man without hurting him too badly, he leaned close.

"Your mistress has nothing to fear from me...but if you don't get out of my way, I will break both your arms."

He smiled, and the footman paled. The poor man looked back at the butler, but Adolfo winced and shrugged. Gideon swept past him without a second glance.

It wasn't until he was at the top of the stairs that he realized he had no idea which room was Amelia's. He was about to start knocking on the nearest one when Carlotta emerged from the last door on the left —the room whose windows would face the garden courtyard.

The tall Italian woman quailed as he approached. Reining his temper, he stepped in front of Amelia's door. He raised his fist to pound on it, but then he remembered Westcliff's and only allowed himself one short knock.

"Amelia," he began, stopping short when he saw the maid was watching and listening to him.

He gestured impatiently and the servant ran down the hall, disappearing. He turned back to the door. "Amelia, I realize what happened downstairs was not what you were expecting. It…it wasn't what I was expecting either. But I didn't mean to hurt you. If I had known you were innocent, things would have been different. I—you and I need to have a long talk."

He broke off, unable to believe that he was explaining this to a closed door.

There was no answer from the other side. "Very well. I will let you gather your thoughts first. I know it's not likely one of your married friends can call at this hour, but there must be at least one married woman on your staff. If you won't talk to me, at least talk to one of them."

Still nothing. The idea that she was behind that door, crying because of him, was killing him by inches.

She believed he hurt her on purpose. Her ignorance of the married state had been total and complete. The magnitude of his crime was starting to dawn on him.

"This conversation is not over. I'll return in the morning. And Amelia—don't think about turning me away."

He sighed and headed for the stairs. His difficult conversations were not over for the night. Amelia did have one confidant. And Gideon was going to get his answers from him.

CHAPTER 13

It was easy to rouse Viscount Worthing from his club. Gideon's note had been short and to the point.

Amelia is hurt.

He didn't sign it. Instead, he stood in the shadows next to the anonymous hack he'd chosen to take him to St. James. He didn't have to wait long.

Gideon caught sight of Worthing emerging from the club a few minutes later. The viscount rushed down the steps with the note in his hand. He looked around wildly, a genuine expression of panic on his face. Stifling a flare of guilt, Gideon reached out and grabbed him by the collar of his coat when he rushed past the carriage.

"What the—"

He shoved the man inside the hack. Worthing landed on the seat with a grunt. Following silently, Gideon climbed inside and sat down across from him.

The carriage lamp was dim, but there was enough light to see Worthing scowling at him. "What is the meaning of this?"

"We are long overdue for a talk, you and I," he replied.

"What about?"

Gideon nodded at the key on his waistcoat. "That pin for starters."

"So this note was just a damned ruse?" Worthing closed his eyes and shook his head as he crumpled the paper in his hand. "I should have known."

He ignored that. "Amelia claims she did not give it to you. Is that true?"

Worthing was silent.

"I'm waiting."

The viscount straightened his waistcoat, sitting up straighter on the bench. "It was a gift from your cousin. I wear it as a keepsake of our friendship."

"Why?"

"Why what?"

"Why did he give it to you?" Gideon said from between gritted teeth. "I know how much Martin valued that pin. I'm supposed to believe he just gave it to you?"

Worthing paused a beat too long. "Actually, it was a forfeit. I claimed it after Martin lost a wager—a drunken dare when we were both in our cups on a wild night in Modena. I offered to give it back the next day, but he said a bet was a bet and insisted I keep it."

Gideon narrowed his eyes, studying the minute details of expression Phineus had taught him to search for when he first joined the war office. Worthing was good, but he was not completely successful at masking his anxiety.

The viscount was lying. But why would he bother over something so inconsequential?

Gideon let the silence stretch to the breaking point. Across from him, Worthing swallowed hard and reached up to cover the pin. At first, he thought the viscount meant to hide it from him. But Worthing didn't cover it. He stroked it with his finger, the same way one would rub a rabbit's foot for luck...or comfort.

The gnawing feeling in the pit of Gideon's stomach grew. Quite suddenly, the truth was there, blazing like a torch in his mind.

"Oh, bloody hell. Amelia called me a fool. She was right. You were never her lover. *You were his.*"

Worthing tried to control his panic, but his eyes betrayed him. His expression was one of stark fear. "Don't be ridiculous. I should call you out for such a slur."

An overwhelming wave of sadness swamped him. *Oh, Martin. Why didn't you tell me?*

Gideon answered his own question aloud. "He never told me because he thought I wouldn't understand."

Tears glinted in Crispin Worthing's eyes. He opened and closed his mouth. "Would you have?" he whispered after a long silence.

Gideon's throat was tight. "I—I like to think so. I am surprised, of course, but if he had told me, well...I trust I would have found better words than I have now," he finished lamely.

Worthing acknowledged that with a tiny nod.

Gideon splayed his hands open. "And his marriage? He and Amelia appeared to care for each other."

The viscount nodded emphatically. "They did! They loved each other...but it was more in the manner of close siblings."

Worthing put his hands on his knees and leaned forward. "Can you imagine what it was like growing up in that house? A boy with Martin's temperament and an intelligent and sensitive girl like Amelia under the thumb of Sir Clarence? And let me tell you—Lady Montgomery was not much better."

"I know. I remember my aunt well," Gideon said, letting himself sink into the cushions of the bench.

Worthing looked chagrined. "Of course. I forgot you spent some time under Clarence's roof as well."

"Only to visit. I didn't have to live there."

"Yes, well, I'm sure I don't have to explain what that sort of depressive atmosphere can do to a child's spirits. I have often marveled that neither Martin nor Amelia was crushed by the experience. But thanks to each other, they came through it by forging the deepest of bonds. When Sir Clarence announced they were to marry, it was a relief to both because it afforded them the opportunity to escape and set up their own household. They planned to live in London."

Gideon frowned. "But they didn't settle in England. They went abroad right after the wedding."

Worthing looked down. "Something happened."

"What was it?"

The viscount picked at his breeches. "Just after the ceremony, Sir Clarence made it clear that if Martin did not produce an heir within a year, then he would take care of the business himself. Indeed, Martin confessed to me that he believed that was his father's plan all along."

He looked up to gauge Gideon's reaction before continuing. "You see, not only was Sir Clarence aware of his son's inclinations, but there were other indications over the years that Sir Clarence had... unnatural feelings for his ward."

Gideon felt paralyzed. For the life of him, he couldn't think of a single thing to say. Icy fingers gripped the back of his neck, but they were soon burned away by powerful rage.

"I'll kill him."

For the first time, Worthing smiled at him. "I considered it myself. However, in the end, I deferred to Martin's wishes on the matter. His priority was Amelia, and she was convinced Sir Clarence's behavior stemmed from greed and his inability to seize her fortune. She either didn't understand or ignored the possibility that some of his obsession might stem from lust. Hardly her fault. Consider the way they were raised. Lady Montgomery thought the word 'stomach' was indelicate. She taught them both to be ashamed of their bodies. There were many things Martin didn't understand about the physical side of affection until we met."

Gideon pressed a hand on his stomach, an instinctive gesture to try to hold himself together. Whatever Sir Clarence had done, his villainy hadn't been complete. Amelia hadn't been violated while under his roof.

She had still been a virgin until tonight. He didn't let himself think about anything else.

"That was in Italy," he prompted. Worthing was finally talking, and he needed to take advantage.

The viscount nodded, his eyes distant and sad. "I fell in love with Martin that very first night in Rome. And he returned my affection.

Amelia was a bit harder to win over. She was suspicious of anyone who threatened her relationship with him. Martin was all she had."

"But you won her over eventually."

He shrugged. "I made him happy. Amelia is too generous a soul to have ever begrudged him that. She…she told me I would always be a part of her family." A tear slipped down his cheek.

Gideon let Worthing recover before asking the impertinent question he most wanted the answer to. "So…they did plan on having children?'

"It would not have been a unique arrangement," Worthing pointed out. "There are many like it in the ton. Martin knew he needed an heir. But given the nature of things between them, they were content to put the thing off. As long as they were abroad, Sir Clarence's threat was inconsequential."

"But they returned before they did their duty," Gideon mused. Another piece of the puzzle fell into place. "You're the reason they came back to England."

His companion's hands dropped limply in his lap. "I ran out of time. My uncle had passed on to his reward, and I inherited the title. Suddenly, I had several estates to run, but Martin and I did not want to part. I asked him to come with me to Kent. He convinced Amelia to settle nearby."

"In a house you owned, according to my inquiries."

Worthing looked surprised, but his expression melted away to one of resignation. "Yes. Before I departed for the continent, I purchased the manor house neighboring my future estate. It was just meant to be an investment, but after meeting Martin and Amelia, I decided it would the ideal home for them. Little did I know…"

Worthing broke off, blinking back tears. "That damn staircase."

Gideon collapsed, sinking back into the cushions. "So, it really was an accident."

"Of course. What else could it have been?"

"And after Martin was gone, you proposed to Amelia to protect her from my uncle."

It wasn't a question, but Worthing nodded again. "It's what he would have wanted. Amelia puts on a brave front, but I know that even after all this time, she's still afraid of Sir Clarence."

With good reason. Sir Clarence's desire to wed Amelia to the impotent Cannonburry was starting to make sense. Old Cannonburry was so desperate for an heir, he might actually agree to someone else siring the babe.

Gideon passed a hand over his face, shoving the rage and indignation he felt away with effort. "I wish Martin had trusted me enough to tell me about his fears for Amelia. I have wasted so much time."

If he'd known the truth, he would have come to her immediately. She wouldn't have had any reason to fear his uncle.

We could be married by now.

A little jolt hit him at that thought. Before he could analyze it, Worthing started speaking again.

"He might have planned to do so, but his time was cut short," he said with a trace of awkwardness. "Then again…"

"What?"

"Well…I believe your cousin wrote you a letter and left it with Amelia's solicitor. It will only be sent to you if a certain set of conditions are met."

He lifted a brow. "What are they?"

"Martin never said."

Gideon suspected Worthing had a very good idea what the conditions were, but he let it pass for the moment. He closed his eyes, guilt flaring again.

"Worthing…Crispin…my note was the truth. Amelia is hurt. I went to see her tonight."

Crispin's face fell. "Oh Lord, did you argue again? I know she was distraught after the words you had at Westcliff's."

How did Gideon explain what he had done tonight? He couldn't. All he could do was promise to fix it.

"I will make it right. In the morning, I will call and explain that I know the truth now. In fact, there's quite a bit I need to explain to her…"

Should he bring some texts from his library? The eastern ones on intimacy he acquired in his travels? Christ, he hoped she'd taken his advice and had spoken to one of her married staff about tonight's events.

Worthing nodded approvingly. "I'm certain she will be relieved to learn you finally know everything. Keeping secrets is always a burden, and this one did a lot to damage her reputation. Everyone assumed we were lovers. A normal woman would have let loose a discreet hint or two out of self-interest. But that's not Amelia. She is fierce about protecting Martin's memory and my own reputation. I will always be grateful to her for that."

Gideon nodded, studying the man his cousin had loved. "Worthing…I want to apologize."

"There is no need. In fact, I want to thank you. Most men in society would brand me a liar or deviant. They would assume the worst about me."

"If my cousin loved you as you say, then that is all I need to know about your character," Gideon said.

Martin had not been a naive innocent at all. In his short life, he'd become well-acquainted with the darker aspect of men's nature thanks to his own father.

Gideon leaned forward. "If there is ever anything you need, all you need do is ask. However, in return, I would ask one favor in return."

"What is it?"

"Stop asking Amelia to marry you."

Worthing coughed, then met Gideon's steady gaze. "I…I think I begin to understand."

"Don't worry. I'll invite you to the wedding."

CHAPTER 14

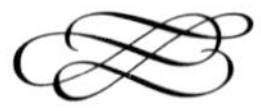

Gideon was pacing his breakfast room, the half-eaten remains of his meal cold and congealed on the table.

He wasn't used to feeling so unsettled. And he'd never left a meal unfinished—not even when he'd been hiding from French agents on the continent. With one eye on the clock, he rehearsed what he was going to say to Amelia.

Gideon had formulated a brilliant speech just before falling asleep at dawn, but for the life of him, he couldn't remember a single word of it now. His efforts to recapture the eloquence of his apology were a spectacular failure.

And it is only growing worse. Bloody hell. By the time he saw Amelia, he'd be incapable of stringing a sentence together.

He was contemplating going to his desk to make sense of his jumbled thoughts with ink and foolscap when his butler announced a visitor. Gideon went to the front hall to meet Viscount Worthing.

The man had been pacing. "I went to see Amelia this morning," Worthing began. "We are sometimes in the habit of taking our breakfast together when one of us is upset. She wasn't there."

Gideon put his hands on his hips. "Where did she go at this hour?"

Worthing ran his hands nervously around the brim of the hat he was holding. "Adolfo, her butler, had a message for me. She extended an invitation to visit her in Devon, at her family home." He grimaced. "According to the man, she had one for you as well if you happened to call, one suggesting you go to a much warmer and...sulfurous location."

Damn. "I should have guessed she would run. I'll have my traveling coach brought around."

Not wasting any time, he called out to his butler to pack a bag before hurrying to his study to pen a note to Clarke.

Worthing followed. When Gideon turned back to him, he was shaking his head. "A change of clothes perhaps, but we cannot waste time waiting for your coach. We must depart with haste."

Alarmed, Gideon rescinded his order for the carriage and asked for his chestnut stallion to be brought round instead. "Why? Do you suspect Sir Clarence is in pursuit?"

"No, you don't understand. Amelia no longer has a home."

CHAPTER 15

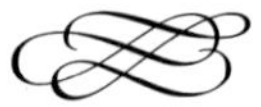

I'm in the wrong place.

"This cannot be right," she whispered, unable to tear her eyes from the ruin at the edge of the cliff in front of her. Behind, the grey ocean stretched out into the horizon, nearly the same color as the sky above.

The neglected Palladian her father had so lovingly restored had been destroyed. The entire left wing had collapsed, and there was a gaping hole in the roof. Soot-blackened debris littered the ground next to the crumbling structure.

"I'm sorry we're not further along, Madame. Your husband sent some funds a while back to start rebuilding. Do y'see over there," Gibson, the caretaker, pointing to some scaffolding on the right. "Made a good start, but then the funds stopped coming and so did the workers."

"When Martin died," she mumbled.

How could he have kept such a secret from her? This had been the home she had shared with her parents—the place where she had known the only true happiness of her life.

There was no pain, only a numbness that spread through her body as if she'd been submerged in an icy bath.

"What was the date?'

"Of the fire, miss? I reckon it was in mid-April of ninety-nine."

That was just over a month after she and Martin had departed to the continent.

"I sent word to the address you left me, the estate of the Italian relation of Mr. Montgomery's," Gibson added.

But the caretaker had directed the missive to her husband, as any employee would once a woman was wed.

True, she should have seen the letter regardless. Martin wasn't the type to maintain a steady correspondence or deal with solicitors. Such details had been her purview.

But Martin had collected the mail. He must have seen the note and hidden it to spare her feelings.

Gibson hadn't done anything wrong, but he was starting to look nervous.

"I would like to be alone if you don't mind," she said quietly.

"Of course, miss. I'll help your coachman settle the horses. The barn is right as rain. It wasn't touched in the blaze. There's plenty of room in the cottage since your father expanded it."

Once Gibson had gone, she moved closer to the ruin, walking over the barren ground where her mother's rose garden had stood. Edging around the house, she found the stone wall that marked the border of the ancient abbey. It had been so well known the property was still called the Abbey, even before the Palladian had been built over the ruins.

She entered the shell of the house without thought. One moment, she was standing in front of the door and the next she was inside, surrounded by the fragments of a once-happy childhood.

It was all a wasteland now.

Picking her way through the charred rooms, she was surprised to see most of the side staircase intact. Her bedroom had been at the top.

Amelia examined the stairs. There was a fleeting question whether they would still bear her weight, but she couldn't hold it in her mind. It didn't matter anyway. She climbed up, lightly leaping over the gap formed by two missing steps.

The damage was much worse upstairs. The hall was under a gaping hole in the roof. Off to the left, the blackened door to her childhood bedroom stood open. The fire had been cruel there. The better part of two walls was missing, exposing a sheer drop of the cliff's edge and the cold ocean beyond it.

Part of the floor was missing as well…if someone wanted to leap out into the sea, they would have to make a running start.

Amelia sidled closer to the edge, holding onto the wall so she wouldn't tumble through the gap. She took off her gloves and slid down until she was seated in the corner—the part of the floor supported by the massive timber beams that were the bones of the house.

Wrapping her hands around her knees, Amelia hugged them tight against her body and rested a cheek on top of them.

The protective fog enveloping her began to melt away. A profound grief overwhelmed her. Part of her felt as if she had already been dashed on the rocks below. For a split second, she thought about making it a reality, but she didn't move. Instead, she let the tears fall. She cried for her mother and father, and for Martin. And she cried for her dead illusions of love.

Gideon must think her such a fool. And in retrospect, he was right. When she thought of the depths of her ignorance, she shuddered. Intimacy between a man and a woman was nothing like she imagined. Her aunt Carol had been right. It was both painful and humiliating, a duty women had to tolerate to please their husbands and lovers.

She squeezed her eyes shut, trying to blot out the look of shock on Gideon's face when he realized she'd been a virgin. And then his explanation…

We were making love.

Mortification inundated her. How could she look him the eye again?

The answer to that was simple. She didn't have to—and no, the answer wasn't dashing herself on the rocks below. Women of means had obligations, responsibilities. Amelia was not about to depart this world and leave her staff to fend for themselves. Almost all had been born abroad, and though most of them were learning English, it would be difficult for them to find new employment even with proper references.

There were also the poor she helped through her charitable endeavors. The school she was building in Paddington, at the edge of the slums, was almost finished. Taking up residence here in Devon wouldn't be possible, but she'd find another home somewhere.

There were so many things she still had to do...but Amelia didn't have to do them yet. For today, and today alone, she could watch the surf below and imagine a new life, one where she wasn't alone.

CHAPTER 16

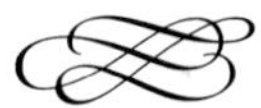

It had grown even colder, but Amelia took little notice. All she knew was that the light was growing dim. She could barely make out the waves as they crashed on the shore now, but she could still hear them—and something else. Men were talking, then shouting.

Had the demon that murdered Martin finally come for her? That was something that should concern her…but at this moment, she was too cold to care.

"*Amelia*! Amelia, look at me. I don't want you to move. Just turn your head and look at me."

She blinked sleepily and shifted, looking up to meet Gideon's waxen face. Was he really there or was it the demon in disguise?

Gideon wouldn't come all this way, not for her. *It's the demon, then.*

"Amelia, I know you've had an upset, but there's no call for this, is there?"

It was the guilt in his tone that pricked her. *A demon probably wouldn't bother with this farce.*

"What?" Her voice was hoarse from disuse and the cold.

"I said there's no call for this. I…I've spoken to Crispin. I brought him with me. Rather, he brought me. He's looking for you downstairs. We came to take you home."

She raised a brow at the irony. "This is my home."

"I meant London, my love. Or we can visit my estate in Derbyshire. You've never seen it. I…I could use some advice on the new agricultural improvements I've been making."

He paused and looked at the floor as if he was contemplating crossing it. She studied the damaged boards lying between the two of them. "I don't think that's a good idea. The floor isn't sound, and you are too heavy."

A little flare of heat crept up her chilled cheeks as she remembered the weight of his body on hers.

"Then can you please come here?" he asked, his voice high and thin. He sounded as if he were being strangled.

"I would prefer it if you left," she replied, turning back to the surf.

"Amelia, please—"

His next words were drowned out by a racket downstairs. Gideon spun and ran to the banister to look over the edge.

"Worthing, hold on!" He turned around. "Crispin's crashed through the floor somehow. I need to go get him. *Please,* please come here!"

Oh, dear Lord, no.

It was probably the only thing that could have roused her. She couldn't lose Crispin. Pins and needles pricked as she got to her feet, wincing as her sore limbs were forced to support her. She rounded the damaged parts of the floor slowly, surprised at how much they creaked under her weight. When she reached Gideon, he grabbed her, pulling her into a crushing embrace.

"*Crispin,*" she reminded him sharply when he didn't let go.

With a show of great reluctance, he released her and she started down the stairs.

"No." He pulled her back. "Let me go first and you'll follow. Here, take my hand."

Amelia rolled her eyes and swept past him. At the gap, she peered down. A sweaty and shaken Crispin waved back at her. Both his legs had gone through the floor, and he appeared to be trapped. With a cluck of her tongue at him, she reached for the railing, sliding along the wide supporting board at the bottom the same way she did as a child.

"*Amelia*!" Gideon yelled

"Do try and not use my name as a swear word," she snapped, rounding the bottom of the stairs and making her way to Crispin, testing the integrity of the floor with each step.

"I'll get him out; get away from there," Gideon said, edging around the open space with a fluid motion. He was down in a heartbeat with almost no noise. It was almost as if he was accustomed to scaling treacherous ruins on a regular basis.

When he tried to approach, she stayed him with a hand. "I told you, you are *too heavy*," she said, over-enunciating her words. "This whole house is built over the ruins of an ancient abbey, and the fire has weakened the floors. It's what gave the house its name. There are numerous chambers below. My father said they were used for storage. I imagine it's a very long drop if you fall through."

"Um, Flint, she may be right," Crispin gasped, almost tripping over his words as he tried to brace himself. His sweaty hands slipped a little on the wood. "Feels as if I'm over the pit of hell itself."

Gideon held up his hands and glowered at them both. "I'm going to run and get some rope. *Do not move*–either of you."

He ran out of the house. Amelia looked down at Crispin with a scowl. "How could you bring him here?"

"The earl was concerned. So was I when I realized you'd come here to Devon."

"So you knew as well, about the fire?" she said, bending and lying flat.

"Yes, I'm sorry, love. Martin was hoping to rebuild before you found out, but he didn't want to ask you for the funds. I offered him the money, but he insisted on using his allowance… Er, darling, what are you doing?"

"Spreading my weight over a larger portion of the floor. I suggest you do the same."

Crispin lay back awkwardly. Pushing herself with her hands, she helped him adjust and then got to work trying to free one of his legs. The first came out with relative ease, but he cried out in pain when she attempted to dislodge the second. A shard of wood the length of her thumb had pierced him in the fleshy muscle under the knee.

"Talk to me, Crispin," she said, trying to distract him. "How could Martin believe he could hide something like this? He had to have known it would take far more than his allowance to rebuild this place."

Crispin winced as her movements jostled his leg. "I believe he was hoping to have most of the work done on credit. He was going to apply to you for funds if some of the small investments he made did not bear fruit."

"He should have told me," she said, a wealth of pain in her voice.

Bloody hell, she would not cry. Not with Gideon nearby. She focused on working the shard of wood free, trying to break off the end.

"Don't take it out! If he's punctured a vein, he'll bleed to death." Gideon had returned.

"*What?*" Crispin's eye's dilated. His pulse throbbed visibly in his neck. Amelia worried he was about to faint.

"Believe it or not, I know that," she snapped at the earl.

She had some experience with injuries and illness. Isobel had been kind enough to teach her how to treat them during their stay in Italy. "Do you have a knife?"

Gideon crouched down a few feet away and slid something to her. The blade was impressively sharp and had a nice heft, although it was a bit heavy for her. Working quickly, she started to saw the shard of wood at the base.

Despite the fact the knife had no teeth, it cut through the thick wood with little effort.

She would have to remember to ask the earl why he carried such a wickedly sharp instrument on his person.

The sound of timber creaking signaled Gideon moving closer. She raised her head to glare at him. "Stay away, my lord," she ordered from between gritted teeth.

A bead of sweat dripped down the side of her face as she returned to her task. Amelia tried to minimize the jostling of the viscount's injured leg as best she could, but she winced each time Crispin panted or groaned.

"I've got it!" she exclaimed as the piece of wood broke off, freeing his leg.

Her eyes gravitated to the darkness exposed by the removal. Her father had been right. This part of the house was over one of the largest of the subterranean rooms. If Crispin had fallen all the way through the floor, he would have plunged to his death.

Ignoring fear for her own safety, she focused on helping Crispin, half-pulling and pushing until they reached Gideon's position near the door.

The earl pulled her to her feet despite her protest he help Crispin first. She was set on the ground in front of the house without a word. Then he went back. He emerged cradling Crispin in his arms like a child.

Gideon carried the other man effortlessly, depositing him in one of the bedrooms of the cottage while she sent Gibson for a physician. The doctor was young, a man she did not recognize because he was new to the area. At Gideon's suggestion, the doctor doused Crispin's wound in strong alcohol before sewing it shut. Then he bound his ankle because it was badly sprained.

Gibson set up a pallet in the kitchen for himself so she and the earl could each take one of the two remaining bedrooms. She retired early, washing and collapsing in bed before the moon was high in the sky. But she couldn't sleep. She lay staring at the sliver of the night sky visible through the window.

Her door opened a short while later. *Gideon could have at least knocked.*

"Amelia?" He was holding a taper.

"I'm sleeping," she said tonelessly, not bothering to turn and look at him.

He sighed and closed the door. But he was on the wrong side.

Amelia should have been outraged, but she was too tired. Her heavy limbs refused to rise from the bed to slap him.

Gideon set the candle on the small table and sat down next to her.

"We need to talk."

"What would be the point?"

"The point is I know the truth about Worthing and Martin. The viscount told me everything."

It should have alarmed her that she had failed to keep Martin's deepest secret, but it was difficult to summon the energy. "Did he tell you why Martin kept the fire a secret?" she asked instead.

"Yes, but first I need to apologize to you. I've been a fool. I allowed myself to be influenced by gossip, rather than my own knowledge of you. I should have believed in you. You're still the principled and compassionate girl I've always known."

"I agree on one point—you are a fool," she said lightly.

His words were fine, but it was still a terrible apology.

He probably has few occasions to apologize to anyone. She really should savor the experience.

Gideon grunted. "You scared the hell out of me today. What possessed you to go inside? Let alone climb those stairs. That could have been you instead of Crispin. He was trying to follow after us when he fell."

He took her hand and lowered his voice. "Amelia, what were you doing in that room with the house falling down around you? If...if something had happened to you, I would never have forgiven myself. I know I hurt you—"

"I was *not* going to jump," Amelia snapped. "I'm not about to do myself in because your lovemaking was not up to snuff," she added with a quirk of her lips, unable to resist.

"It's not funny! You took ten years off my life. Martin will never forgive me for what I've done. I will never forgive myself."

His apology was no longer amusing. *I can't blame him for what happened—as much as I want to.*

"Gideon...you did nothing wrong. Naturally, you assumed I was a woman of experience. And I had a few delusions about the act itself. There, now I have absolved you. Please leave so I may go to sleep."

"No." He gripped her hand tighter. "I need to explain about what happened between us. You see…er…when a man and a woman—"

Amelia shook his hand off. "Don't you dare condescend to me! I am not a child, nor am I an imbecile."

He scowled at her. "I'm aware of that. But you were ign—uninformed. The first time is always difficult for a virgin, but it improves. Under the right circumstances, it can be very pleasurable for the female."

Amelia threw herself back on the bed. "I cannot believe we are having this conversation."

"Love, it's long overdue." His eyes bored down at her. "Why did you say we weren't making love? What were you expecting? Did you think kissing was the extent of it?"

"I am not so completely ignorant, my lord! I have been kissed—twice. A Frenchman took a liberty at a ball once, but Martin thrashed him soundly. As for intimate relations, I have seen it firsthand…but I should have realized it would be different between a man and a woman."

Gideon's lips parted, and he stared at her for a long moment. "You saw Martin and Worthing together?"

She sighed and nodded. "Accidentally. I returned unexpectedly to our rooms one day, and I stumbled upon them."

Gideon looked rather red in the candlelight. He coughed. "What were they doing?"

Amelia threw up her hands. "They were making love!"

"Sweetling, there are many ways to make love."

She let the endearment pass, acknowledging the truth with a nod. "Yes, well…they were…" Amelia trailed off, embarrassed, but Gideon nodded at her encouragingly. "They were using their mouths, or rather, Crispin was using his mouth on Martin…you know…down there."

Amelia gestured with her hand at the junction of her legs. Her face was flaming wildly, but she kept her tone nonchalant. "Apparently, that is not how it's done when one of the party is female," she added with a sniff.

Gideon opened and closed his mouth a few times as if struggling to find the right words.

"What you saw is one of the variations of lovemaking, even between a man and women. But it's not the only way. What happened between us is another. Some would say it's the more conventional technique," he explained a little haltingly.

Amelia's mouth pursed. "I suppose it makes sense…anatomically."

The earl released a strangled bark of laughter before abruptly cutting it short. "Agreed. Your body was designed to accommodate mine in exactly that fashion. Do you understand why?"

She frowned at him. Gideon looked distinctly uncomfortable.

"What we did—it is how I would plant my seed in your womb."

Amelia stared at him, dumbfounded. Then her eyes widened in horror.

"It's all right, love!" he said reassuringly. "It's not likely I got you with child, not yet. Things did not proceed to completion if you get my meaning. But…if you conceived, that would be perfectly fine."

Fine? Her heart was pounding in her chest. "How can you say that? It would be a disaster."

Gideon frowned. "Amelia, surely you realize we have to marry now regardless of whether you fall pregnant?"

"*What*? Why?"

He stared at her as if she'd grown horns. "A gentleman does not dally with an innocent without doing the honorable thing."

Amelia rolled her eyes. "Well, in that case, I have excellent news. In the eyes of the ton, I am far from innocent. A dalliance between us, however fleeting, is quite in keeping with my reputation."

His expression darkened. "I don't give a bloody damn about what the ton thinks." She raised a brow, and he had the grace to cringe. "Not anymore, anyway. My sole purpose in this whole charade was to discover the truth behind my cousin's death. I did not plan what happened between us, but I am not about to walk away because society would excuse me. I will *not* shirk my duty just because everyone is acting the fool."

His duty. "How romantic, truly," she said drily.

Gideon narrowed his eyes and leaned in close. If she didn't know any better, she would have thought he was trying to intimidate her. "Amelia, you and I will be married. Neither of us has a choice anymore. I know that's not the romantic proposal a girl dreams of, but consider this—even when I thought you had a hand in Martin's death, I couldn't keep away from you."

"Only because you were determined to find me guilty!"

His jaw firmed. "No, it was because I wanted you. I still want you. And you want me. Now make room on that bed."

Stunned, her mouth dropped open. "Gideon!"

He held up his hands. "I'm not going to ravish you. Not tonight in any case. But if the last few weeks have taught me anything, it's that I cannot let you out of my sight. So, from now on, I won't."

With quick efficient movements, he removed his waistcoat and cravat. One boot dropped on the floor. It was swiftly followed by the other. He kept everything else on and pulled up the bedclothes just enough to slide in next to her.

Amelia had no choice but to move to the side to give him room. He was a big man. She tried to make herself as small as possible, scooting to the side until she was almost hanging off the edge of the mattress.

Gideon reached out and hauled her close. He sighed, his body relaxing completely. She considered slapping his face…but she didn't want to.

It would just be for tonight. Her bone-deep weariness had dissipated during their conversation, but it was back now. And the heat from the earl's body was so inviting. With a little exhalation, she lay her head on his shoulder and cuddled against him.

There would be ample opportunity to rail at Gideon tomorrow. But first…

"Sir Clarence burned down my home, didn't he?"

Gideon sucked in a breath and began to rub his hand up and down her back. "I believe he did. It must have been retaliation for when you and Martin left England."

Tears pricked at her eyes. "Why couldn't Sir Clarence have been content with my dowry? I made sure he had the entire sum before we left."

She waited, but Gideon made no response. That was just as well; she already knew the answer was greed.

"I suppose Martin thought he had plenty of time to rebuild, and that's why he didn't tell me," she continued, trying not to blame her husband. He'd only been trying to protect her. "However, even rebuilt, the house will never be the same. It won't be the home I shared with my parents."

Gideon was quiet for so long she thought he had fallen asleep, but then he said something.

He couldn't see her frown in the dark. His murmur had been close to unintelligible, but it sounded like. "My home is wherever you are."

Exhausted, she gave up on further conversation and fell asleep.

CHAPTER 17

Gideon opened his eyes to full darkness. Shifting, he felt the warm weight of Amelia nestled against him, sleeping soundly. She hadn't moved in all that time or he would have woken earlier. He was a light sleeper.

He would have gone back to sleep, but a stray thought prodded him to full consciousness. Amelia had no trouble sleeping with him because she was accustomed to having someone else in her bed.

Martin, of course.

A flare of jealousy caught him off guard. He told himself he was being an ass—*again.*

The pair might not have been lovers but with all the traveling they had done, it was only natural they shared a bed. Indeed, they wouldn't have had a choice. Martin couldn't have left Amelia unprotected in all those inns and foreign homes they visited during their travels.

How odd it must have been for the two of them to be forced into a charade where they had to pretend all the time.

Rather like spies. He snorted at the irony.

Amelia shifted and raised her head. "What is it?" Her voice was confused and husky with sleep.

He winced. "I'm sorry, I didn't mean to wake you. It's still a few hours till dawn. Go back to sleep," he whispered.

She nodded and settled back into the pillows but didn't close her eyes. He couldn't see their blue shade in the moonlight, but he knew they were studying him.

When she continued to watch him, Gideon couldn't resist reaching out to trace the smooth line of her cheek, following the path down her neck with his fingertips.

Amelia closed her eyes and shivered. Hoping it was excitement that caused her reaction, he leaned over her until his lips were a hairsbreadth from hers. Given her ample time to pull away, he closed the distance.

It was meant to be a brief caress, a test of sorts, to see if she would respond to him. But his restraint burned away the second he realized she wasn't going to push him away. He teased her lips with his tongue until they parted and let him inside. Her taste was addictive and exotic, more intoxicating than any wine.

Gideon pulled her closer, deepening the kiss. She shivered again and put her arms around his neck. His skin tingled, and a groan escaped as her soft warmth enveloped him.

Amelia responded to his caresses with an untutored and honest passion. Gideon spared a thought to thank the stars. He hadn't destroyed her sweet desire with his impatient blundering during their first disastrous experience together. But he needed to proceed cautiously, to open her mind and body to the pleasure of physical intimacy.

He shifted, pressing his heavily aroused lower half against her. Amelia's eyes flew open, and she broke off the kiss to look up at him with anxious eyes. He bent to kiss the silken skin next to her ear.

"I promised not to ravish you. I intend to keep my word, but it only seems fair that I fulfill some of your expectations about lovemaking…"

~

AMELIA GASPED as Gideon moved down her body, lifting the blankets away. He arranged her legs on either side of him and smiled at her, a flirtatious grin that stirred her blood.

Her body heated, a telltale slippery warmth concentrated between her legs.

"Gideon, I don't think—"

"I strongly advise against that. Stop thinking," he interrupted, pushing the fine lawn cotton of her nightgown up above her knees before pausing. "Unless the issue is one of trust. Do you trust me, Amelia?"

"Of course I trust you," she said immediately, trying to find the words to explain why he should stop. It was difficult to find any, impossible in fact.

He waited a beat longer. "*Good.*"

Amelia yelped when he pulled her lower, removing her drawers with startling efficiency. The chilly air hit her heated core, but she didn't have time to feel uncomfortable. Her body was in flames the second Gideon's mouth touched her.

He pressed a kiss to her heated flesh and she whimpered, reflexively trying to close her legs. Gideon held her down with his hands, parting them to fully expose her to his caress. His tongue tasted and teased, stroking her like rough velvet.

Amelia squirmed helplessly, but she was unable to move because she was held fast to the bed. Gideon continued his gentle assault, using his hands to touch and probe while teeth abraded the pearl crowning her sex. His mouth moved over her lips and bud in a ragged pattern that devastated her senses.

Moaning, she buried her trembling hands in his hair. The little ripples of pleasure built upon one another until they were a rolling wave that swept from her head to the tips of her toes. Her skin felt alive, every nerve clamoring for more—more touch, more *heat*. She was drowning in sensation and just when she thought she would die from the pleasure, Gideon moved one hand up to cover her breast.

The rosy tip swelled and beaded under his hand, sending sparks of lightning directly to her heated core as he caressed and stroked.

"Gideon, I can't stand it," she gasped, pleading.

But he was merciless. He tweaked and pinched one nipple just as his tongue plunged inside her. Her body seized as her sheath closed around him and spasmed violently. His tongue worked in and out of her, one hand stroking her breast while the other moved over her bud, pushing and extending the ecstasy consuming her body. Each touch was magnified, a ripple of energy that made her writhe and moan until she dissolved in a blazing radiance of light.

When her awareness returned, her body was whole once more. She felt like a wrung-out mop, but there was strength in her hands. They were holding onto Gideon's shoulders. She couldn't let him go, not even when she realized his breeches were open, completely exposing him.

"*Amelia, don't.* You have to release me," he protested, even as the hard length of his manhood stroked and ground against her slippery folds.

He wanted her badly. She could feel the force of his desire not just in the tension of his body but in the way he could barely catch his breath. Marveling at his restraint, she whispered in his ear. "It's all right. I want you to have your satisfaction too."

"No, I promised I wouldn't," he said from between gritted teeth. His body, however, continued to respond—his hips were still pumping.

She moved her hand down, intending to guide his arousal, but he was coated with the moisture from her body and he slipped easily back and forth under her palm.

Gideon hissed. "Yes, hold me against you like that," he said, adjusting her hand so he was pressed firmly against her without checking his movement. "I won't enter you, but you can watch. I want you to see everything—to understand."

Her lips parted, and she nodded, utterly taken with the idea.

That part of him was so hot, like heated iron, but the skin was so smooth. She stared wide-eyed as his erection slipped up and down against her, striking her nub on the upstroke. Each time it happened, another tickle of sensual energy would shoot through her body.

Amelia watched in fascination as Gideon's staff swelled and jerked. He threw his head back as the last convulsions racked his body and a pearlescent liquid spilled across her belly like hot candle wax. He collapsed to the side, his chest working like a bellows. After a few moments, he swore under his breath.

"I didn't expect that to be so…satisfying."

Her lips curled up, and he returned her smile. "Seeing you watching me, taking it all in, was very arousing," he confessed, an amused bewilderment in his expression before he moved away.

Gideon bent over the edge of the mattress, retrieving a handkerchief from his coat without leaving the bed. He began to clean her. Before he could wipe away all traces, Amelia touched one of the drops on her stomach with her fingers.

"This is your seed," she said, rubbing her fingers to test the texture. "How can this grow into a baby?"

"It has to take root in your body, and that only happens at a specific time," he said, bracing himself on his forearms.

He explained how a woman's fertility was tied to the monthly cycle of her courses, something Amelia had been aware of, although the details had never been laid bare.

Blushing like mad, she asked him one question and then another. Before Gideon knew it, he was delivering a lecture on anatomy and sexuality using himself as a real-life model. He did it as matter-of-factly as he could until she grew comfortable enough to ask him anything.

Gideon answered every question she put to him with clarity and deference. Not once did he belittle her intelligence, even when he laid to rest some of her more ignorant assumptions.

The one thing that did surprise him was that she'd never taken it upon herself to learn about the issue on her own.

"I think Martin did you a disservice by not even broaching the topic of sex," he confessed. "If you were planning on having children, he should have explained some of this."

Amelia had put her head close to his as they lay on their sides facing each other on the bed. "You mustn't blame him. It was my decision to set such discussions aside. Martin had met Crispin early in our marriage, and I could see the pair were falling in love. At the time, it seemed wise to disregard any personal considerations until they could be indulged."

He frowned at her. "I know a wife is expected to do whatever she can to ensure her husband's happiness, but burying your own needs and desires hardly seems fair."

She lifted one white shoulder. "As I said, it was my decision. I had ample opportunity to educate myself as it were, had I chosen to do so. While abroad, I had to actively discourage the attentions of several gentlemen who would have only been too happy to be of service in that regard."

"I'm sure there were," he growled before kissing her with a hard hunger. "Be prepared—any man who dares volunteer to be at your service now will have to answer to me."

Gideon pulled her closer, his blatant possessiveness on open display. She should have chided him for it, but instead, she curled her body against his, stroking his chest with her hand until she fell asleep.

His life, his future, was literally in his arms. Gideon swept a hand over Amelia's waist and hips with the lightest touch so he wouldn't wake her.

A confused riot of emotions stirred in his breast. Guilt was predominant among them. His current prospects for a marriage based on love and respect had come at a high price—the life of his cousin.

Deep down, a part of him knew that this had been inevitable. He had lied to himself and to Clarke when he said he hadn't seen Amelia since she was a child. She had been sixteen, almost seventeen, and already a stunning beauty.

Almost eight years her senior, he had been stirred even then. Instinctively, Gideon had known she could be dangerous to his heart. From them on, he had avoided her and Martin, telling himself he would visit the following year or the year after.

He hadn't wanted to be anywhere near Amelia, to be forced to confront his feelings for her, especially after she and Martin had married. Consequently, he had been unaware she was in danger from his predatory uncle.

Then there was Martin…what if there had been a way to prevent his accident? And if his cousin had lived, would the truth of their marriage have been enough for Gideon to set aside his honor so he could selfishly claim Amelia for his own?

I would have still wanted her, even if I had met her as his wife. He was honest enough to admit the truth.

Unlike other men of the ton, Gideon did not dally with married women, restricting his brief liaisons to widows and once a member of the demimonde. Though those women had not asked for fidelity, he had given it to them as long as the liaison had lasted. The only time he had flirted with someone's wife had been in France, under the auspices of the war office. But he had never been the reason a woman broke her wedding vows.

Violating the sanctity of marriage—even one as complicated as his cousin's—would have been a stain on his honor. He had never questioned whether he was capable of such a sin until now.

He had to stop thinking like this. The sad fact was, Martin was gone. They had mourned him for over a year, but not even the harshest grand dame would expect a widow as young as Amelia to devote her life to his memory and wear black for the rest of her days.

No, the ton was anticipating a second marriage for her. The fact she would be marrying him and not Lord Worthing would set tongue's wagging, but Gideon didn't give a damn about the gossip. As long as Amelia was his, society could hang.

The moon was too bright. At this rate, he would spend all night staring at Amelia if he didn't close the curtains. Gideon turned, soundlessly extracting himself from her sleeping form. He was at the window when he saw it—a pair of glowing eyes not ten feet away in the shadow of some trees.

His mind tried to dismiss it, but the apparition did not fade. In fact, it moved, the eyes shifting position as if they were meeting his gaze. Then they winked out. The head had turned away.

Gideon was shocked into immobility by the strange sight. But the sound of Amelia shifting on the bed spurred him. He stormed into action. Snatching up his coat, he threw it on, dismissing the rest of his clothing. He hesitated over his boots but decided to go without—there was no time to waste pulling on the tight calf-length Hessians.

Taking advantage of being on the ground floor, he threw open the window and jumped over the windowsill. He took care to close it behind him before running toward the spot where he'd seen the intruder. If the villain got past him, he would have to take the time to open it again if he wanted to get to Amelia.

Gideon wouldn't let that happen.

He narrowed his eyes and drew his pistol out of his coat pocket, squinting into the darkness under the tree canopy. By the time his eyes adjusted, he knew he was alone. His finely honed senses didn't detect the presence of another.

There was no hint of a hidden person breathing in the shadows, no sound of running feet. Indeed, there was no noise at all. None of the normal sounds of the night could be heard. All was silent. Whoever or whatever had been out here was gone, but the unnatural quiet marked the spot. Something had stood here under the trees, watching him.

Gideon checked the perimeter of the house in his bare feet, careful to keep the gun ready in his hand. With only his coat as cover the cold bit at his exposed skin, but there was no way in hell he was going back inside if there was a chance the intruder was still about.

What the devil had it been? He stood outside, practically naked, until he accepted that the eyes were well and truly gone.

Shaking his head, Gideon crawled back through the window, fastening it shut with a tiny metallic scrape. He'd only been gone a matter of minutes. Amelia was still sleeping soundly in bed. Despite his rapid action, he'd left the room with practiced stealth, quiet enough to avoid waking her—at least until he slipped back under the covers, bringing the night's cold with him.

Startled, she stirred and pulled away from his chilled body. "What? Wh—"

Blast. "Shh. Everything is fine. I—I had to go outside," he said in a murmur.

"Why?" Amelia muttered, her eyes drifting closed.

"It was nothing," he murmured absently, his thoughts on the nightmarish vision he'd seen.

It had to be a trick of some kind. "I thought I saw something is all," he said, wrapping one arm around her protectively.

Amelia murmured something he couldn't catch, but then her voice strengthened and she raised her head. "Was it the demon?"

He watched her for a long moment. "What demon?" he asked, his throat tight.

She yawned and put her head back down on the pillow. He shook her. "Amelia, what demon?"

"The one that killed Martin."

CHAPTER 18

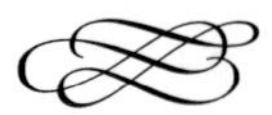

Gideon paced outside impatiently. He'd risen at dawn and dressed quickly, determined to examine the area around the house as soon as he could. A weighty resoluteness settled in his breast when he saw the traces of giant footprints under the trees.

Forcing himself to focus, Gideon followed the prints until they faded some hundred yards from the cottage. They ended well before the ruin of the main house, but after checking the lower floors of the burned building, he was certain last night's visitor had been there, too.

He clenched his jaw, taking a steadying breath before heading back to the cottage. If what Amelia had said last night was true, then someone—or something—had been responsible for his cousin's death. And it was following her.

A demon. Gideon didn't believe in such things, but that was what Amelia had said while half-asleep. After what he'd seen last night, he didn't question her choice of words—not that she'd elaborated. Despite his poking and prodding, Amelia had slipped back into slumber without further explanation. He'd decided the discussion could wait until the light of day.

It was difficult to credit, but the threat to Amelia had taken an occult turn. Or at least it was what someone wanted him to believe.

Despite the strain and distance in their relationship, Sir Clarence would not have harmed Martin. Though he had been frustrated with his son at times, Gideon knew from past conversations that his overbearing relative had loved Martin.

Clarence's feelings for Amelia were another story. Nevertheless, connecting Sir Clarence to these events didn't wash, not if last night's visitor had something to do with Martin's death.

Gideon tracked the position of the sun in the sky, wondering if it was too early to wake Amelia. He needed to question her. She could no longer afford to keep any secrets from him. He couldn't let her.

The sound of carriage wheels cut his rumination short. He reached for his pistol before he recognized the man peering out the vehicle's window as it stopped a few dozen yards down the drive.

Clarke stepped down and greeted him with a frown. "I received your note. What in the blazes happened here?' he asked, gesturing to the house.

Gideon explained his suspicions about the cause of the fire tersely, thanking the impulse that led him to ask his friend to follow him. Clarke had arrived via the most expedient route, traveling on the mail coach and then hiring a carriage in a nearby town.

"How badly is the viscount hurt?" Clarke asked after Gideon detailed the accident.

"I'm not certain. But it's fortunate you're here. I'd appreciate if you could examine his injuries and make an assessment. We had a doctor look over him last night, but he was quite young and struck me as still wet behind the ears."

He hadn't mentioned this observation to Amelia last night. There had been no reason to distress her further—and he'd known Clarke was on the way. His friend had medical training and had even sewn shut one of his knife wounds after a particularly eventful night in Toulon.

Clarke nodded and dismissed the driver and postilion with a handsome tip, letting them take the hired chaise back to the posting inn. "I'll look in on the patient straightaway, but perhaps you'd like to explain why you and the viscount are suddenly on good enough terms to tear across the country together? Not that I question the wisdom of the trip," he added with a nod at the ruined Palladian.

Gideon hesitated, weighing disclosing the truth about Worthing and Martin. It was the conflict of a moment. He trusted Clarke with his life—and Worthing's. They had been keeping too many secrets as it was.

Clarke was surprised, but not appalled to hear of Martin's proclivities. He grew quiet and thoughtful before promising not to breathe a word of the truth to anyone. His only exclamation came when Gideon showed him the footprints and described what he saw, but he cut him short—they'd discuss the situation again once he'd spoken to Amelia.

He sent Clarke to wake Worthing and examine the viscount's injury before going in search of the caretaker. Now that Clarke was here, they might need more provisions for breakfast.

The old venerable was one step ahead of him. Gibson had sent messages to the local taproom and the nearest baker. An assortment of freshly baked breads and pies were on their way. Gideon was about to go and wake Amelia when she stumbled into the kitchen of her own accord.

Somehow, she'd managed to wash and dress in a fresh gown without the aid of a maid. Still blinking sleepily at him, she allowed him to usher her to the table without argument. He'd just informed her of Clarke's arrival when his friend joined them in the kitchen and the caretaker retreated to check on the horses.

Clarke greeted Amelia with a warm smile, and then took her hand in a sure sign something was wrong. He didn't prevaricate, promptly sharing what was bothering him.

"Viscount Worthing is doing well enough under the circumstance, but his convalescence may be long if he's not cared for properly. He's determined to return to London, to the care of his personal physician. Normally I'd advise against moving him, but given the distance to the nearest neighbors and the relative isolation here, I think it would be prudent to accede to his wishes..."

Amelia's eyes had darkened as he explained. "Of course, we'll depart for town as soon as he's ready," she said, rising from her seat.

"After breakfast is soon enough," Gideon murmured, urging her back down. He waited for her to finish before fetching her pelisse.

Then he took her out to the space under the trees. He didn't say anything, watching silently as Amelia's lips parted. Her creamy skin paled, the horror in her eyes growing until he pulled her into his arms, trying to envelop her with his strength.

"You've seen these before, haven't you?" he asked quietly.

Her chin rubbed his chest as she nodded. The noise of the carriage stirred her. Clarke was helping Worthing into his carriage.

"No, put him in Amelia's coach," he called out. "It's bigger and he'll be able to stretch out more comfortably." He turned back to her. "Clarke will ride with him. We'll take Worthing's coach back alone so we can talk. You are going to confide in me now, aren't you?"

"I…yes. It's time." She inhaled audibly and pulled away, but was checked by the hold he kept on her arm. Reluctantly, he released her so she could speak to the servants. Once her trunk was loaded, they departed.

Miles passed in silence. "It's not a demon," he began.

Her blue gaze searched his face in shock, confirming she'd been asleep and had no memory of what she'd said.

"That is what you said last night. I went out to investigate our trespasser last night and you asked if it was the demon that killed Martin."

Amelia averted her gaze, her hands fisting in her lap. He waited and she laughed to keep from crying. "I've seen things…things that cannot possibly exist in a sane world. I thought I was going mad."

"You're not mad, but I think someone is trying to convince you that you are. You need to tell me everything. Start when Martin died."

She nodded, but her gaze was fixed on her lap, her expression remote. "It was the worst day of my entire life. I had paid a few calls and then attended a tea. We were new to the area, but Crispin had introduced us to all the major landowners—he'd thrown a ball in our honor. He made certain the local gentry embraced us, so I was always being invited to some event or another." She paused, a trace of a smile on her face. It faded quickly.

"Everything was going well. Crispin and Martin were happy, and I had met some like-minded females who devoted themselves to charitable causes. I was with the ladies' auxiliary discussing ways to raise funds to expand the local school…and then I came home and found him."

Her eyes filled with tears, and he fought the impulse to yank her back into his arms. He needed her to tell him everything, even if it meant letting her face the agony of her memories alone. The most he could do was take her hand, which he gripped tightly.

"His head had struck the marble floor. There was blood everywhere," she continued in a whisper. "I didn't know what to do so I took him in my arms. The servants tried to make me let go, but I refused…The creature was watching from the top of the stairs. By the time I noticed it, the sun had set and it was dark. All I saw was its eyes —they glowed like the fires of hell. And then I blinked and it was gone. Afterward, I was convinced the shock had momentarily unhinged me. Nothing happened while I was in mourning. But then Crispin convinced me I needed to go up to town…"

She stopped speaking, her eyes growing bleak and distant.

"You've seen it since then," he prompted when she remained silent. "Was it at Westcliff's?"

Amelia shook her head. "No, it was at the Duke of Marlboro's ball. The demon was watching from the musician's balcony."

That explains it. "It was why you fainted," he murmured, marveling at the arrogance of the villain, to attempt such a thing in full view of half the ton. "Did you get a good look at it?"

"No, again, I only caught a glimpse of the eyes."

"Where else have you seen it?"

"That was the only other time I saw it physically, but I also found similar marks in the soil of my garden in town. And there have been other…disturbances."

"What kind of disturbances?"

Her blue eyes clouded with uncertainty. "It's not the same. You'll say it's my imagination."

"No, I won't." Gideon stroked her palm with his thumb. "What I saw last night looked demonic. I'm not so much of a braggart that I'd deny it nearly made me piss myself."

Amelia scoffed, wiping a tear from the corner of her eye.

"It's true," he assured her. "But I think the force behind this monstrous vision is a person. One who is trying to frighten you—and they're doing a fine damn job of it. If this villain is willing to taunt and intimidate you at a major ball, then it stands to reason they've made other attempts. This bastard is without morals or scruples and they're devilishly inventive."

Amelia failed to repress a shudder. "I've heard voices coming from empty rooms, and have seen shadows cast by nothing at all. Thrice now I've been walking in the hallway and caught movement out of the corner of my eye, but when I turn the corner, there's nothing there."

"What else?" He knew from the way she was avoiding his eyes that there was more.

"I keep finding things at the bottom of the stairs. Dead things. It used to be roses, but the last was a rodent of some sort. Gideon—"

"What?" he asked, perplexed.

"You're hurting me," she said, gesturing to the hand holding hers with a now-painful grip.

"Oh, good God." He relaxed his hold, rubbing her fingers gently. He was losing control. He needed to refocus.

"Why did you say it was your fault?" he asked, aware he was holding his breath.

She frowned, her confusion apparent.

"I had your servants questioned," he said, apologizing when her eyes flared. "When you found Martin's body, you said it was your fault. That's the reason I suspected you to begin with. Why would you say such a thing?"

Amelia's lips parted, and she began to speak before hesitating and beginning again. "I don't recall saying it…but I do know what I meant. You see, I have often thought those words since that day."

She raised her eyes to his, the crystalline blue sparkling behind a pool of unshed tears. "If I hadn't agreed to come back to England, Martin would be alive today. I didn't want to return. This place—the peerage—had nothing but contempt for my father—a man who built a fortune out of nothing. My father was brilliant and kind. He had more nobility of spirit than any blue blood born to a title… but any fat slovenly lord thinks he can spit on his memory because he wasn't titled. *They're not fit to even speak his name*," she hissed.

Gideon knew enough of the haute ton's secrets to agree with her. He winced. "I know you may not believe this, given my recent ascension, but for some I've met, I am in complete agreement."

Amelia snorted lightly and took a shaky breath. "My plan was to make our life in Italy near Isobel and her family. Although he missed England at times, Martin agreed. We were free on the continent in a way that simply wasn't possible here. It was like I could breathe for the first time. He felt the same way…until he didn't."

"Because Martin met Lord Worthing," he said, filling in the blanks. "And the viscount had to return home to attend to his estates. He convinced the two of you to come with him."

"Yes."

They stared at each other for a long moment. She squeezed his hand. "I know you don't agree that what we saw is a demon, and maybe it isn't, but whatever its true nature, it *is* evil. Perhaps there is a person behind all these incidents, but if so, then they are in league with something unnatural and occult."

Oh dear. She really believed that…

It wasn't her fault, of course; the villain had done his job too well. What Gideon had seen had made him question reality, too. But demons and mysticism was the realm of charlatans. "Whoever the culprit is, they are both ruthless and clever. But they are not magical—there are no supernatural forces at work here."

One corner of her mouth turned down and he moved to sit down next to her, giving in to his impulse to hold her in his arms.

"I'm going to find this person, and I'm going to stop them. I promise you that."

Gideon waited for her to agree with him, to express some faith in his ability to take care of her. He was still waiting when they arrived in London.

CHAPTER 19

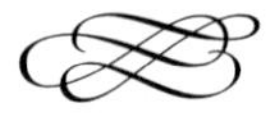

Amelia watched in fascination as Gideon got down on his hands and knees.

"Was it here that you fell?"

She nodded mechanically, forgetting he couldn't see her in his near-prone position on the floor of her salon.

"Yes," she confirmed as he felt along the ornate floral pattern of the Aubusson carpet. He appeared determined to touch every fiber of the weave.

Gideon had already examined the shelves and moldings. She had explained that everything appeared to have shifted and warped, but all had been righted before she woke the following day. There was no sign of what happened save for a bit of tell-tale streaking in the windows she was sure hadn't been there before.

The earl was not convinced by the glass, telling her that the expense of the house did not always correspond with the quality of its glazing. He was certain she had been drugged somehow.

Gideon had been determined to interrogate all the servants. He was convicted one of them had slipped her something, but she'd sworn she hadn't taken a drop or eaten a bite after returning from the ball. He'd conceded poison by food or drink unlikely then, and instead began to look for toxic substances on every surface and in the individual threads of her carpet...

Crispin had been delivered to his townhouse by an attentive Mr. Clarke. Amelia had insisted on stopping there as well, so she could make the arrangements for his convalescence. She had been prepared to organize the servants and to send for Crispin's family physician, only to find that Mr. Clarke had taken it upon himself to coordinate everything to the last detail.

By the time she and Gideon had arrived, Crispin was freshly bathed and dressed in his night rail. He had been deposited on a makeshift bed in the library, having expressed a strong preference to be surrounded by his books.

Mr. Clarke had acceded to each one of Crispin's requests, fussing over him with such care and consideration that Amelia had felt superfluous when the doctor arrived. She had let Gideon usher her away, unaware he would start turning her home over the minute he walked into the door.

"Would you care for some refreshment?" she asked as he crawled across the carpet.

He grunted, his face inches from the floor. Amelia sighed. After standing there a moment longer, she went to the kitchen to ask for a cold collation to be sent to the salon. She was heading to the stairs when Gideon charged into the hallway, sweeping her into a tight embrace.

"Where did you go?"

"To the kitchen!" She gasped. "I was asking Cook to prepare us something to eat."

Chagrined, Gideon winced and released her. "My apologies. I tend to get lost in my investigations."

Despite the fright he had just given her, she had to suppress a smile. "I see... Does this mean you found something?"

"No, but that doesn't mean there was nothing there. If someone coated one of your vases or the fabric of your settee with some toxin or hallucinogen, it is entirely possible that there would be no trace of it now. Many such substances would only be efficacious for a short while before losing potency."

"Wouldn't I have noticed such a thing?"

He shrugged "Even trace amounts of a liquid or a powder could have done the trick."

Amelia nodded placatingly. She hadn't expected him to find anything. She knew in her bones the attack had been occult in nature. But men like the earl required facts and evidence.

Would he be leaving now? Her heart constricted. She took a deep breath and braced herself for the inevitable parting. "Well, thank you for going to the trouble to look over the salon."

Gideon's mouth firmed. "Amelia, I haven't finished. I intend on examining every inch of this house and garden. In between, I will speak to all the servants from the butler to the lowliest scullery maid. They may not have slipped something into your tea, but it doesn't absolve them of this. It's also possible one of them saw something relevant and is afraid to speak."

Every inch of the house? He had just taken over an hour in the salon! How long was he planning on staying?

"But I was just about to retire to bed…" She trailed off as his expression softened.

"I promised to get to the bottom of this. Until I have, I'm not leaving you alone. I can sleep on the floor if you wish."

"You *can't* sleep on the floor."

He scoffed. "Believe me, I've slept in more uncomfortable places."

Feeling self-conscious, Amelia stared at him. He was so handsome, so protective…

Because of her marriage, she had denied her own needs and desires for so long it was now second nature. But last night with Gideon, she had a taste of nirvana—just enough to know there was more to feel and experience.

Feeling very warm and very daring, Amelia put her hand on his arm. "I think you should continue with your inquiries upstairs…in my bedroom."

Gideon blinked. Clearly, she had caught him off guard with her blatant invitation. He leaned back. "Well, in that case, I think I can postpone my search of the rest of the house until the morrow."

Amelia was tempted to giggle to cover her awkwardness but ended up gasping instead when Gideon swept her into his arms and up the stairs.

~

THERE WAS no fire in the bedroom. She should have been cold, but Amelia didn't feel the chill in the air. If anything, she was flushed and overheated.

The warmth came from within. It burned inside her as Gideon undressed her, removing her dress and stays until she was in nothing but her thin chemise.

"Take it off for me," he whispered.

Grateful that there was only the moonlight to reveal her, she wriggled, pulling the almost transparent linen over her head.

Gideon sucked in a deep breath, his hand reaching out and touching the skin of her décolletage as if he couldn't help himself. He ran his hand all the way down the side of her waist and over her backside, palming it and pulling her closer to him.

She would have complained that he was still dressed were it not for the explosion of sensation when her skin encountered the rough wool of his breeches.

He embraced her, lifting her off her toes and laying her gently on the mattress. He stripped off his boots and waistcoat, but only managed to open his shirt before giving in to the temptation of joining her on the bed.

Amelia opened her arms, hugging him to her, a move that made him laugh.

"I think you'll enjoy it more if you let me move."

She pressed a hot kiss to his neck, tugging off the cravat he'd been too impatient to remove. "I don't think it can get better than this."

Gideon raised his head, meeting her eyes with a hot intent gaze. "Oh, it will. I swear it."

He pulled the rest of his clothing off and guided her legs around him, making her shiver as the delicate skin of her inner thighs met his hard hips. His mouth took possession of her, stroking her tongue with his own until she was mimicking him in perfect concert.

Though practically a novice, Amelia knew enough to realize she was in the hands of a master. Her misgivings and self-doubt disappeared as Gideon touched her, stroking every inch of her body and alternatively lathing and sucking the tips of her breasts.

Nearly insensible with lust, Amelia gave over control of her body, moving when Gideon moved, responding to his touch instinctively. She gloried in his touch, using her own hands to learn his body, the way he was hard and soft at the same time.

Licking a spot under his ear made him shiver, sending a shaft of satisfaction through her. Her victory was short-lived when Gideon pinned her wrists with one hand, urging her legs apart.

His hard staff rubbed against her, priming in her liquid heat. Consumed by hunger, she twisted and pulled him closer until he was pushing inside.

It wasn't like their first joining. That had been so jarring and unexpected. This time, she was ready and eager for her body to become one with his. Amelia wanted to hold him inside her, to meld the very fabric of their beings.

An involuntary cry was ripped from her throat as his cock slowly forged inside, pushing to the hilt. Murmuring sweet nonsense, Gideon soothed her until she had absorbed the shock of his intrusion. He kissed and nibbled at her lips, one hand moving up to cradle her head as his hips moved with minute precision and Herculean patience.

His advance and retreat was carefully orchestrated—a dance that built in speed and tempo until she writhed, clinging breathlessly, with her arms wrapped around his chest. It was as if his member was coated in some magic elixir that turned friction into ecstasy.

Sensation built as he continued to pump in and out of her. She did her best to touch him back, using unfamiliar muscles in her channel to caress and gratify him in turn.

Amelia knew her campaign to give as much pleasure as she received was succeeding when Gideon's breath hitched. His grip on her head tightened briefly before he shifted to brace his weight on his forearms. His chest pressed down against her breasts firmly as he closed the distance between them. The only space he allowed was the one required to withdraw, and only so he could surge forward with inexorable strength.

She could feel that about him—his power and potency. It was in the definition of arms and chest, and the lines of his body. He could use that vigor against her. In many other men, his strength would become a weapon. But as Gideon rocked into her, his deep pulsing rhythm stuttering as he finally began to lose control, she knew he would never hurt her.

Amelia gave him all she could, trusting him as she had no other. The deep twinges of pleasure coalesced, rolling on top of each other. Moaning, she rode the wave, her inner muscles fluttering rapidly with her climax.

Gideon gasped and threw his head back, pumping out of control until he was grinding against her. His staff firmed until it was impossibly hard, a velvet-covered stone phallus that jerked and pulsed as he spilled his seed at the entrance of her womb.

His breath ragged, Gideon collapsed to the side, pulling her on top of him so he wouldn't lose the skin-to-skin contact as he recovered.

Wrung out and replete, Amelia rested her head just below Gideon's chin.

She could barely move. Every muscle in her body was lax, save for the one still racing in her chest.

Sexual relations were supposed to be pleasurable, even gluttonous at times. Amelia knew that from watching others, the way lovers in first flush acted with one another. But she hadn't expected it to be beautiful.

After long minutes, Gideon sighed drowsily. He pressed a kiss to her forehead. "I love you, too," he whispered before slipping into a deep sleep.

It took her heart longer to calm than it should have after that. She hadn't meant to tell him she loved him, but apparently that was what she had done. He had read the truth in her response to him, her every touch betraying her most deeply hidden secret.

She should have known better. Gideon had always been able to read her, to see straight through to her soul. Now he knew she loved him, that she probably always had.

But he just claimed to love you in return. Could she take him at his word?

Amelia knew the depth of Gideon's honor. If he said he loved her, then he believed it. But what if it was simple infatuation—or worse? What if deep down, he felt obligated to return her affection because of their familial ties?

Yes, he desired her. But how often had a man confused lust with love? Her library shelves were full of such cautionary tales.

Like the snake in the garden, Gideon would offer Amelia her heart's desire. Marriage. A life at his side. She knew him too well to believe it would be otherwise. As a husband, he would be faithful. His honor would demand no less. But honor was not the same as love.

Could she live with an imitation of her longest-held dream?

She lay awake many hours, trying to convince herself she could.

CHAPTER 20

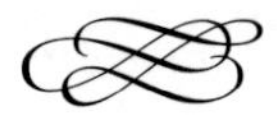

Whispers dragged her from sleep. Still pleasantly weighted down by the effects of last night's lovemaking, Amelia was reluctant to move. However, there was a rushed quality to the muted conversation taking place on the other side of the curtains that roused her to full wakefulness.

Why were the curtains around the bed drawn? "Gideon?"

The rapid buzz ceased and Gideon appeared at her side through the opening, holding her grey pelisse. He was already dressed save for his cravat.

"Finally awake! Good," he exclaimed. "Come, come, I'm starving."

He threw the pelisse over her nude body.

"What are you doing? Who is out there?" she asked, gesturing beyond the curtain.

"It's only your maid Carlotta, going about her business." He pulled her to the edge of the bed, trying to put one of her arms through the sleeve of the garment.

She struggled out of his hold. "Gideon, stop."

He frowned. "Wouldn't you rather be covered while we breakfast? Personally, I'd prefer your male servants didn't get to see you like this, but I'm rather selfish that way."

Amelia blushed. By now, the entire household staff must be aware of her overnight guest.

As a widow, she had every right to entertain a male like his lordship, but she wasn't keen on parading him before every footman and chambermaid.

"I think we should stay here and send for a tray."

"But you have such a lovely morning room!" he protested. "Wouldn't you like to eat there instead?"

Not content to wait for an affirmative answer, he tugged her out of bed with an eager air, ushering her to the bedroom door in only her pelisse.

"At least let me get dressed!"

If he was so concerned about modesty, then he could bloody well wait till Carlotta was free to help her don a proper morning gown. She pulled away from him, intent on asking her maid for assistance.

"Amelia, wait!"

But it was too late. In a few steps, she could see Carlotta on her hands and knees on the floor at the foot of the bed. Tears were streaming down her maid's cheeks as she scrubbed at an enormous blood stain on the carpet.

Amelia's breath stuttered to a stop.

"I—I left the window open," Gideon broke in, rushing to her side to take her hand. "An injured bird flew in and died. I took it outside. Why don't we go downstairs while Carlotta cleans in here?"

She put a horrified hand over her mouth before kneeling to take the distraught maid in her arms.

Amelia didn't believe Gideon for a moment. The stain was too large for any bird or even a small animal. Only a big animal—or a person—could account for its size.

Wrapping her hands tighter, she pulled Carlotta in close enough to whisper in her ear. "Tell me quick, was it a person—a child?" she asked in Italian.

"*No, un cane.*" Carlotta sobbed.

"Carlotta!" Gideon scolded, hauling both to their feet.

"Don't yell at her, Gideon. You should have known you could

never hide such a thing from me," she said, holding and comforting the other woman.

It was easier than dealing with the storm of emotion roiling in her breast.

Gideon rubbed his hands roughly over his face. "Of course, I apologize to you both. Carlotta, I'm sorry. Please, help your mistress to get dressed," he said, giving them a little shove toward her wardrobe.

"Gideon…" she began.

"Do not worry. I'll take care of this," he interrupted, waving at the stain. "We're getting rid of the lot—the entire carpet has to go."

"That's not what I was going to say," she protested as Carlotta rinsed her own hands in the washbasin.

The water turned pink, and Carlotta excused herself with a murmur to empty the basin and refill the pitcher for Amelia's use.

Gideon waited till Carlotta left the room. "I know, love," he said softly. "But I think we should put off any discussion until I'm certain the household is secure. Once you've dressed, I will have your driver drop you at Lord Worthing's house. I'm going to ask Clarke to meet you there. He'll keep watch over you and Carlotta while I deal with an important matter."

He wanted Carlotta to go as well? "I'm not in the habit of taking my maid to call on Crispin."

"She's had a fright. I think it would settle her nerves to accompany you."

Amelia suspected he was more concerned with having another set of eyes on her than her maid's sensibilities but didn't make an issue of it. "Where will you go? What is this important matter?"

Gideon averted his eyes. "I'll be making a few stops—Bow Street chief among them."

He stopped, his gaze flickering over the stain and the bed beyond. His head shook a fraction as if he was arguing with himself. "I don't understand how I could have slept through this," he muttered.

Gideon turned back to her, putting his arms on her shoulders. "I'm going to hire a few runners to watch the house from the outside. I'll also enlist their aid to conduct systematic interviews of your staff. One of them must have seen or heard something."

"You will need Adolfo to translate then. Most of them speak English poorly," she said as Carlotta came back in.

"A sound plan. I'll go speak to him now," he replied before kissing her hard and quitting the room.

Amelia wrapped her arms around herself and stared at the dark stain on her carpet. She pushed it away in her mind.

Gideon is right. The entire carpet needed to be discarded. Carlotta interrupted her reverie with a signal all was in readiness.

Moving mechanically, she performed her ablutions and dressed. Her mind was quiet and strangely detached, as if she was watching everything from a distance.

When Gideon bundled her and Carlotta into her town coach without breakfast, she didn't complain. Nor did she utter a single word of reproach when he saw her to the door and then hurried away with a promise that Clarke would be joining them shortly. She was too busy formulating a plan.

Crispin was still indisposed when his butler let her into his townhouse.

"Don't worry Jefferson. I can hardly expect him to come down on a broken leg. I'll just show myself up."

Leaving Carlotta to visit with her friends in the kitchen, Amelia went up to the second story. She entered Lord Worthing's bedroom after a perfunctory knock and stopped short.

Mr. Clarke was sitting on the bed at Crispin's side. Their heads were close together, and Crispin's hand was resting over Clarke's.

Mr. Clarke noticed her first. He broke away, getting to his feet quickly.

"Excuse me, Mrs. Montgomery," he said before bowing.

Clarke's formality betrayed his unease. Just yesterday, he'd been very familiar with her, greeting her with a hug and quick pat on the back.

"Err...I suppose you are surprised to see me here," he said. "After yesterday's mishap, I decided to call round early to see our patient."

Our patient?

"How kind of you," she said. "I did expect you, but not so soon. Gideon sent word to your house asking you to come here."

Clarke's expression changed, an alert expression lightening his eyes. "Oh, I see. Then I'll have a quick word with Lord Worthing's staff. Gideon's notes will have been brought round here by my staff."

He excused himself with another bow.

"Amelia..." Crispin held out his hand. She gave herself a little shake and went to his side, noting his slight blush.

"How are you feeling, dear?" she asked, sitting on the bed.

"Fine, fine," he said. "Um, about what you just saw..."

Amelia squeezed his hand. "Don't worry, my friend. There is no need to explain. Martin wouldn't have wanted you to spend the rest of your days alone either."

The viscount looked down at his hands and sniffed, his chin dimpling as he fought not to cry. "I will never stop loving Martin. Quite frankly, I am surprised to be feeling this way—and this may not be mutual. I find Mr. Clarke a bit difficult to read."

She did not share Crispin's opinion. Clarke's behavior just now had been telling, but perhaps it was easier for an outside observer to understand it. *Plus, I've seen someone fall in love with Crispin before...*

"I have no doubts," she assured him. "There is something there."

Crispin leaned closer. "Do you really think so?"

She nodded. "I do...And I hope you forgive my selfishness, but I will be trading on your recent attachment to achieve the impossible."

"Hmm." Crispin leaned back on the pillows. "Does this impossible task involve a certain determined earl?"

"It does, and I will explain every detail once I've secured Mr. Clarke's assistance."

"Ah, I think I understand," he said with a sage nod. "Then I suggest you go down and find him straightaway because I want my curiosity satisfied as quickly as possible."

Amelia hadn't thought herself capable of a genuine smile this morning, but it came anyway. She excused herself from her friend, buoyed by his manner and unquestioned support.

If Mr. Clarke was surprised by her request for a private conference, he did not betray it in any way. It wasn't until she'd sat him down in the library that she truly shocked him.

"I received Gideon's note," he began, reaching out to pat her gloved hand. "I want you to rest assured that you are well looked after. No harm will come to you while you're in my care."

"Thank you, but my life is not in danger. It's Gideon who will die if you don't help me."

Clarke frowned. "Mrs. Montgomery, Amelia, you've been through an ordeal. I assure you—"

"Crispin will also die," she interrupted. "And most likely you as well if you don't listen to me now."

She took both his hands in hers and began to explain.

CHAPTER 21

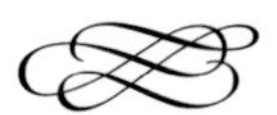

Gideon was furious. Since waking to a bloodstained mess in Amelia's bedroom this morning, nothing had gone right.

He had lied to her, of course. A visit to Bow Street had been low on his list of priorities that morning. His chief purpose in leaving her that day had been to find Sir Clarence and wring his bloody neck.

He had stormed to his uncle's townhouse, ready to tear him apart. But his plans to exact a painful retribution had been put on hold when he was told his relative was out of town.

Gideon had been so put out the housekeeper had shown him in, fetching his mistress to confirm that Sir Clarence was indeed away on business.

Only Mrs. Spencer's genuine surprise had convinced him to quit Clarence's house. Spoiling for a fight, he had gone back to Amelia's to interview her staff. He was certain Clarence had bribed one of them to terrorize Amelia. Unfortunately, he had failed to materialize a single suspect.

Perhaps it had been the language barrier, or the fact there were so many of them, but when no one had broken down with a confession or come forward with a helpful clue, he had lost his temper. He'd stormed out of the house to Bow Street, where he'd hired not one but two runners to watch over the house. He also resolved to ask Amelia to send some of the staff away to one of his country estates—preferably all of them.

Gideon was no fool. There was no way Amelia would dismiss any of them outright, but he needed smaller numbers to deal with right now. Besides, they'd be combining households once they were married.

All those plans and suggestions he was about to make were for naught.

He'd returned to Amelia's house after a few hours absence. His steward had sent an urgent message, relaying a minor kerfuffle between tenants on his country estate. Believing Amelia to be securely ensconced under Clarke's watchful eye, he had taken the time to write detailed instructions to his man on how he wished the problem handled.

Then he'd taken himself off to Doctors Commons to secure a special license. Gideon wanted to be married right away.

When he'd gone to collect Amelia at Worthing's, he was told she had already gone home. Gideon swore under his breath the entire way, hoping Adolfo had faithfully executed his order to replace the carpet in the bedroom. But he didn't find out if the butler obeyed him.

Amelia had barred him from the house. No one answered his knock. When he tried to open them, he found she had added bars to the exterior doors and extra locks to the windows. To the outside observer, the house appeared empty.

He knew it wasn't. The Bow Street runners reported movement behind the drawn curtains. Additionally, both Amelia's town carriage and travel coach were still in the mews.

Gideon ignored the snickers of the Bow Street runners when they realized he was locked out.

"A fine toff like you can find another bit o' muslin," the one named Owen suggested helpfully.

The burly man scrambled out of his way when Gideon turned on him with a black look.

"Just do what I'm paying you for," he ordered. "Watch for anyone approaching the house—and I mean anyone. I even want to know when the night man visits and how long he stays."

The two runners exchanged a look but agreed. He was paying them too much for them to do otherwise. To their credit, they didn't laugh aloud when he was forced to scale the back garden wall to access the rear balcony of the house.

He broke into one of the salons and stalked down the hall to her bedrooms, intending to confront Amelia straight away.

No carpet, but also no Amelia. Nothing in the other rooms as well. The house was almost empty. The few servants left only spoke Italian. After a stilted but productive conversation, he learned they had been instructed to pack their belongings—theirs, but not Amelia's. While they were being sent to the country for their protection, their mistress was selflessly staying on in town.

Knowing better than to wait for Amelia to come to him of her own accord, he sent out notes to his informants. Ten pounds to the man, woman, or child who could give him Amelia's whereabouts.

The answer came in a record twenty minutes. Amelia was at a ball.

CHAPTER 22

Lord Durney studied the list Amelia had copied from Isobel's letter. His expression was paternalistic and shrewd. "You know most of these volumes are very dear."

He pointed to a title on the list. "This one alone is quite costly. It's worth more than my wife's jewels."

Amelia smiled politely in the direction of the Lady Durney. The lady's modest string of pearls was probably paste, but she didn't dare mention that. "I imagine most genuine occult volumes are expensive, but if the text is on this list, then money is no object. Not for me. If you procure these volumes for me, I am prepared to pay a generous commission. Say twenty percent?"

Durney leaned in closer, a spark of eagerness lighting his eyes briefly before it dimmed. "But that commission alone would be hundreds of pounds on some of these," he warned, his head bobbing between her and the list.

"As I said, money is of no consequence. Speed is essential. If you can get me those books this week, I'll be pleased to compensate you for any additional expenses you might incur."

She put her gloved hand on his wrinkled one. "My dear friend the

Contessa Garibaldi specifically recommended you as the man I needed for this task."

Amelia had given up on receiving any aid from her former governess. Her appeal for advice had been sent weeks ago when she first encountered Gideon again. When she didn't hear anything, Amelia assumed her letter had been lost. With the recent outbreak of war with France, the mail service abroad had been thoroughly disrupted. But by some miracle, Isobel's letter had been waiting for her when she returned from Devon.

Amelia felt loved when she read the letter. Isobel was distraught over her predicament. Her former governess had expressed regret at being unable to come to her because of the perils of traveling in wartime. Nevertheless, Isobel managed to convey in a few simple words her concern and affection for her former charge.

More importantly, Isobel had practical advice to offer—just as Amelia had hoped. It contained an extensive list of books and several names.

Lord Durney had been at the top of the list. A brief inquiry via her solicitor revealed him to be an aficionado of rare and antique books. Isobel had also sent the names of a handful of other collectors, as well as an apothecary and another of a midwife.

Amelia wasn't certain how the latter was supposed to help with her current predicament, but at least she had a place to start her inquiries into the supernatural.

Durney pulled his collar away from his neck. He was blushing. "The Contessa is generous with her praise. She's a discerning collector. But while I'm familiar with most of these volumes, I should warn you that most are in private collections much like my own. Some of their owners may not wish to part with them for any price," he added anxiously.

Disappointment threaded through her. Amelia bit her lip. She had expected this part to be simple. "If they won't sell, perhaps they would consider letting the volumes."

"Letting the books?" Gurney guffawed. "These are hardly the type of works one finds in a lending library." His aristocratic tone was filled with disdain.

For a man of modest means, the old collector was certainly high in the instep, but Amelia didn't let her annoyance show on her face. The idea of renting out their books might strike some of them as one step too close to being in trade. Amelia knew many in the genteel class would rather starve than stoop so low.

She took Durney's arm and prodded him to walk with her around the edge of the Trenglove's ballroom. "They shouldn't think of it that way," she said with a dismissive wave. "It would be more like being a patron who lends a work of art for an exhibition. The difference is it won't be a painting, but a book and the audience will be considerably smaller. Namely myself and possibly a friend."

"A patron, you say? I hadn't thought of it in such a light." Durney puffed up. "Well, I do think some of the collectors involved might be moved to become patrons for your special project. An index of the supernatural is a Herculean task, but with your resources, you are advantageously positioned to make a better than decent start."

Amelia thanked him, promising to consult him if she had any difficulties understanding the books he had already agreed to part with—something he seemed preoccupied with. She bristled at such condescension but held her tongue. She knew nothing about the occult and Durney was an expert, although strictly in an academic sense.

Though he was only one of half a dozen collectors she had to consult, Amelia felt better than she had in ages. It was good to be *doing* something rather than wait for the next horror to befall her. She turned the corner, intending to find the exit now that her business was concluded.

The familiar hand that snaked out, pulling her into the dark corner, was so quick she didn't even have a chance to scream. Not that Gideon gave her a chance. His hand covered her mouth.

Amelia blinked up at him. How had he even found her? Though the Folsom ball was well attended, it wasn't considered the most fashionable of events. Their hosts were too old to be considered high-flyers, their music and refreshments tired and uninspired.

She didn't have the opportunity to question Gideon about his spy network. He kept his hand on her mouth and caught her up in his arms. Moving like a cat, he melted deeper into the shadows, abducting her from the ballroom with next to no effort.

There was no hue and cry in their wake. He managed to snatch her from under the ton's nose without anyone being the wiser. Marveling at his skill and the blindness of the other guests, Amelia waited until he had taken them to a dark and empty sitting room.

"Damn it, Gideon! You can't just carry me off without so much as a by your leave!"

Gideon's grip on her arms was firm. "And you can't seriously believe changing a few locks is going to keep me away from you."

Amelia shivered involuntarily, but it wasn't fear she felt. *Stop it*. She couldn't afford to be alone with him anymore.

"I have to leave." She tried to break his hold, but he wouldn't release her. In fact, he pulled her closer, wrapping his arms around her until she was crushed against his chest.

His scent enveloped her, and her body reacted predictably. Her breasts swelled, moisture pooling low in her body.

He stroked one of her curls. "Amelia, why are you trying to do this alone?"

"You know why!"

He winced. "As unfortunate as this morning's incident was—"

"It was more than an incident!"

Gideon held up a hand. "I know. But it changes nothing."

He lifted her chin, meeting her eyes imploringly. "Amelia, I know you may have some doubts. Someone is trying to intimidate you and last night, I slept through their latest assault. I understand your faith in me might be shaken now, but it's not a mistake I will make again. I can and will protect you."

She shook her head. "No, you need to stay away from me. The dead dog wasn't just intimidation. It was a message—a warning."

"Amelia..." he began.

She pushed against him, clutching at his waistcoat. "No, you must listen to me. That poor creature died because the monster wants me to know you're next."

"*Me?*" Gideon scowled. "No, my love. *You* are the one in danger."

The casual endearment nearly derailed her argument. She cleared her throat and stood her ground.

"If the monster wanted me dead, I would be dead," she declared firmly. "It has had ample opportunity to do away with me. Nothing occurred the entire year I spent in mourning. It wasn't until I returned to society that this nightmare began."

She put her hands on his chest. "Gideon. It doesn't *want* to kill me. It wants me to be alone. You're the one who will die if you continue to associate with me."

Gideon's jaw went slack as he followed her reasoning. But then he blinked, stubbornly jutting his chin out. "No. This must be part of Sir Clarence's plan. He's trying to force your hand. He wants you to marry Cannonburry. You told me so yourself. I would have confirmation of that now if Sir Clarence was still in town. The minute he returns, I'll *beat* the truth from him."

Amelia wanted to scream in frustration. Though there had been occasions when she wished ill for her authoritarian guardian, she knew Gideon would only be worsening the situation if he stooped to such violence.

"I would sooner marry Cannonburry than let anything happen to you."

The words were out before she could even think about them. If she'd spared a second to consider Gideon's reaction, she would have never uttered them.

She couldn't see much detail beyond the outline of his features in the dim light, but she didn't need a candle to know how he was reacting. The very air around them heated and seemed to vibrate. Amelia felt as if she had stumbled upon a predator in his lair, possibly a bear.

Holding her breath, she cautiously began to retreat. Gideon's arm shot out, yanking her against him.

"Don't even *think* about such a thing."

She struggled against his hold. "Damn it, Gideon! Can't you see I'm trying to save your life? What more do you want from me?"

"Everything. I want *everything*."

His lips came down on hers, hard and demanding as his arms wrapped around her, pulling until she was pressed against him, the tips of her breasts rubbing against his chest through the thin cloth of her bodice.

Gideon's kiss was like a fire blasting through her, burning away her resolve. Her willpower crumbled to dust against the intensity of his desire. She felt almost battered by the force of it, and the almost violent response of her own passion.

Hanging onto the last thread of her resistance, she pushed away. "No—we mustn't."

Breath harsh, he tugged her to the left, pinning her against the wall of the salon. "You want me as much as I want you."

It was a statement of fact, irrefutable. Amelia couldn't lie to him even as much as she wanted to.

"No one can know," she decided.

That demand was not well received. His hand slashed the air. "Amelia, you're nonsensical. We're about to be married."

"*No*, we are not. Not until this is over and we find the person or—or thing—behind all this."

"Am—"

"*Promise me*." She threw herself against him. "No one can know about the two of us until it's over."

Despite what he believed, Amelia knew in her heart his life depended on this—and she was not above pleading. She would beg if she had to.

The monster behind this was not all knowing. That would be too much to bear, but there was no evidence that was the case. Whoever was bedeviling her was acting and reacting to what he or she observed.

If Gideon wouldn't forsake her, then their liaison would have to remain a secret for his protection.

The earl looked up at the ceiling as if asking the heavens for patience. She knew he was marveling over her stubborn attachment to a belief he viewed as an irrational and superstitious conclusion.

"If you don't promise me, I'll run off to Gretna Green with Lord Cannonburry, my hand to God."

Her blasphemy amused him. "Cannonburry can't run anywhere, love."

Amelia tugged at the lapels of his tailcoat. Tears threaded through her voice. "*Do not laugh at me.*"

Gideon instantly sobered. "I will do as you ask on one condition."

She wiped surreptitiously at one cheek, hoping he hadn't noticed the tear in the dimness. "What is it?"

"You are not to sacrifice your safety for mine or anyone else's. No more haring off on your own. Even if the ton believes you to be unattached, you must consent to be guarded day and night, even if you are moving about socially."

"Gideon, you can't escort me about town. It would defeat the entire purpose."

"Then take your maid and footmen when appropriate. If it's necessary to attend a ball, notify me in advance and I'll be there as well, or Clarke if it pleases you. Even if I can't be with you, I can still watch over you from a distance. And you never sleep alone at night. I will be with you if I can help it—otherwise, your maid must sleep in your room."

This was like arguing with a brick wall. "You know very well you can't share my bed. Not when the creature enters my room to watch me sleep. And I can't subject Carlotta to that kind of danger. I'm sending her away, along with most of the staff. If I need help with the household duties, I will hire day servants—only I will sleep there after dark."

Gideon sighed heavily, but he didn't acknowledge the wisdom of her plans. "There's one more thing you must agree to."

Good God, there was more? "What is it?"

His hand rose to trace the line of her jaw. "Once this perceived danger passes, you will marry me with all haste."

It was on the tip of her tongue to agree, but she checked herself.

Gideon did not appreciate her hesitation. He leaned over her. "Promise me," he ordered, throwing back her words at her.

"If the danger has truly passed, then yes, I will marry you."

She could see his mouth curve just before he kissed her again. This time, she willingly melted into his embrace, grateful for the privacy of this small unused salon.

Amelia expected more of his potently drugging kisses. But suddenly, Gideon bent down on one knee. For a moment, she thought he was going to formally declare for her hand—up until the moment he tossed the hem of her skirt up.

"My lord! What are you doing?"

In fact, what he was up to was obvious. Gideon burrowed under her skirts, parting her legs and throwing one of them over his shoulder.

"Gideon, we are at a ball!"

She shivered as his busy hands ran up her stockings, stroking the bare skin between her garters.

His touch was sure and devilishly possessive. Amelia held on to his shoulders as he pushed her legs further apart to accommodate him. Cotton rent as he ruthlessly tore the slit in her drawers wider, exposing her most secret flesh to him.

Gideon's hands pinned her against the wall. She couldn't see his face under her skirts, but she could feel his smile against her before his lips parted. His tongue and fingers rubbed and licked, quickly establishing a rhythm that stole her breath.

Amelia moaned, dark pulsing pleasure rolled through her as little flames licked and bit at her sex. She made one last weak effort to push him away, but it was no more effective than melted candle wax. "Gideon, we must stop."

His grip tightened. Teeth bit down gently on her straining pearl. Her broken gasp of ecstasy became a moan. Amelia had to focus what little strength she had on remaining upright. Hips pistoning reflexively, she held onto his shoulders as two of his fingers delved inside her. Then the pattern changed. It was as if his fingers were searching for something, but she didn't know what.

Enlightenment came with a throb of pleasure. Gideon worked a magical little spot while his tongue lathed the pearl at the top of her sex over and over until she convulsed.

Amelia slid down the wall, limp and replete. The only thing she felt —was aware of—were those last throbs of velvet pleasure still echoing through her body.

It was the feel of Gideon's harsh breath on her cheek that brought her back to herself. She was in his arms, still pinned to the wall but now her legs were wrapped around him. His steely cock was probing, pushing at her swollen folds, demanding entrance.

"Someone will come in," she whispered, clinging to him. She had to hold on. Without his support, she would have crumpled to the floor.

His mouth pressed to her cheek and he inhaled, drawing her scent deep into his lungs.

"I locked the door." He took her mouth, his tongue plunging deep at the same time as he found her entrance and began to push inside.

Overwhelmed by his size and strength, Amelia broke off, throwing her head back and gasping as he drove his broad shaft home. She wrapped her arms around him, holding on for dear life as he with-drew and then thrust back home.

Nothing should feel that good. Trembling, Amelia gasped, biting down on his neck.

He laughed, appearing to enjoy her response. "That's it, love. You can take me now. Take all of me."

His words—the plaintive desperate note buried deep in his author-itarian demand—stoked the fire higher. She shuddered and pulled him into a deep kiss while he continued to move within her, rocking her into the wall.

Clamping down on him, she fought to hold him tight, fighting him as he pushed in as if to prove her will was a match for his. Gideon groaned and flexed, his grip on her legs and hips tightening. He moved with greater determination, thrusting deeper and faster until he had to move his hand to protect her head from being slammed against the wall.

Pinned helplessly, Amelia accepted his thrusts, crying out when his rhythm stuttered and broke. His hips ground into her one last time, pushing her over the edge into a violent and blinding orgasm. Inside her, he jerked, spilling his seed in hard jets.

This time, it was Gideon who crumpled weakly. He'd poured every bit of his strength and vitality into her. She took it, absorbed it, cradling it and him to her like a precious gift.

Gideon seemed surprised when he came to on the floor. By then, she had rearranged her clothing and repaired her coiffure. Her drawers were a total loss, so she'd stuffed them into her beaded reticule.

"Where are you going?" he asked, lifting his head from the floor when she made for the door.

Amelia stood straight, trying to project a strength of will and determination she did not actually possess.

"Home," she said firmly. "Don't follow me. From this moment on, I sleep alone."

She waited for his acknowledgment and agreement, but neither came. Instead, he just grinned, a flash of white in the darkness. Amelia decided to retreat before he recovered enough to argue with her.

If they did, she would lose and he knew it.

GIDEON WAITED until Sir Clarence was close enough to strangle before striking the match and lighting the taper on the side table.

"Hello, Uncle."

A red-faced and bleary-eyed Clarence whirled to face him, almost losing his balance in the process. "*What*? What are you doing here, boy?"

He stumbled to the bed against the wall in the spare, but elegantly appointed room.

Gideon resisted the urge to wrinkle his nose as a waft of stale wine breath hit him. "I've been waiting for you. For several weeks, in fact."

"Eh?" Sir Clarence, obviously relaxed, hiccupped and patted his paunch. "Oh, well…been out of town. I have many business interests. Things to attend to…"

Gideon had to strain to hear those last words. Sir Clarence was slurring. He pushed him onto the bed before the portly man fell over.

Would thrashing a drunk man be a stain on his honor?

"I called on you several times these weeks past, only to be told by the charming Mrs. Spencer that you were away. She didn't know where. None of your friends knew either. I even sent a man to your Northumberland estate. Imagine my surprise to learn you've been sleeping here in your club for the last week, instead of your comfortable townhouse."

One of the few I don't happen to be a member of…

"Hmm," Sir Clarence hummed, his heavy lids drifting down.

Gideon leaned over and yanked out one of his protruding nose hairs. Sir Clarence yelped, sitting up straight.

"As I was saying," Gideon continued as if there was no interruption. "No one knew where you were. I believe Mrs. Spencer was becoming quite annoyed with me toward the end there."

Seemingly confused as to what had happened Clarence rubbed his face with the palm of his hand. "S'bit annoyed with me too. Tis why I'm sleeping here."

Gideon nodded understandingly. The hesitation in the elder's manner that followed the nose-hair yank dissipated and he slumped again, clearly not recognizing the threat across from him.

Sir Clarence coughed and spat on the floor next to the bed. He stretched. "Um-hum, well, thank you for checking in on me."

Gideon's smile grew several degrees colder. "I'm afraid my motive is not so altruistic. I'm actually here to threaten your life, my dear uncle."

Sir Clarence blinked and cocked his head at him. "Sorry?"

In a snap, Gideon hauled the older man to his feet. "The only reason I don't kill you where you stand is because you didn't rape her all those years ago."

Clarence was sober now. His hands scrabbled against Gideon's grip. "I don't know what you're talking about," he said, blinking, then contradicted himself. "Whatever Amelia's told you—"

"It wasn't her. Amelia never speaks about her time in your home. I think she prefers to let the past lie." He lifted Clarence off his toes. *"I am not so generous."*

Despite his precarious position, his relative's bone-deep sense of superiority was undaunted. "I've done nothing wrong," he spat. "I gave that girl a home! I provided for her—a cit's daughter no less."

Gideon scoffed. "One worth a fortune. Amelia insists it's the reason behind this ridiculous attempt to strong-arm her into a marriage with that doddering old fool Cannonburry. But we both know what is really behind it. Is Cannonburry really so desperate for an heir he'll overlook someone else fathering it?"

Releasing his uncle, Gideon gave him a little push, sending him crashing onto the bed.

"Save your excuses and explanations. I have the whole picture now—save for one piece." He inhaled and released it slowly. "Did you have anything to do with Martin's death?"

Clarence's mouth went slack. He sputtered incoherently, whiskers quivering, before finding his tongue. "How dare you suggest I had anything to do with that! My own *son*."

Gideon studied him carefully, drawing on all his knowledge of interrogation and dissimulation. Drunk or no, the indignation was genuine. He bent to meet Clarence's eyes on the same level.

"Then the mysterious man you hired to terrorize Amelia—the giant who leaves behind clay shards—he's not the same one who threw Martin down the stairs?"

Sir Clarence blinked at him. "No, that's not right. My boy fell down the stairs. Tripped on the runner," he whispered.

Gideon noticed he didn't deny the charge someone was intimidating Amelia at his behest, but this was confusing. The suggestions that Martin's death was not an accident elicited a reaction of surprise and shock…perhaps even pain.

Though he could never be called a warm or loving parent, Sir

Clarence had some paternal regard for Martin, if only because he was an only child and a son.

Less certain now about his accusations, Gideon continued. "The damage was too great for a simple fall. I spoke to one of the witnesses who heard it happen. Martin's body was found too far from the bottom of the stairs, too far unless he'd been hurled by someone very strong. This same someone left large and deep impressions in the carpet and traces of brown dust—probably clay."

His uncle reddened. "You're lying! There was no dust. It was a simple accident. Trying to imply anything else is disgraceful, a sham."

Clarence slashed at the air, pointing an accusing finger at Gideon. "You're just trying to deflect from your scandalous affair with your cousin's widow." He waited for a reaction before making a fist. "Oh, yes, I know all about it. Tongues are wagging all over town. I can't even escape it here in my own club. If I didn't know better, I'd say you had…"

He stopped short and lapsed into a sullen silence.

"That I rid myself of Martin so I could be with Amelia? Why would that have even been necessary? It's not like theirs was a true marriage," he pointed out. "Additionally, you are well aware I was abroad at the time of his death."

Gideon crossed his arms and looked down his nose at the older man. "Fortunately, you don't need to concern yourself with the rumors. The furor will die down once Amelia and I are married."

Sir Clarence's head snapped up. "But you can't!"

"I assure you I can. Furthermore, I want to."

"But you're a bloody earl now. Think of your title. You can't marry a *cit's* daughter."

"I can do whatever I damn well please. As it happens, I am marrying a lady. A loving and generous one."

"Men in your position don't marry for love! They marry unstained virgins fresh out of the schoolroom, well-dowered chits of good breeding."

"My bride has enough natural grace and breeding for the both us."

And until he got his hands on her, she'd been as pure as the driven snow.

"Pffaw. That hardly matters." Sir Clarence said. "She's a bloody widow and a tradesman's get. It's simply not the done thing."

Gideon was getting tired of the circuitous argument. "Nevertheless, I *am* marrying Amelia, and soon. I just stopped by to give you fair warning—cease this pointless harassment. Stop trying to draw Amelia into your sordid arrangements. She is out of your reach now."

Sir Clarence's eyes flicked away. "Told you. I don't have an arrangement with Cannonburry. As for these other accusations, I know nothing about them."

Gideon should have expected the pugnacious reply, but it still irked him. He leaned close, forcing Sir Clarence to draw back until his shoulders touched the wall on the other side of the bed.

"Thrashing a drunkard is considered bad form, so I'll take my leave of you now, but make no mistake. If you or your giant so much as sneezes in Amelia's direction, I will call you out—blood relation or no."

Checking the impulse to continue making threats he exited the room, nodding to the now ashen-faced porter he'd bribed for entry to the club's inner sanctum.

Gideon didn't think the details could be made out through the thick doors and walls of the bedroom wing. Nevertheless, he tipped the porter an extra pound for his discretion on the way out. Truthfully, he didn't mind if the entire ton knew what he thought of his uncle, except for the fact it would also drag Amelia's name into the mud once more. And he knew society was only too quick to blame the woman, no matter how innocent she was.

As I did.

Gideon shook himself as he reached the street. He wouldn't make that mistake again. From this moment on, he would give short shrift to those pernicious societal whispers the ton thrived on.

Of course, some of those rumors were true now. He and Amelia *were* engaged in a scandalous affair. Clarence wasn't wrong about the scandal. Even the most staid gentlemen at his clubs were commenting about it, according to Clarke. Fortunately for them, no one dared to cut Amelia directly over it. As far as he could tell, she was oblivious to the situation. Her mind was fixed elsewhere these days. However, he could not count on his reprieve to last.

Gideon sincerely hoped tonight's visit would be the end of the harassment plaguing Amelia. Though he had no direct evidence, he knew in his bones Clarence was responsible. Except...

His uncle *had* been shaken when Gideon related what he'd learned in his investigation, especially the detail about the dust. Turning over Sir Clarence's reaction in his mind, he dismissed his doubts.

I'm not wrong. It was him.

And marriage would silence the current gossip. These kind of scandals were forgotten the moment the couple in question said, 'I do.' Such was the way of the ton.

With luck, Amelia would consent to marry him soon. In the meantime, he decided to go and find her at the Porter bash. His mind raced ahead, wondering where he would find the seclusion required to seduce her. Gideon didn't really have a choice in the matter.

Despite his attempts to convince her otherwise, Amelia had put her dainty foot down about them sharing a bed at night. Convinced that her mysterious monster would return when they slept, she had taken the unprecedented step of giving up the master bedroom of her home. Alone in the house at night save for Adolfo—who refused to leave her—Amelia slept in a narrow cot in the servant's hall.

Her reasoning was faultless. Who would expect the lady of the house to be in a lowly chambermaid's quarters?

However, Amelia's brilliant maneuver meant Gideon had to wait for her to fall asleep every night before he silently crept inside the room and stretched out on the floor next to her. He would rise and depart just before the day servants arrived.

The situation would have been laughable if it weren't so frustrating.

Just another quiet week, perhaps two, and she'll see it's over. Gideon was certain. In the meantime, there was the orangery in the Porter's garden...

CHAPTER 23

Amelia perched at the edge of her chair at the edge of the ballroom. She listened with rapt attention to the impromptu lecture she'd prodded Lady Lewin into giving her.

A noted bluestocking and eccentric, Lady Lewin was an expert in demonology, one who needed little prompting to wax enthusiastic on her favorite subject. It was the reason the other old biddies in this, the chaperone's seating area, were giving them a wide berth.

Amelia had been apprehensive about approaching her. The spinster wasn't one of the scholar and collectors recommended by Isobel. Relatively new to town, Lady Lewin hadn't interacted with the contessa before—probably because she was much younger than Amelia had initially supposed—her early forties at most. There was also the fact that, as a woman, Lady Lewin was not held in high regard in the exclusive circle of experts Amelia had been consulting.

That was exactly why Amelia had sought her out. She was not disappointed.

"While Barrett's demon classification is quite popular with Gurney and his cronies, I'm fond of the King James' simpler arrangement, the one detailed in his *Daemonologie* series. His way doesn't fuss with names and ranks but organizes them according to their modus operandi—the specific behavior demon's display when bedeviling humans. Of course, his thesis was incorrect. King James believed spirits and demonic influences were the cause of all maladies and illnesses. Now we know they are caused by an imbalance of the humors."

Amelia nodded. "That seems a far more practicable approach. After all, these entities have the names people gave them, but in reality, one name could describe any number of demons and vice versa."

She didn't want to think about the alternative scenario where the demon *shared* its name with a human. "Would it trouble you if I wrote this down?" she asked, reaching into her unfashionably large reticule for a small pad and pencil.

Lady Lewin blinked and beamed at her. "No, by all means go ahead," she said before complimenting Amelia on her foresight.

"A commendable practice. I should do the same. These affairs are so deadly dull—well, they normally are with no one to talk to," she added, patting Amelia on the hand before pulling the drawstring of her own reticule.

Lady Lewin pulled out a copy of Mrs. Moore's latest horror novel.

Amelia laughed. "I love Mrs. Moore as well. Her books are so... atmospheric." She trailed off and looked down at her notes.

Lady Lewin was a remarkable woman, with a breadth of understanding for the occult and esoteric. And like Amelia, she was a bit of an outsider in their rigid society.

She felt a kinship to the older woman, the sort that came from a mutual lack of acceptance from their peers.

Amelia slid to the edge of her chair, casting a quick glance around before asking what she didn't dare ask any of the other priggish scholars she'd been interviewing. "Would you be familiar with the types of entities one could call on to act on someone's behalf?"

Lady Lewin's bright expression sobered. "Now, my dear, I realize some of the ton may be a bit too tart-tongued when it comes to you, but summoning the dark forces to do your bidding is not the answer...not that I would know how. My interest is strictly academic."

Amelia flushed. "No, that is not—"

Lady Lewin tsked maternally. "Believe me, my dear, I have wished for the ability to crush my detractors now and again. But calling on demons is a dangerous business, even if one knows what one is about and you as a mere novice..."

Amelia held up a hand, trying to stop the gentle reprimand before any passersby heard them. Her voice dropped to a thready whisper. "I have no interest in calling a demon; on the contrary, I want to...I wish to rid myself of one."

"*Oh.*" Lady Lewin paled. She took hold of Amelia's hand and held it tight. "Er, I wish I could help you, my dear..."

Amelia smiled despite tears stinging at her eyes. Lady Lewin was definitely a kindred spirit.

"I understand, your interest is strictly academic. But all I want is information. I need to know about those entities that can act in our world, giants with glowing eyes," she whispered.

Lady Lewin's mouth turned down. "According to my studies, that would not be a demon. You see, the latter are creatures of spirit—they do not possess a physical body. I've never heard of one that could manifest itself on this plane."

It was Amelia's turn to frown. "But if they don't have bodies, how do they act?"

"By using others, influencing the weak-willed or through outright possession. Truth be told, I've had more than one nightmare imagining who on my staff might be possessed. It's hardly a rational fear. From what I've read, a possessed person is barely functional, and they grow sickly as if the demon feeds off them. The afflicted could not do a servant's work for very long."

She caught Amelia's dismayed expression. "Though they are rare, there are other nefarious creatures in the world, those with corporeal form. You may not be dealing with a demon at all."

Amelia bit her lip. If the giant wasn't a demon, then what was it? "What could it be?"

Lady Lewin gaze sharpened, a determined glint in her eye. "Why don't you call on me in a few days? I can delve into my library and try to come up with a list. I suggest you do the same with the books you've already collected."

Trying to take heart, Amelia nodded. It was what she'd been doing, but her focus had been on demons. If Lady Lewin was correct, then none of her meticulously listed research had any relevance.

They spoke a half hour more until there was a commotion at the door. People began to whisper and throw them sideways glances.

Amelia didn't need to be told what had captured their attention. Gideon had arrived. Hurriedly, she rose, preparing to excuse herself.

Lady Lewin gave her a knowing glance before turning in her seat, craning her neck to see across the room. "No need for explanations, my dear. If I had that man at my beck and call, I'd head for the nearest orangery as well."

Dumbstruck, Amelia stared at her, embarrassment flooding her cheeks.

Lady Lewin was too busy looking at Gideon to notice her chagrin. "My, my," the older woman breathed, snapping her fan open and waving it over herself. "Look at those shoulders. I imagine that's what gladiators used to look like in the Roman arena…"

Amelia choked back unwilling laughter. Face flaming, she bid Lady Lewin a hasty goodbye. It would do no good to deny the affair at this point.

Despite her entreaties, Gideon insisted on appearing at every event she attended. Though he would never do more than give her a civil greeting before their avid audience, people had inevitably noticed when they would disappear together.

She had insisted on not being seen with him, and the earl had obeyed her instructions to the letter. However, he always managed to find that one moment when no one was watching to waylay her. Once, he'd snatched her in the empty hallway outside of the ladies receiving room at the Trent rout. At the Kenneth ball, he'd managed to grab her from an alcove just a few steps away from the crowded dance floor.

This time, Amelia got no further than the hall outside the ballroom. She was looking for a footman to fetch her cloak when Gideon appeared at her back, his hands burning through the delicately embroidered organza cloth at her waistline.

"Come with me," he whispered in her ear.

"*No*, Gideon."

Her protest fell on deaf ears. He rushed her to a narrow hallway and through a series of darkened rooms before tapping on the wall, revealing an opening in an otherwise unexceptional oak panel.

"A hidden door!" she said, enchanted despite herself. It was just like a Mrs. Moore novel.

"Shh," he chided with a flash of his white teeth.

Amelia bit her tongue when she saw where they were.

The room opened directly off the main ballroom. The only thing that hid them from view was an ornate metal grillwork she had barely noticed from the other side.

She would never have imagined there was a room behind that decorative screen. Between it and the ballroom proper was a wide corridor encircling the entire room. At the sides were private alcoves where couples would retreat for a few moments of privacy, but this small space was completely obscured by the screen and its repetitive floral pattern.

It was the perfect place to observe the ball in secret. Gideon led her to the front of the room so they could observe the milling crowd. The low strains of a waltz rose and strengthened.

"The band is just behind that pillar," he whispered into her ear. His lips pressed to the side of her neck, making her shiver. "That is why no one is standing so close to the screen. But I would advise you to be quiet as you can be. You tend to lose yourself when I'm buried deep inside you."

He couldn't be serious. Amelia opened her mouth to protest, but Gideon silenced her with his lips. His tongue teased, robbing her of her good sense.

It was always this way when they were alone—and sometimes when they weren't. Gideon could send her into flames with the lightest of touches or a single smoldering glance.

Cool air on her chest alerted her to the fact her bodice had been undone.

"My lord, we must stop." She could see the whirling couples on the dance floor. What if she cried out in her passion? She couldn't trust herself with him.

Amelia trembled in his arms as his hot mouth closed over the taut buds of her breasts. He circled her waist with one arm. Holding her upright, he lathed and bit at her nipple, pulling up her skirts with his other hand.

She melted against him, her resolve in cinders. Being in Gideon's arms was worth the loss of her pride, which was somewhere down around her ankles along with her drawers.

Amelia raised her arm and curled it around his neck as one of Gideon's big hands palmed her breast. His sheer size was exciting, the way he could hold her, lifting her as if she weighed nothing.

But Gideon didn't enfold her in his embrace. Instead, he turned her away from him, placing her hands on the crossbars of the screen. His mouth flamed up her neck, holding her still when she tried to turn to him again.

"Don't move," he ordered, using his knee to nudge her legs farther apart.

Cool air caressed her skin as he lifted her skirts, exposing her bare bottom to his touch. One hand gripped her waist as the other caressed and probed. Amelia's hands tightened reflexively on the screen as his cock parted her heated folds.

Thick steel pushed past her constricted entrance. Impatient, she backed against him, urging him inside with a whimper. The sensation nearly made her scream. She had never wanted anyone or anything so badly.

Gideon pulled her tight against him, pushing and retreating as he stroked faster and faster. Her fingers flexed on the screen and she trembled, moving mindlessly and unconsciously where he led.

Exquisite pleasure pulsed through her. She felt like one of the musical instruments being played just a few feet away. Amelia was a violin, and Gideon was a virtuoso, the master plucking at her strings.

A swell in the music reminded her she was only a few feet from discovery. What if someone could see them through the screen? It was a heavy grill, but *she* could see the ballroom. If one of the other guests focused in their direction they might be able to make out their bodies locked in an illicit embrace.

"*Gideon.*" Her cry was involuntary and probably much louder to her ears than it actually was.

Nevertheless, Gideon chuckled. "You have to be quiet love."

That was more easily said than done. "I don't think I can be," she gasped and moaned when he thrust his full length into her again.

"Then I'll help you," he whispered, covering her mouth with his hand and pinning her against him as he continued to plunder, the relentless drive of his hips into her sheath calling forth an answering throb of primitive joy.

Amelia was on the edge, clinging to the screen as a sharp hunger swelled and clawed for release. Her backside moved up and down against him, totally under his control.

Relief finally came when Gideon forced her head back with the hand over her mouth. He stroked in hard twice and then ground hard against her. She shattered, her entire body throbbing and convulsing in his tight hold.

When she recovered, she found herself cradled in Gideon's lap on a settee she hadn't even noticed in the dim light. He'd even managed to right her clothing, but she could still feel his shaft, no longer rock hard, but still large and firm against her bare bottom.

"Lady Lewin was right. You *are* a gladiator."

His deep-throated chuckle sent a frisson down her spine, but it was only an echo of the thrilling and sharp euphoria of a few minutes before.

"Does that mean you would have been the proper Roman lady who requested my services to stud?"

She turned to him with wide eyes. "They did not do that!"

"I assure you they did. High-ranking Roman women could pretty much do as they pleased. They were like men that way. And most of the time, the gladiator was happy to oblige. If the lady was pleased with him, she might intervene on his behalf and he wouldn't have to fight in the arena again…although I believe men purchased gladiators with greater frequency."

Amelia huffed a light laugh. "Well, of all people, I understand the men's inclination to do so, but that they acted openly…"

"In ancient Rome, the sexual arts were not proscribed the way they are at present. One can only hope attitudes will shift once more in the future so people can be free to love as they are wont," he said, nuzzling at her ear. "In the meantime, *your* gladiator serves his lady with discretion. I have my coach waiting on the other side of the garden wall. We can make our way through the adjoining passage and the back rooms of the house without much danger of being seen."

"You certainly know this house well."

He nodded, taking her hand to lead her out. "I was advised by a friend to become acquainted with the secrets of Mayfair homes before I went abroad. I practiced my intelligence gathering for the war department in these very ballrooms and in my clubs. What I learned served me well on the continent."

With that, he led her to his coach, delivering her to her townhouse via the back alley. The kiss at the back garden door was brief, but he didn't argue when she bid him goodnight. A little disappointed he'd let her go without a fight, she consoled herself with the lengths he was willing to go to while following the restrictions she'd imposed on their affair.

Of course, those restrictions hadn't done much to quell the rumors about them. If an eccentric like Lady Lewin knew about them, then everyone did.

Amelia sighed unhappily and prepared for bed in her room before retiring to the empty staff quarters. She had been sleeping in Carlotta's narrow little room for the past few weeks. It wasn't the most comfortable of situations, but it made her feel more secure.

Gideon would laugh if he could see her in this rickety little bed. He certainly couldn't join her here. Then again…

She fell asleep, remembering each of the inventive ways the earl had made love to her all over town. It would not be wise to underestimate him.

Loud knocking and footsteps played at the edge of her consciousness. Someone shook her by the arm. "Amelia, wake up!"

Groggily, she shifted and cracked her eyelids open. "*Gideon*? What are you doing here?"

Oh, dear God. Something had happened. "Is it Crispin? Or Mr. Clarke?" she asked, her heart in her mouth.

"No, they are meeting us at Flint House. Hurry, you need to get dressed."

He tugged her out of the cot, his urgency propelling her up the stairs. Panic and the remnants of sleep jumbled her thoughts. It didn't help that Gideon was acting as if they were under siege.

He had no weapon, but his massive body was alert and battle ready. He approached the window with caution, flattening himself against the wall to peek through the curtains at the garden below.

"Is someone there?" she asked anxiously. "What is going on?"

She had never seen Gideon behave this way. Frightened despite her resolve to remain calm, she fumbled with the buttons of her gown.

Gideon was silent so long she thought he wasn't going to answer her. "Sir Clarence is dead."

"*What?*"

"Clarke sent word just a few minutes ago. Sir Clarence was found dead in his townhouse less than an hour ago. Now hurry, we don't have much time."

Trembling, Amelia threw on the rest of her clothes and slipped her feet into a pair of kid half-boots. Gideon was taking her to his townhouse, but from there, they might end up anywhere.

"Was *it* there?" Had the demon been found?

"No. No one saw the murderer. Mrs. Spencer and the servants said Clarence retired to his study with a bottle of spirits. He was found a few hours later when he did not join his mistress upstairs."

Gideon threw her cloak over her and tugged her downstairs to the kitchen door. "Could it have been an attack of apoplexy or his heart?" she asked

"*No.*"

Amelia's breath stuttered. There was a wealth of meaning in that one syllable. She no longer wanted to know the details of how Sir Clarence had been found. Her imagination was more than up to the task.

Trying to block out the gruesome images, she reached for Gideon's hand and held it tight.

"Do you think it will come after us?" she asked once they were in the privacy of his coach.

"On the contrary," Gideon said, his shoulders dropping visibly in the moonlight filtering in from the window. "I think our problem is over. I had a talk with Clarence at one of his clubs a few days ago. I warned him against further action against you. I can only guess he took my threat to heart and called off his giant. The man must have been enraged over his dismissal—Sir Clarence has never been known for his diplomacy."

Amelia's mind struggled to keep up. Sir Clarence was *dead*. Gideon still didn't believe the servant was supernatural in nature, but did that matter? If Sir Clarence had been involved—and his death certainly suggested as much—would this be the end of it?

"Where could the murderer be? Will it come for us?"

Gideon focused on her, his expression softening. "I'm sorry, love. I know I've frightened you pulling you out of bed so abruptly. But it's unlikely Sir Clarence's henchman has stuck around. Even in the stews, a man of his size and description won't blend in. He probably hied it out of London just after the murder."

Amelia's uncertainty must have been written all over her face because Gideon stepped across the coach to pull her into his side. "I really believe it is over my love. I would stake my life on it...and do you remember what you promised to do when the danger had passed?"

Shock held her immobile for a few seconds. He couldn't be serious! "Gideon. There's been a murder!"

He squeezed her hand. "And I'm not going to wait for you to finish mourning Sir Clarence to marry you."

Her head drew back. "I will *not* mourn that man."

His lips twisted with resignation. "I won't either, not in my heart. But in public, I think we must given the circumstances."

Gideon forestalled her diatribe with a raised hand. "There is more. The watch was summoned to the scene of the murder. And given the state of the body, there will be no question it was a murder. The news of my argument with Clarence is making the rounds at the clubs. I never intended to hide it, but truthfully, I did not foresee Sir Clarence's death."

Her blood chilled as she began to understand his meaning. "You believe you'll be a suspect." It wasn't a question.

His shrug was infuriatingly casual. Did he not take this seriously? They could hang him for murder!

"They will tread carefully, of course, but it's only a matter of time before they come to interview me. I don't expect anything to come of it. I can account for my whereabouts to the minute. My title will help, but it's still necessary for us to marry as soon as possible."

"But why? There is no prohibition to marrying while in mourning. Aside from the impropriety, that is, which given what we've been doing the last few weeks, seems of little importance."

He stroked her palm with his thumb. "Love, it's only a matter of time before they draw you into this investigation as well. Despite my best efforts to quell the rumors, enough people have guessed you are the reason behind my quarrel with Clarence. And I'm not going let anyone near you until you are the Countess of Flint, with all the dignity and protection that position affords."

Amelia scoffed. "I don't need that kind of protection! You're the one who will be implicated in the murder—unless you're willing to explain about the giant."

Gideon eyed her cautiously. "We'll tell the authorities enough to satisfy them, but I don't think it's wise to go into detail about the particulars, love, should they insist on speaking to you. In fact, leaving out all mention of demons and the occult would be best."

She bit her lip. He was correct. They would think she was mad…

The carriage arrived at Flint House. They exited in a flurry of movement, but she hesitated at the front door.

"Amelia."

She looked up to meet his eyes in the moonlight. "Yes?"

"This is not the way I would have chosen to do this, but I do love you and I want you to be my wife."

It felt as if the ground had given way underneath her. He smiled as he steadied her on her feet. "Please, say you will marry me…right now."

"*Now?*" She looked at the door, and then back to him.

"Yes. Clarke and Crispin are waiting with the minister."

"But the banns—"

"I have a special license. I've had one for weeks."

"*Oh.*"

Gideon held out his hand. Amelia stared at it for a long moment. Breathing deeply, she took it with both of her own. She walked into the house with him, into her future.

CHAPTER 24

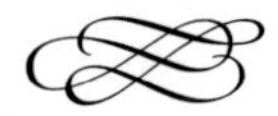

The interview with the authorities was going exactly as Gideon had predicted.

"And when was the last time you spoke to your guardian?" Inspector Hayes asked.

"If you recall when it was, that is," Sir Lennon interjected. The small rotund man fingered his cravat, trying to loosen it. The neck-piece was tied so elaborately she had to wonder if he could turn his head.

Sitting in the chair to Sir Lennon's right, Hayes rolled his eyes but stopped short when he glanced behind her where Gideon was standing.

She was sitting behind her husband's desk in the study at Flint House. A few days had passed since their hasty marriage.

News of their union, coming so close on the heels of Sir Clarence's murder, spread like wildfire across the entire ton. It was the scandal of the moment, but Amelia saw firsthand what Gideon had meant about weddings wiping away all sins.

Since the announcement of their marriage in the Times, they had received a flood of invitations and cards. While Amelia had been next to a pariah as Widow Montgomery, as the Countess of Flint, she was all the rage. Her fortune and beauty, previously viewed as the sinister lures she used to ensnare men, were now assets for her husband to enjoy. Gideon was—hypocritically in her view—openly congratulated for securing her hand. The connection to a gruesome murder only seemed to add to their mystique.

So many callers had lined up at the door Gideon put his foot down and closed the house to visitors, complaining viciously about parasites and rumor mongers. Amelia hadn't liked entertaining any of their callers either, but she had met one or two genuinely kind ladies hauled to her door by their social-climbing connections.

"It was several weeks ago. I saw him at a garden party," Amelia replied, choosing to omit the details of the conversation.

"I was very sorry to hear of his passing," she added with genuine feeling. Whatever his sins, no one deserved to die as he had—not that her husband had chosen to share the details with her. But she'd heard enough from her callers to surmise it had been a bloody and painful end.

Sir Lennon thanked her and reached inside his waistcoat for a handkerchief. He wiped his sweaty brow, his eyes sliding over her shoulder to Gideon as if he couldn't help himself.

No doubt her husband was wearing a terrifyingly forbidding expression because both men were cautious and on edge, though Hayes' seemed a touch resentful. Amelia didn't know if it was because he felt hamstrung by the presence of the earl or if it was because the local magistrate had insisted on sitting in on the conversation.

"And you didn't see him on the eleventh, on the day he died?" Inspector Hayes asked, looking as if he half-expected Gideon to interject.

Her husband shifted his weight. She glanced over her shoulder to see him stone-faced with his arms crossed, but he didn't interrupt.

"No, as I said, the last time was at the Wescott's garden party."

Hayes glanced at her suspiciously. "You were also married on the eleventh."

Amelia nodded, a hint of a smile on her face. Despite her reservations, she had loved the impromptu celebration Gideon and Crispin had thrown together. Every day since had only gotten better. "Yes, we were. It was in—"

"That afternoon," Gideon supplied smoothly, putting a hand on her shoulder.

Hayes noted the possessive gesture and Amelia nodded placidly in agreement with her husband.

Sir Lennon, obviously concerned the young Inspector was going to offend the new Earl of Flint, threw him a censorious glare.

But Hayes was undeterred. "I understood there was a disagreement at Sir Clarence's club," he said, his eyes narrowing on Gideon's face. According to the club's majordomo you and your uncle had some words, the evening of the eighth, and your bride, his former ward, was the subject."

"That is not precisely true," Gideon said easily. "Yes, we did argue and my wife's name was mentioned, but *she* was not the true subject of the argument. Her inheritance was."

"Oh, I see." Hayes' eyes lit in understanding. He focused on Amelia. "As your guardian, he held your purse strings—at least until your marriage. Was Sir Clarence loath to give up control of your fortune?"

Amelia shook her head. "While it's true Sir Clarence was once my guardian, he was never the executor of my trust. I have always controlled that, even as a child, although it was managed by my father's attorney Tolbert Callaghan until my first marriage. Callaghan still manages my affairs today but at my direction."

"My wife's fortune is still under her control." Gideon confirmed, "She manages it with great skill. I plan on consulting her on the Flint family holdings and investments. With her counsel, the estate can't not prosper."

Inspector Hayes blinked. "*Oh*. How forward thinking of you." He leaned forward in his chair and made a quick note in his pad.

Even Sir Lennon was surprised. "An unusual arrangement," he said with a bemused nod. Amelia raised her brow and he cleared his throat. "But a wise one on the part of your father," he assured her. "Especially in light of your guardian's greed."

"Well, I don't like to speak ill of the dead..." Amelia trailed off with genuine discomfort.

"Of course you don't," Sir Lennon said with a paternal little nod of approval for her delicate sensibilities.

"Perhaps you should apologize for offending my wife's delicate sensibilities," Gideon suggested softly, returning to stand next to her in a pointed show of support.

Amelia flicked her eyes at him, giving him a half-hearted little smack on the chest as if to say *stop it*. Sir Lennon was pompous and a touch condescending, but he meant well.

"Countess Flint, did you love your first husband, Martin Montgomery?" Inspector Hayes asked.

Sir Lennon reddened and coughed so violently Amelia was concerned he was having an apoplectic fit.

"Are you all right? Should I ring for tea?" she asked with a furrowed brow.

Sir Lennon wheezed, tugging at his cravat. He waved away her concern. "You don't have to answer that," he said between coughs.

"It's fine." She turned to Hayes, meeting his mulish expression with equanimity. "I loved Martin with all my heart. He was my closest friend. I miss him every day."

Her words rang with sincerity.

Amelia looked up at Gideon, anxious to forestall his inevitable explosion, but he was watching her with a somber, sympathetic expression. For a moment, they simply stared at each other in a moment of shared grief. Then he took her hand and gripped it tightly.

When she looked back at Hayes, the martial light in his eyes disappeared. He looked down with a little nod to himself, seemingly convinced of the genuineness of their unintended display. He glanced at Gideon but wisely decided not to ask if he missed his cousin.

"Well, I think we have all the information we need," Sir Lennon announced, rising with an abrupt *let-us-depart* gesture in Hayes direction.

The young Inspector rose to his feet slowly, looking thoughtful. He turned back at the threshold. "Just one more thing. Are you familiar with Sir Clarence's houseguest, his friend Mrs. Ellen Spencer?" he asked in a low voice.

"Only slightly," Gideon said in a repressive tone reserved for discussing another man's mistress.

This time, Hayes appeared chastised. He shifted on the balls of his feet. "Yes, well, I just thought you should know she's been…er…"

"Making accusations?" Gideon asked pointedly. "Because I stopped by to ask after him when he was away a few weeks ago."

The inspector paused, appearing to choose his words with care for a change. "It's more like she is trying hard not to make them…strategically, if I might add," Hayes said, one corner of his mouth pulling down.

"Yes," Sir Lennon sniffed disapprovingly. "The woman has been making the rounds at all the major events. Murders lend a certain cachet to the people associated with the victims. Needless to say, she's all the crack at the moment."

He noted the wrinkle of Amelia's nose. "Don't concern yourself with that sort of cheap display, my dear. Mrs. Spencer will find this sort of popularity wanes quickly as soon as a new scandal crops up to occupy the ton."

Gideon murmured his gratitude to the two men, thanking Hayes with surprising warmth. They eyed each other over a firm handshake, the tension of a few moments ago seemingly forgotten.

Kindred spirits, Amelia noted to herself before turning her attention to the pile of correspondence on Gideon's desk as he walked the two men to the door.

Gideon had generously offered to share his office with her until her private parlor was redecorated. It was part of a series of improvements planned. Flint House was a spacious and drafty mansion with many outdated features. Gideon had always intended to conduct a top-to-bottom renovation, but hadn't started any of the improvements before their marriage.

"I was too focused on you and my investigation," he admitted with an abashed grin when they discovered the chimney in the master bedroom smoked. He'd thrown open the window and turned to her.

"But now that you're here, we can make the improvements together, and choose new furnishings for the drawing room and whatever else your heart desires."

And so the work renovating Flint House had begun. They had started in the master bedroom, spending every night in the adjoining chamber meant for the lady of the house. Though both rooms were being redecorated, Gideon had already declared they would share his once it was finished. Theirs would not be a fashionable ton marriage.

"Get used to living in each other's pockets," he'd declared that morning near dawn, after spending most of the night making love to her. He fell asleep with his arms wrapped around her.

Feeling more secure and loved than she had her entire life, she had slept peacefully.

Marriage to Gideon was everything he had promised. Amelia was spoiled and cosseted at every turn. Their wedding vows hadn't diminished their passion. If anything, that aspect had strengthened. Living together allowed Gideon the opportunity to lavish affection on her, while taking advantage of his ready access to satisfy his seemingly insatiable appetites.

Her husband's fixation with her—the intensity with which he loved her—governed her days. He was demanding and generous and wilder than anything she'd ever known. His hunger extended far beyond the marriage bed. He wanted to know everything about her, what she liked, disliked, and hated.

Gideon seduced her at every turn…and nearly every room, including this one.

"Are you thinking about what we did on that desk a few days ago?"

She blushed. "How did you know?"

"An educated guess based on the fact your quill is dripping ink all over my estate reports."

Amelia looked down and cursed. "I'm so sorry!"

Gideon laughed. "Leave it," he said, setting the ink safely out of reach in a drawer.

She put her hands to her face and rubbed before changing the subject. "They asked all the questions you said they would. I'm surprised you let me answer them."

Gideon removed his cravat, leaning carelessly against the desk. "I wasn't raised to privilege, and I've only been an earl a brief time. There's no need to beat them over the head with my title. From my own experience making inquiries, I know it would only make Hayes more suspicious to deny him access. He'd give up on finding the real killer all the sooner, and I want him to keep looking."

If that were true, then he might have mentioned the giant. *No, the omission made sense because a giant as murderer sounds mad,* she reminded herself.

There had been no disturbances since Sir Clarence's death. It had been so quiet since that she was forced to concede Gideon had likely been correct about her former guardian's role. Sir Clarence had been the one behind the strange disturbances and attacks on her.

"What if Inspector Hayes interviews the minister?" she asked, remembering Gideon's unexpected falsehood regarding the hour they had married.

"Old Lessig has been amply compensated to tell the same story."

She frowned. "But it's not even necessary. Your friend Mr. Clarke confirmed Sir Clarence died in the evening."

He bent to nibble on her ear. "At this point, I believe you can safely lay claim to Clarke's friendship as well. He's become a great advocate of yours. Also, it seems he and Lord Worthing have struck up a friendship."

Amelia held her breath, waiting for Gideon to comment further on Crispin and Clarke's relationship, but he seemed too engrossed with toying with the fine curls of hair next to her ear.

"And, yes," he continued. "The murder was most likely when we were together at the Vernon's, making love in the ballroom."

"We were behind a screen!" she protested.

"I know. I simply like making you blush," he teased before leaning over and picking her up. He pushed the papers on the crowded desk's surface to make room to set her down.

"What did the inspector mean about Mrs. Spencer?" she asked, running her fingers through his thick dark hair.

Gideon's mouth compressed. "Don't worry about her."

Amelia stopped him with a finger on his lips. "What is she doing, Gideon?"

Her husband sighed and sat back in his chair. "It seems the vivacious Mrs. Spencer has been making the rounds attending all the major balls and parties—all the ones we haven't accepted invitations to that is. According to Clarke, she's stoking the fires of public opinion against me, rather artfully, I might add. She knows better to state outright I murdered Sir Clarence, but she has dropped hints about my visit to Sir Clarence's townhouse while he was away, painting it in the darkest light."

Amelia was incensed. "Gideon, we can't let her get away with that! How dare she impugn your honor? Why, I want to call her out myself. I may not know how to use a pistol, but I used to fence with Martin when we were younger. Get me your sword!"

He chuckled. "My bloodthirsty little wife."

"Your loyal wife," she corrected, pushing his nose with her index finger. "And most of the time, I could disarm Martin, so don't make me angry."

This time, he laughed outright. "I'll remember that, but believe me when I say we don't need to be concerned about Mrs. Spencer. Sir Lennon was right. Her proximity to the murder makes her fashionable, but it's temporary…and I've already taken steps to dampen her cachet."

"How?" she asked suspiciously.

Gideon began to fiddle with the ties of her bodice. "By exposing Sir Clarence's dirty dealings. With the help of a few friends in the war office, I've dug deeper into my uncle's business affairs. His reputation was that of a scrupulous and savvy investor, but we've found evidence of some unsavory connections and underhanded tactics. A few things were technically illegal."

Amelia sniffed. "I suspected as much about Sir Clarence, but how will exposing those details hurt Mrs. Spencer?"

"Well, to be blunt, her reputation is tied to his. Before his death, he was considered spotless, a bit of prig really. But once his reputation is tarnished, hers will be by association. It's not fair, but neither are her insinuations. Also, Clarke is already seeding doubts about the lady herself."

"Such as?"

Gideon spread his arms as if addressing an audience. "Who is she? Ellen Spencer appeared on Clarence's arm this season, but she never speaks of her people. No one knows anything about her. The sticklers in the ton have begun to question her background."

He paused and rubbed his chin. "There is more. As Sir Clarence's closest relation, I inherit his estate. His lawyers have contacted me. I've had them send word to Mrs. Spencer that I'll be giving up the lease on his townhouse, but she is welcome to stay until the end of the season. If she is wise, she'll make other arrangements soon. Without Sir Clarence's fortune to sustain her, I expect she'll leave town."

"That's quite generous under the circumstances." Amelia crossed her arms. "What if she finds another protector instead?"

He shrugged. "Even if she does, the power of her words will be greatly diminished by the time my campaign is over. Have a little faith. Manipulating information was my stock in trade up until a few months ago."

"Very well, I will trust your judgment on this," she said, reaching out to him again.

He came eagerly, wrapping his arms around her. The next few minutes passed in a blur of heated kisses and caresses. She was about to suggest they retire to their room when Gideon exposed her breasts and pressed a soft kiss to one hardened bud as he began to fiddle with the fastening of his breeches.

Apparently, they would be staying where they were. *Which reminds me...*

"Do we still have to stay in town? You said we could leave after being interviewed by the authorities."

Gideon reluctantly lifted his head. "Yes, but I don't want to make the connection obvious so I think we should stay on till the weekend.

There is a vote in the House of Lords on Friday. Hayes and the others will assume we stayed on for that."

He returned his attention to her décolletage. Amelia had to tug his hair to get his attention again. "What is the vote regarding?"

His head dropped back to look at the ceiling as if searching his memory. "Something to do with munitions and supplies for the war effort, nothing critical," he said before eagerly drawing up her skirts.

Amelia stayed his hand. "Nothing critical! My lord, that issue is of extreme importance." She pushed him away and hopped off the desk.

"You must tell me which suppliers are being considered for government contracts," she said, hurrying to the stack of ledgers she'd brought over from her townhouse. "There are entirely too many corrupt ones vying to be suppliers—poor workmanship of weapons and uniforms or tainted food. Even gunpowder is not safe. There was one case of adulterated powder supplied to the Navy. When they needed it for the cannons, it failed and the ship was taken. We must learn everything about the companies being considered. It's urgent. The safety and well-being of our soldiers is at stake."

Gideon sighed and fastened his breeches with a wistful grin. "As you wish, my love. But let's do hurry..."

CHAPTER 25

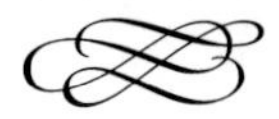

The rapid whispering grew louder as she approached the library.

At first, Amelia believed Clarke and Crispin had dropped by to wish them well on their trip. She and Gideon were about to leave for Tarryhall, the Earl of Flint's principal seat. They would spend a week there so Gideon could catch up on estate business with his steward before leaving for Devon.

While helping Gideon with the correspondence for his far-flung estates, Amelia had been thrilled to learn he owned a small property a stone's throw from her father's country home. After verifying that the cottage was in good repair, Gideon had offered to take her there as part of a larger bridal tour of his new properties.

She was so excited, she'd been unable to sleep the night before their scheduled departure. Not that Gideon allowed her much opportunity for sleep at night.

What good was a brand-new marriage bed if one didn't use it? he'd asked.

The rogue, she thought with a small private smile. It had become necessary to nap for several hours each afternoon to keep up with his demands. And the reason their bed hadn't seen much use was because

Gideon was usually too impatient to go upstairs. The staff had quickly learned to make themselves scarce when they were together.

Blushing at her memories, she hurried to the library to say goodbye to their friends. But Amelia found Gideon alone, his face granite-hard. He spun around to face her, his hand in a fist.

"Gideon, what's wrong?"

Relaxing his fist, her husband made a visible effort to calm down. He took a deep breath and cleared his throat. "Nothing."

Dread pooled like bile in her stomach. "Don't—I could hear the voices from the hall. It's happening to you now, isn't it?"

It was as if Gideon closed in on himself. She could see him withdrawing, his expression metamorphosing into a careless mien.

"Of course not," he said dismissively with a hint of a smile. "What you heard was the servants speaking upstairs through the chimney. I told you this place was in bad repair," he added, gesturing at the hearth. "This needs to be rebricked, that is all."

Well, she supposed that could be true. The renovations were taking longer than she'd assumed they would. It was such a large house, and like all of Gideon's properties, it had been neglected for some time.

He narrowed his eyes and looked at her from head to toe. "You were ill this morning. How are you feeling now?"

She waved away his concern. "Much better. It's just taking a little time to grow accustomed to your French chef. His meals are delicious but too rich… Are you certain it was the servants? The voices were loud as if there were multiple people in here with you."

"Darling, the maids are busy closing the rooms upstairs. Now, have you finished packing, love?"

"I have. My apologies for the delay. I didn't realize how many trunks I would need and had to send out for another from my former residence."

"Well, if you didn't insist on taking so many books with you… We have to use a second carriage as it is."

Crestfallen, she stepped closer to him. "Oh Gideon, I need all those books!"

Gideon put his big hands on her upper arms. "Amelia, darling, I know what those books are for. And we don't need them. Not anymore."

But what if he was wrong? *It really sounded as if the voices were coming from the library.* "I need them," she insisted.

"My lord!" Footsteps pounded in the hallway. Young John, Gideon's tiger, and Adolfo appeared, sweaty and winded.

"What's wrong?" he asked, rushing forward.

"It's the grey mare, one of the matched pair. It's dead."

AMELIA COVERED her hand with her mouth. She wanted to weep. "That poor animal."

Gideon hadn't been able to keep her from the stables. Intent on seeing the horse, he'd given up trying to make her stay in the library.

"Don't look at it," Gideon growled, shoving her behind him to obstruct her view. "Was it poisoned?"

"No, my lord," the stable master said in disbelief. "Can't you see—"

"I think it was poisoned. The same thing happened to Lord Stanley's last month when he didn't pay the staff's wages for the quarter and he dismissed a groom for complaining. Notify the relevant authorities and have it hauled away."

"But, my lord—"

"*I said have it taken away.* Hitch the chestnut to the carriage instead. It's the closest in size to the dappled grey. We leave within the hour."

The stable master tried to hide his dubious expression. He and his subordinates hurried to their lord's bidding.

"Gideon!" Amelia scolded. "You know very well the animal was strangled. Look at its neck."

The air around them grew thick with tension. Disbelieving, she stared at him, wondering how he could be so obtuse. But he was in earnest—so much so that the cords on his neck stood out.

"It was *poisoned*."

She threw up her hands. “Damn it, Gideon, you can’t bury your head in the sand and pretend the giant hasn’t returned.”

He put his hands on his hips and walked in a circle, then turned and stared at her.

She waited for him to acknowledge reality. It was suddenly painful to breathe. Was he about to assert his prerogative as her lord and master and dismiss her truth?

Amelia didn’t know what she would do if that happened.

Gideon’s eyes flicked to her waist. Without a word, he opened his arms. Relieved, she flew into them and waited.

“We’re still leaving,” he muttered into her hair. “The air in town is not good for you, and I have put off attending to my estates long enough. But we’ll travel with a few more outriders than I originally planned.”

He led her out of the stable and hailed Adolfo, who was watching the men readying the carriage.

“Yes, my lord?”

Gideon leaned toward him. “Adolfo, I’m going to write a quick note to Inspector Hayes. I’d like you to deliver it. Keep the horse’s body long enough for him to see it.”

“Yes, my lord. I take it you want me to deliver it after you have left?”

He nodded. “We won’t be delaying our departure. Find me in my library in five minutes.”

He turned to Amelia. “Come, my love. Our departure from London is long overdue.”

CHAPTER 26

"Amelia, love, where are you?"

Gideon stepped around a stack of books, trying to find his wife. She'd been locked in Tarryhall's immense library since breakfast and was now officially ten minutes late for lunch.

Despite his initial plan to visit all his estates as part of their bridal tour, they hadn't stirred past Derbyshire for the past three weeks.

Once they'd arrived, he had taken a good look at the estate and decided to stay longer. Despite the size of the holding, and the neglect it had suffered after changing hands so many times, the house itself and surrounding pleasure gardens were sound and imminently defendable—almost a fortress.

If the giant was coming for them, it would have a hell of a time getting to them here.

Fortunately, they had sent most of Amelia's extra staff to Tarryhall. As it happened his estate manager had a few positions to fill, posts his predecessors had left vacant far too long. Grateful for the help, the rest of the staff absorbed the foreign-born servants with surprising open-mindedness.

But there were still superfluous footmen he could now employ as guards for the house and grounds. He also quietly assigned four guards to watch over Amelia whenever she left the house to pay calls or visit his tenants. Since they were all members of her former staff, she hadn't quibbled about his overprotectiveness—not once he hinted he'd been at a loss to find other occupations for them. Rather than see any of her people dismissed, she'd accepted the guards with no complaint.

There had been no further disturbances of the kind he experienced in London, but he wasn't willing to risk his wife—or the child he believed she was carrying.

He found Amelia curled up on a couch in a corner of the library surrounded by leather-bound volumes. She'd insisted on bringing her complete collection of occult books to Derbyshire and had taken over the library for her research.

Amelia had even added a few texts related to the supernatural from Tarryhall's own shelves. Apparently, one or more of his predecessors had been an enthusiast of the occult.

Gideon knelt and tried to shake her awake, but she was fast asleep. He stroked her cheek, deciding to give her more time.

Amelia continued to ascribe her fatigue and occasional bouts of illnesses to the long journey and his country cook's preference for heavy local dishes. Privately, he found her sweet ignorance endearing, but it also made him a little sad that nothing in her upbringing had prepared her to consider pregnancy as a cause.

Selfishly, Gideon hadn't been sorry she was carrying his child. When she first showed signs of illness, he'd been concerned she was being poisoned. Then it dawned on him she was only sick in the morning. He'd welcomed the idea of a baby with relief. But the more he thought about it, the more concerned he became.

Amelia was so small and he was a big man. It stood to reason his babe would be large. Childbirth might be difficult for her.

At least those strange occurrences have stopped plaguing her. The voices and strange visions, and the horse's death—those had been directed at him. It was difficult for him to accept, but Amelia had been correct about the supernatural aspect to the harassment. No wonder she had believed she was going mad.

Gideon stood and rolled his shoulders. Whatever else was true, he still believed Sir Clarence was behind the initial attacks. But he hadn't conducted them on his own. There was the giant, the one that turned on him, and possibly someone else. A person able to cast spells.

There simply wasn't another explanation for everything he'd seen.

"Gideon?"

He turned to find a sleepy Amelia blinking up at him. "You slept through lunch, my love. I came to find you, but now I have a better idea. Why don't I have cook prepare us a hamper and we can dine outside? A little fresh air should help if you're still feeling poorly."

Her soft smile curled around his heart. "I'm much improved, thank you, but a picnic sounds lovely."

He nodded, touched by her enthusiasm. She was so easy to please, and he loved spoiling her. "I thought we could find that little stream on the other side of the orchard again."

Amelia beamed and gave him her hands. She didn't appear to have an issue with dizziness, he noted as she got to her feet. Nevertheless, he would keep a watchful eye on her…

"This choice of picnic spots was inspired," Amelia said, falling back on the blanket with a satisfied sigh after they had finished their meal. "What is it about the sound of running water that relaxes one so?"

"Hmm, I don't know, though I agree," Gideon said, pushing away the plates so he could stretch out beside her. He leaned on one elbow and ran his finger down her cheek. "I'm just grateful for the unseasonably warm weather; otherwise, I couldn't do this…"

He opened the ties at the front of her gown, undoing her bodice.

"Gideon, we are out of doors!"

"On *my* estate." He laughed, bending to tease her lips with a series of nibbling kisses.

"Yes, but the tenants—"

"Better stay away if they know what's good for them," he said, tossing up her skirts with a grin.

"What about the guards? Don't think I don't know you've had all my footmen shadowing my every step. They'll be able to hear us."

"Which is why I asked them to keep a wide berth this afternoon.

None of them are near enough to hear us if we don't shout…or rather, if *you* don't shout."

Wrinkling her nose, she pinched him. "You are louder than I am!"

"Fibbing is a sin, love." He snickered, blocking her little fists when they flew at him. "But have no fear. The men *are* far enough away. Plus, I secreted a brace of pistols in that hamper. We are perfectly secure here."

Amelia's lips parted at the news there were arms within reach, but she didn't seem disturbed. Instead, she dismissed them with a shrug and opened her arms to him.

With a husky laugh, he crawled over her, his hands gravitating under her skirts. After a few feverish minutes, he'd managed to rid her of her gown, leaving only her gossamer shift. Gideon loved the way her beautiful body appeared through the sheer silk fabric.

But not as much as I love touching her through it. He opened his shirt and pressed his chest against her swollen breasts as he shifted down to kiss and suckle them.

"Oh, oh, stop. It's too much!" Amelia said. Her hands trembled as she tried to shift him away.

Of course, they're too sensitive! "Sorry, love," he murmured, drifting down to pay court between her legs instead. There his mouth was more than welcome.

Amelia moaned, arching under his touch. The sound heated his blood, and he increased the pressure of his lips, using his teeth to gently graze her soft inner lips and swollen bud.

She cried out, writhing in an attempt to escape, but he held her firm. Her taste was indescribable—and subtly different now. Combined with her other symptoms, there was only one conclusion. She was most assuredly with child.

"Gideon, please stop," she panted, shaking her head. "I can't…I…"

"Yes, you can love. Now open your legs a little wider," he ordered, nudging them with his broad shoulders. Twisting her bud slightly with his teeth, he worked two of his fingers in her sheath, curling them forward to stroke the special little spot inside.

Amelia gasped and put her hand over her mouth to muffle her

own scream, so the guards beyond the orchard wouldn't hear her. She was still trembling when he pulled open his breeches and drove into her.

"My lord!" she sobbed, her arms clawing at his shoulder.

Gideon didn't know if it was praise or a plea. The moment his shaft entered her hot clinging passage, all thought had ceased. His lips parted as he slid to the hilt. It was like a velvet vise, the only home he'd ever known or wanted.

"Hold me tight, little love," he said, withdrawing and surging back inside, driven by the hungry fire she effortlessly stoked in him.

"Yes, yes," she breathed, her hips straining to meet his.

Gideon fisted a hand in her hair. The wanton flush staining her cheeks and lips was a personal victory. He loved her unbridled response, the way she gave herself to him. It was a sign of her trust in him, one he would never take for granted.

Soon, his breath shortened, the ragged sound joining the chorus of moans that Amelia fought to hold back. But he wouldn't let her.

"That's it, little love," he whispered. "Take all of me, feel me filling you."

She sobbed again, pressing a hot openmouthed kiss as she clenched him tight, her thighs shaking with the effort to keep up with the relentless drive of his hips.

"You're all mine," he hissed. "Every bit of you—mind, body, and soul. It's all *mine*."

"And you're mine," she said, craning her neck to bite his lip, surprising him.

Her small show of aggression was enough to break down what little restraint he had left. He stroked faster and faster, glorying in her pulsing, throbbing heat.

Gideon wanted to pound and grind against her, but the thought of his child held him in check. Amelia, however, cared nothing for his self-discipline. She met him thrust for thrust, using her hands to pull him close as she twisted and rocked to caress his length with her body.

It was too much. He waited until she shuddered, climaxing with a sharp intake of breath before thrusting one more time and finally letting go. The tight coil of pain and pleasure unraveled and he poured himself into her, his seed jetting hard against the entrance to her womb.

An unwilling groan was ripped from his throat as he expended his last bit of strength to try and roll away. Amelia wouldn't let him. She held him with shaking limbs, effortlessly managing to keep him in place despite the disparity in their strengths. He gave up and resettled his weight to avoid crushing her, enjoying the feel of her hands running through his hair.

They lay joined together for so long, he wondered if she had gone numb from his weight, but she didn't complain. He lifted his head, parting his lips to ask, and saw *it* watching them.

The demon.

The deep mud-brown creature stared at them, the raging fires of hell in its eyes. It was massive, standing two heads taller than him with strangely misshapen arms.

"Amelia, get up!" he shouted, pulling from her body and scrambling to his feet. He dragged her up and forced her behind him.

That moment of inattention was enough to give the monster the advantage. The few seconds Gideon spent trying to secure Amelia allowed it to approach. He had no time to move before the creature backhanded him, sending him sprawling to the floor with a strange hissing sound.

Gideon winced, biting back a shout as his manhood was abraded on the rough ground. He shot back up, ignoring the pain as he spared a moment to tuck himself back in. He went back after the beast, which was steadily advancing on Amelia.

"No! Stay away from her!" He threw himself at it, landing on its back.

The creature brushed him off like an annoying gnat. He landed on his back, the force knocking the air from his lungs. Sucking in a big breath, he stood, a little more slowly.

"Gideon."

He couldn't see his wife. The size of the giant hid her from his sight. Panting for a new reason, he rounded on the beast, spinning to get between it and Amelia.

"Gideon, what do I do?" Amelia asked, clinging to his back.

"Run!" he yelled, bracing his booted feet against the ground to keep the monster from advancing.

It didn't work. The creature was too strong. The soles of his boot's slid helplessly back as it continued to advance. He didn't see the arm lift, but he felt the impact—a glancing blow to the side of his head strong enough to send him crumbling to the ground.

Amelia's scream was distant and tinny. His ears were ringing like that time he'd stood too close to a cannon being fired.

"Amelia, run!" She was still there. He could hear her screaming.

His heart felt as if it was being ripped out of his chest. The piercing agony of that cry reverberated in his soul. Gideon had never felt more helpless in his entire life.

"Run," Gideon repeated, but his voice sounded half-strangled. His attempt to stand failed, so he crawled.

He blinked, trying to clear his blurred vision. The small pink and cream form against the tree was his wife, the brown mountain the beast moving toward her.

"Don't."

Amelia cowered against the trunk, her hands up to cover her face for the inevitable blow.

Staggering to his feet, Gideon watched, transfixed, as it reached out. But it didn't hit Amelia. It *fondled* her.

Amelia's dumbstruck expression was as shocked as his. The creature was touching her breast, roughly rubbing its massive hand across the rosy-tipped peak clearly visible through the translucent material of her shift. And then it got worse.

The human-shaped hand trailed down, stroking to the shadowy cleft between Amelia's legs.

Face appalled, Amelia shrank down against the tree, slapping at the violating fingers.

The pistols. Blood surged, and Gideon fought to stand, only to fall when he dived for the basket. But the guns were loaded; he just needed to squeeze the trigger.

Holding his aching head with one arm, he climbed back up and staggered forward, squeezing between his wife and the monster. Aiming for the head, Gideon fired at point-blank range—*and missed.*

Somehow, the creature managed to jerk its head out of the way. The monster reared back, hissing that strange whistling sound again.

Clutching the back of his shirt, Amelia sobbed. The creature reacted, jerking again. It stood still for a heartbeat and then spun on its misshapen heel, stalking away.

Gideon released a shaky breath, pushing the pain in his head to the back of his mind. Steadying his arm, he took aim, calling on his instincts and the skill he'd honed with hours of practice at Manton's.

The blast caught the hand, blowing off a chunk. Fingers exploded into dust and shards of pottery. Then it began to move away, heading for the tree line.

Gideon tried to follow but the tug on his shirt reminded him of Amelia. He couldn't leave her unprotected. In the blink of an eye, the creature was gone, having melted into the trees.

CHAPTER 27

"*Will you stop touching it?*" Clarke scolded.

Crispin glanced up with a guilty expression, his hand hovering above the still-recognizable clay finger.

Gideon glanced up from the book he was perusing, surprised at the vehemence in his friend's voice. "It's completely harmless now," he assured him.

He should know. He'd been turning the thing over and over since the day the creature had attacked.

At first, Gideon had insisted on decamping, but Amelia wouldn't hear of them leaving Tarryhall. He could barely walk in the immediate aftermath. His ears rang for days—a side effect of the blow the creature had dealt him.

Once the monster had gone, Amelia called their guards for assistance—chiding him for insisting she throw her gown over her head for modesty's sake before the men saw her in *dishabille*.

It took two of them to help him to the house. He only remembered fragments of the trip back. His next clear recollection was of being in his study, undergoing an examination by the surgeon Amelia had insisted upon.

The doctor had proscribed travel by carriage for at least two weeks. He'd been prepared to disregard the medical edict, but Amelia hadn't. By the time he could think clearly enough to argue with her, she'd organized the staff against him. The male servants were split into teams that guarded the house day and night. And the maids or Amelia herself attended to him at all hours, making sure he didn't exert himself, while cook prepared tonics and enough fortifying dishes for an army.

Amelia had also sent for Clarke. Lord Worthing had accompanied him. Despite the injury to his leg, the viscount had stoically endured hours of carriage travel to come to their side. His presence had comforted Amelia, so Gideon was grateful, but he was a little surprised Clarke had allowed it.

Though social in ton terms, his old friend had few close confidantes. In fact, before Lord Worthing, Gideon had believed himself to be the only one. But in a short amount of time, Clarke and Worthing had become fast friends. Their ease with each other was like those who'd known each other from the cradle.

He was still marveling over the change in Clarke's usually reserved disposition when Amelia appeared around a tall library shelf with several books in her arms.

"I've found it!" she exclaimed.

She hurried to the central table and laid down the volumes, indicating a small dusty volume on top with a flourish.

Lord Worthing glanced down. "The Maharal of Prague, a history and dissertation." He frowned, squinting at the smaller text on the pocket-sized leather volume. "A rabbinic text? I thought we were meant to be searching for our monster in these occult volumes."

"And that's where we—or more specifically I—went wrong." She turned to Gideon. "You were correct, my lord, it is not a demon."

Gideon frowned and she cradled the book excitedly.

"You called it a giant and in some respects, that is true," she elaborated so quickly her words almost ran together. "I remembered something I had read, a legend about a rabbi creating a man made of earth to protect his people after the sitting pope ordered they be expelled or killed. I couldn't recall the details, but fortunately for us, one of your predecessors was an ecclesiastical scholar with varied interests, for these were in *your* library."

Gideon nodded, leaning forward. "That would have been Edwin. He was earl a few decades ago—the Duchess of Marlboro's particular friend."

"Edwin, bless his heart, may have saved us all," Amelia said, sitting at the table. "This book details the story of the Golem of Prague."

"A golem? What is a golem?" Lord Worthing asked before Gideon could.

"It's a creature made of earth or clay, animated by magic. It's a part of Hasidic folklore," Clarke said.

Heads turned to him in surprise. He shrugged. "A few of my informants are Jewish, though they don't advertise the fact. I dined at the house of one once. He told his misbehaving children the golem would punish them if they did not stop making noise. But he didn't mention Prague."

Amelia shoved another book toward them. "I found the pope I was thinking of in this one. It was Rudolf II, the Holy Roman emperor and the rabbi in question was named Loew. The rabbi brought the golem to life through rituals and secret incantations and kept it alive by placing holy words on a piece of paper either in its mouth or forehead. In some accounts, the holy words are written on the forehead."

"Our golem definitely does not have words on its forehead," Gideon growled. "If this creature is meant for protection, why in the bloody hell is it bedeviling us—and why did it touch you?"

Amelia blushed, but she had been the one to insist their friends know all the disturbing details so she didn't prevaricate.

"Protection was its purpose in Prague, but there are many tales where it was simply used for labor. These are usually framed as cautionary tales because the golem follows instruction letter by letter. For example, if it was supposed to dig a ditch, but never told to stop, it keeps digging endlessly."

"So it follows orders?"

"Yes, and very literally. And they must be simple instructions. That is the salient feature of golems. There are many tales about them, some even outside the Jewish tradition. You tell a golem what to do and it obeys, even if your orders are nonsensical or..."

"A perversion?" The flames in Gideon's eyes could have set fire to the curtains. "I still say Sir Clarence is our chief suspect, especially considering the way it behaved the last time, but he *is* dead. I saw his body."

"You did?" Amelia asked.

Gideon hadn't told her that before, but after what had just occurred, there was little point in protecting her anymore.

He nodded. "I was summoned as his next of kin. The body had been removed from his home by then. It was at the local icehouse, but I did see him and he is most assuredly deceased...so he can't be controlling this monster."

Frustrated, he threw up his hands. "Where would he even learn about such a thing? There was never a bigger prig in the whole of England than Clarence. How would he know about rituals and witchcraft?"

Amelia hummed and looked away. He narrowed his eyes at her. "What is it?"

"Er...Sir Clarence might have had occasion to learn about the occult. Not a golem per se, but he encountered magic long ago if my guess is right."

"*When*? And how?"

"I can't explain in too much detail because I'd be revealing the confidence of someone I love, but Sir Clarence witnessed a demonic possession and encountered a witch years ago."

He gaped at her. "*It's Isobel.* Bloody hell, she's a witch!"

Amelia blinked and smacked him on the shoulder. "How did you guess?"

Gideon stared at her incredulously. "The only other people you love are in this room."

"*Oh.*" Her abashed expression was so adorable he couldn't stop himself from leaning close and stealing a kiss.

His cousin Matteo's wife was a witch. *Imagine that.* "Tell me everything," he ordered.

"Later," she promised. "What's relevant here is finding who is controlling the golem. Though he knew about witchcraft and spells, I don't believe Sir Clarence could create them on his own. Isobel would have said if that was the case."

"That is reasonable," Worthing said. "But who else could it be? Is it possible he commissioned it, the way you would have a builder make something? And now it's running loose, out of control?"

"I suppose it's possible," Amelia replied. "There are tales of golems breaking down and going on a murderous rampage. However, that doesn't explain who created it in the first place…and to me, the answer is obvious."

She paused, flicking her eyes from him to the other two men.

"Don't keep us in suspense," Clarke said. "Who is it?

"Mrs. Ellie Spencer."

THE MEN STARED AT HER. Each was wearing some variation of a frown, although she noticed Clarke's was contemplative as if he was mulling over her idea.

Gideon, she noticed, did not look convinced. "Are you certain? Ellie Spencer always struck me as…simply ornamental. A charming companion for Sir Clarence in his old age. I've never seen her do anything out of line."

She scowled at him. "Except for spreading rumors about you murdering Sir Clarence."

"Ah, yes, well in my view that's something quite in character for a member of the ton."

"Isn't that the truth?" Crispin said with a snort.

"I think I see some of Amelia's logic," Clarke said. "It always struck me as a bit odd that someone as conscious of the proprieties as Sir

Clarence would have his mistress living with him openly in town. Few said anything because of their respective ages—Mrs. Spencer is hardly a debutante and she claimed to be a widow. When she first arrived in town, Sir Clarence kept a hired companion on hand to observe the proprieties, but once the sticklers became accustomed to Mrs. Spencer, the old woman was quietly dismissed and no one batted an eye."

"Tightfisted Clarence wouldn't pay an additional servant wage if he could get away with it," Crispin observed, and Amelia nodded. "Even to stop the tongues wagging—after all, it's Mrs. Spencer who would have been savaged by the gossips, not himself."

"Regardless of whether he was concerned with his own reputation, why would Sir Clarence ally himself with a woman like Mrs. Spencer?" Amelia pointed out. "As attractive and presentable as she is, she has no fortune, no connections to any notable families. No one knows anything about her. And I don't believe Sir Clarence would sponsor any mistress, no matter how charming, unless it benefited him in some way."

Gideon pursed his lips. "Love, I understand you've been a bit sheltered, but there are many ways a woman like Mrs. Spencer can make herself indispensable to a man."

"Really?" she asked with sarcasm. "To a man like Sir Clarence—the man you called the biggest prig in all England?"

He shrugged. "The thing about prigs is that they tend to be hypocrites as well."

Amelia sighed. She knew she was correct about Mrs. Spencer, but men—even her loving husband—did tend to underestimate the females around them. Including herself.

"I believe Amelia may be right," Mr. Clarke said, his eyes distant. "There isn't another reasonable candidate. Sir Clarence had no friends aside from a few cronies at his clubs, and from all accounts, those relationships were superficial. In the last months of his life, when we were keeping a close watch on him, he had no visitors of note, no tradesmen who came and went with any regularity. And it makes sense his magical mercenary was someone he kept close at hand. And

Amelia's point about Mrs. Spencer's background is a valid one. She's known to be tight-lipped about her family and only mentioned in a vague way she was from Somerset."

"A magical mercenary and mistress in one. You may be right," Gideon told Amelia, rubbing his chin. "That's a convenience even a miser like Sir Clarence would value, enough to sponsor a woman through the high cost of the season. Mrs. Spencer always dressed in the height of fashion—a very expensive proposition for someone like Clarence. And clearly, Mrs. Spencer benefited from the arrangement in other ways. She was accepted in the best homes and was seen everywhere. Though of mysterious and most likely humble origins, she has taken to the ton like a duck to water and would be loath to leave town."

That fit with what Amelia knew of her. "Which means she should be easy to find, surely?"

Clarke held up a hand. "I'm afraid I have some bad news. As you know my information network is still hard at work. They've been monitoring Mrs. Spencer, and she disappeared from town around the same time you departed. At least she was not seen afterward. Enough people noticed for them to make a few more nasty insinuations about you," he said with a nod to her husband.

Gideon humphed. "This makes sense. She may have realized she overplayed her hand by using her golem to strangle one of my greys." He drummed his fingers on the table. "Sir Clarence said he met her in Bath. Is there any chance that's where she is now?"

Clarke conceded the point with a nod. "I would guess so. Most people retreat to familiar stomping grounds when they run from trouble. We do have some connections in Bath and can send more men to do some discreet questioning. One thing working to our advantage—I doubt Mrs. Spencer will attempt to live quietly wherever she is."

Amelia hoped that was the case. Privately, she didn't agree about the reason for Mrs. Spencer's sudden departure from town. Her instinct told her the woman had lost control of the creature she had raised. It made more sense that she had run from *it*—and not out of fear for a single earl's wrath.

If they were correct, Mrs. Ellie Spencer was a witch, one unprincipled enough to harass an innocent member of her own sex. Amelia doubted someone like that would decamp from her hard-won position in the ton over guilt or fear of reprisal. Nevertheless, she couldn't argue with the plan.

The witch had to be found.

CHAPTER 28

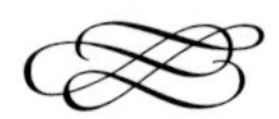

"Are you certain she's in there?" Gideon asked.

"According to the tradesmen, she is. She's been using Sir Clarence's existing accounts, though she hasn't been spending freely or lavishly," Clarke confirmed.

"No. If she did, they'd suspect Sir Clarence was not actually authorizing the purchases. She can't do anything too out of character lest they ask questions. As it stands, I'm surprised she hasn't been discovered in the lie before. Sir Clarence's murder was in the papers."

"She must have some ready cash, enough to keep up appearances," Clarke guessed.

Mrs. Spencer's hideaway was a suite of apartments in Bath, a place she had frequented with Sir Clarence years ago, one in keeping with his uncle's spendthrift ways. The street was not the most fashionable, but that didn't seem to concern Mrs. Spencer.

While many in Bath were aware of Sir Clarence's death, Mrs. Spencer hadn't done anything to call attention to it the way she had in London. Indeed, she was living quietly, but in plain view. She had not done any entertaining since arriving in town.

"Funny that," he commented before sharing his observation with the others.

"It doesn't surprise me," Amelia murmured next to him in the carriage.

She didn't need to explain why. His brilliant wife was of a mind Mrs. Spencer had lost control of her creation. *And she may be right.* The current circumstances certainly suggested as much.

So did that make Amelia safer at this moment or less? Gideon was almost certain she was carrying his child. Intent on protecting them both he had initially insisted she remain in their apartments, but she had argued with him, playing on his insecurities regarding the footmen and Manning's ability to defend against a creature such as a golem.

"And really, it's not likely Mrs. Spencer has the golem secreted in her closet," she pointed out. "Not in the middle of Bath."

Gideon reminded her the Golem of Prague was rumored to be stored in an attic, but eventually, he relented. Letting Amelia out of his sight would cause him more distress than taking her with him, especially since he didn't go anywhere without a cache of loaded pistols.

Gideon was carrying two on his person, same as Clarke. Given that Lord Worthing was still lame in one leg, requiring the use of a cane, he only carried one. But the footmen and outriders they traveled with everywhere were also heavily armed.

Manning approached the carriage window. "She's there," his manservant said.

"Are the other men in position?"

"Yes, my lord. They're all around the house and the corners of the neighboring streets."

He nodded approvingly. "Good. Remember, if she gets past us, don't let her escape. Do whatever you need to do to prevent it. We can't let her slip through our net."

They wasted no more time.

As tempting as it was to kick the door down, Gideon settled for the more socially expedient knock. For a long minute, no one answered, but the curtains on the upper story twitched.

He signaled his men, telling them to get ready. He was about to rap again when to his shock, Mrs. Spencer answered the door herself.

"Oh, thank the Lord," she exclaimed, appearing genuinely relieved to see him.

"I was worried you were dead," she told them, a wild look in her eye as she turned her head right and left, searching the street.

Mrs. Spencer backed away from the threshold, waving them inside with a hasty "*Come*".

Amelia threw him a triumphant glance as she took his arm to cross the threshold. They entered the darkened suite.

It was much smaller than he had originally supposed. And darker. Was Mrs. Spencer in such desperate need of funds she couldn't afford lamp oil or tapers? Or had she picked up Sir Clarence's miserly ways?

Suspicious, Gideon pulled Amelia to his left, putting himself between her and the witch.

Mrs. Spencer perched at the edge of a chair. Now that they were all safely inside, her eyes flitted from his face to the others in a manic fashion.

Her behavior was far different from the socially assured woman he'd seen moving through London on Sir Clarence's arm.

"We know you're a witch and that you control the golem," Amelia announced.

Gideon and Clarke looked at each other. They had agreed beforehand to let Amelia start the questioning, assuming Mrs. Spencer would feel less threatened that way. If she refused to speak, then he would step in and take over.

Mrs. Spencer sucked in a breath. "Yes, and no. In a way, no one is controlling it now."

"So you admit you raised a golem." Gideon's voice cold, but far less harsh than the tone he wanted to use with her. "Is it here in Bath?"

"No, I don't believe so, although..." Her eyes flicked to Amelia. "It is unpredictable now."

Amelia was about to ask another question when he touched her arm surreptitiously. She looked at him and he shook his head a tiny fraction. It was interrogation technique Phineus had taught him.

Establish the facts and let the silence stretch. The person being questioned usually filled in the blanks.

An unseen clock ticked away somewhere behind them. *Usually*.

"I met Sir Clarence here in Bath," Ellie Spencer said, smoothing her hands over her skirts. "He knew witchcraft existed and had been in search of a practitioner to hire for some time. I was making my living telling fortunes and conducting séances, but the baronet had grander plans for me."

Finally, they were getting somewhere.

"What sort of plans?" Amelia asked. Her voice was mild, but her grip on his hand was tight.

Mrs. Spencer looked down. "It varied. In the beginning, he wanted information for his investments. It was not the sort of thing I was accustomed to providing for my clients—oh, I might have insinuated things about windfalls and the like, but no one can tell the future. Before when a client was dissatisfied, I would use a confusion spell on them and send them on their way. It always worked before Sir Clarence. He wouldn't take no for an answer. When that didn't work, he offered me hundreds of pounds.

"It was more money than I'd ever seen in my life. I tried to muddle along, however, what he asked wasn't possible. I couldn't pull the information he wanted out of thin air. I needed to move in his circles, to find and question the relevant parties. Eventually, I came clean about my limitations, thinking it would be the end of it."

"But it wasn't, was it? Sir Clarence had found a witch and he wasn't ready to give you up."

Mrs. Spencer nodded. "He was angry when he realized I needed to move in society as he did. Nevertheless, he was sufficiently motivated to provide me with the education and wardrobe I would need... The speech and accent were not difficult. My mother was the result a liaison between a chambermaid and Clyde Burgess, the son of a prominent family in Somerset.

She seemed to be waiting for something. "I've heard of the family," Gideon acknowledged with a nod.

Mrs. Spencer appeared satisfied. "My grandfather provided for my mother's education, but by the time I came around, he had passed on and there was no more money. But I had enough knowledge to accurately emulate a genteel lady with a little guidance.

"And Sir Clarence provided that guidance?" There was a tiny pucker between Amelia's brows as if she was surprised he would exert himself to such a degree.

"He hired a companion and told her I was a long-lost relative that needed be polished for the season. It didn't take me long to capture her mannerisms—all those unconscious little movements the ladies of the upper class are taught from birth. Sir Clarence took me to country parties and we began to work together on his business schemes."

"More confusion spells?" he asked, remembering the strange disorientation he and Amelia had experienced.

Another nod. "When it seemed expedient. I could hypnotize some of his business partners or other investors. But when information was not enough, then he would ask me to intimidate them."

"And you didn't have an issue with that?" Amelia's voice was hard. Gideon gave her hand a warning squeeze. He didn't want Mrs. Spencer to stop speaking.

Mrs. Spencer picked at her skirts. She wouldn't look them in the face. "Honestly, I didn't think too much about what I was doing. My abilities had never been challenged before. Now they were. I was learning more and more and being rewarded for it. And...by then Sir Clarence and I had become intimate. He promised me if I continued to make myself useful, we would marry."

Her eyes swung up to Amelia with an almost accusatory expression. "But then you and his son came home."

She blinked and looked up at the ceiling, face hard. "I didn't understand Sir Clarence's obsession at first. It seemed quite natural for him to gripe about the two of you settling so far from his home in Northumberland. When you chose to stay in Kent instead of partaking of the season in London, he wanted me to do something about it. But I had heard his valet talking to the coachman one day. The two implied his son would do well to keep his young bride out of Sir Clarence's grasp. I understood then there was more to his complaints than a desire to be close to his son. So...I read his journal."

Her face twisted, and she said no more.

"You read about his plan to sire his son's heir." Gideon said it as matter-of-factly as he could, but inside, his stomach roiled.

Mrs. Spencer sniffed and glanced at Lord Worthing out of the corner of her eye, making Gideon wonder if Sir Clarence had written about his son's lover. "I was angry with Clarence. Despite all I did for him, he had stopped speaking of marriage. Instead, he carped about finding some way to bring his son to heel.

"I knew about golems from my time as a fortune-teller. One of my clients was a wealthy Jew who liked to tell stories. I had traded him my services for some texts on the subject, but they were written in Hebrew and I couldn't use them—not until I had access to the libraries of the ton. Rich scholars commission translations. I found other texts in English that detailed rituals on various mystical rites, including how to raise a golem for labor. I had been experimenting on how to alter the ritual when Sir Clarence stormed in and demanded I do something to make his son obey him. It was the first time he'd mentioned Amelia, Mrs. Montgomery, by name."

The witch's chin firmed mulishly. "I could practically see him salivating. He wrote down fantasies he had about her while she was living in his home when she was younger. He wanted her in easy reach again, seemingly certain that he would be the one to claim her innocence—as if she hadn't taken lovers abroad while her Sodomite of a husband amused himself."

The tension in the room heightened with those bitter words, but they didn't say anything as Mrs. Spencer attempted to catch hold of her temper. "I vowed then and there that Sir Clarence would never accomplish this goal."

Gideon finally lost his temper. "How did killing Martin with the golem help? Without him to protect her, Amelia was even more vulnerable to Sir Clarence's schemes."

"That was an *accident*," Mrs. Spencer cried, bursting into tears. "I had just succeeded in raising the golem but was disappointed to learn how stupid it was. It was incapable of following anything but the simplest of commands. But I found a way to overcome that. With the right incantations and a small sacrifice, I could put my mind inside it, see what it saw and touch what it touched."

Gideon stiffened. A flash of the golem stroking his wife's nearly naked body rose ran through his mind. He wanted to jump up and shake the woman. Amelia sensed that. Her grip on his hand altered, pressing down to effectively keep him in his seat.

After a few deep bracing breaths, he calmed down. Mrs. Spencer was continuing of her own volition, the words spilling out almost as if she had been waiting to confess all her sins.

"I was only trying to scare Mr. Montgomery into leaving England again, but it all went wrong." Her hand shook as she raised her arms and then snapped them back to wring her hands in her lap instead. "My control of the creature was tenuous at best so early on. I could not judge the dimensions properly. I did not mean to kill him, but he simply flew over that railing."

Amelia was stone-faced, staring at the woman in disbelief. "Martin never harmed a living thing in his entire life. He was the sweetest, kindest man that ever walked this earth."

Mrs. Spencer said nothing, her eyes on her skirts.

"Sir Clarence took over the golem later, didn't he?" Gideon asked before the woman decided to stop speaking altogether.

After a time, she continued. "Because of his preoccupation with Mrs. Montgomery—the countess I mean—Sir Clarence had stopped coming to my bed. We also stopped planning schemes together. He left me to my own devices for a while, but unbeknownst to me, he would periodically go through my papers. It was there he learned about my experiments with the golem. He was thrilled. He demanded I summon one he could control."

"And you did," Amelia supplied tonelessly.

"Yes," Mrs. Spencer said, exhaling sharply. "Over time he became quite adept at managing it. When the countess began to move in society again he was ready."

"By this time, I knew he would never marry me. I had begun to look for another protector...but I was still angry." She looked at Amelia. "I hated you and Clarence both."

"So you plagued with Sir Clarence's blessing and didn't care how it affected her," Viscount Worthing said.

Mrs. Spencer grew red in the face. She fixed her attention on the darkened window and didn't answer.

"How did it go wrong?" Gideon asked.

"It was about *her,* of course," she said, gesturing at Amelia. "He wanted finer control over the creature, and over larger distances. One had to be quite close to manipulate it. By then, you had made your intentions clear. You were going to make Amelia your countess. But Sir Clarence intended to stop you."

She broke off and shrugged. "I don't know if he planned to kill you with the golem or simply carry Amelia away. We quarreled over his plans. I reminded him of his promises to wed and he *spat* on me. He told me he'd never marry Amelia, a cit's daughter, so why would he wed gutter trash like me?"

Her eyes were blazing, hurt fueling her words. "In a rage, I raised the golem and I strangled him with it."

Gideon glanced at Amelia, but her face was impassive. He knew Mrs. Spencer was leaving some details out. He'd seen the body and Sir Clarence hadn't been merely *strangled*.

"But he's a part of it now, isn't he?" Gideon asked.

The words hung in the air, unacknowledged, but he knew he was right. Some part of Clarence lived in the beast now. The way it reacted to Amelia in the woods—the way it had touched her was proof.

The witch opened her mouth. "I didn't know that could happen. I still don't know how...except..."

"Except what?" His temper strained, making the words clipped.

"Part of the ritual giving Clarence control over the golem involved using his blood. We used it to write the words that fuel it, a mixture of the holy and the profane. His name is also part of the script we placed in the creature's mouth." She shook her head. "Consequently, the creature possessed a bit of his *anima*. That is how he controlled it."

"And when you used it to kill him, it took more of this *anima?*" That would explain the creature's behavior.

If it absorbed even a fraction of Sir Clarence's twisted desire for Amelia… Gideon's jaw clenched tight as he suppressed a shudder.

Her shrug was infuriating, but he fought hard not to let it show. "I believe so. It stopped responding to my commands then and there. It's wild now. I don't know how to stop it."

Those last words cast a pall over the others in the room. They had come here hoping for answers and a way to put an end to the menace once and for all. Answers they now had, but not a solution.

Everything Mrs. Spencer had told them confirmed his worst fears —there was a monster out there, and it wanted his wife.

"What about the sacred words? Can't we simply remove them?" Amelia asked.

Mrs. Spencer's eyes flared. "I tried. It wouldn't let me near its mouth."

Gideon stood and began to pace. "No. If there are some of Clarence's memories in there—and it appears there are—then it would guard against that." He stopped and removed the rough pottery finger from the pocket of his waistcoat and held it up.

"What about this? I shot this off with a pistol. Can it regrow fingers or limbs?"

Mrs. Spencer frowned. "I don't think there are enough pistols in the world…but no, it can't regrow itself. But if it remembers what Sir Clarence remembers, then perhaps it could try to repair itself."

Gideon held up a hand. "But what if it had a big enough shock and was shattered all at once?"

"If the blows destroyed the head as well, then yes, but I have to believe that it would fight back." Mrs. Spencer raised her arm and drew her sleeve up, revealing a string of deep black bruises.

His mind went to the fingerprint marks Sir Clarence had left on Amelia's arms all those months ago. These were bigger, more misshapen, but the similarity was there.

Hell was too good for his uncle.

"We could try and gather a group of men with axes," Clarke said, speaking for the first time.

"I doubt you'd find enough that wouldn't run for cover if they saw such a thing in the flesh—or clay as it were," Lord Worthing said.

"We only need a few brave souls."

Amelia swung to face him. "A few? My Lord, we need an army."

"Which conveniently we have," he pointed out. "Between the two of us we employ enough servants to make a stand against a besieging army, but we won't need them to fight. I have something else in mind."

He glanced at Mrs. Spencer, unsure if he could trust her enough to detail his plans in her presence.

She seemed to understand his reservations. "What about me? Are you going to have me hung? Or burned at the stake?" she asked bluntly.

Gideon and Amelia exchanged a glance. Part of him wanted to absolve the witch. If not for Sir Clarence, she wouldn't have ended up on this twisted path. But if he was reading her reactions correctly she had taken some pleasure in casting her nefarious spells. She wasn't remorseful for the damage she had inflected—only for getting caught.

Amelia watched him with her hands folded in her lap. Like the others, she waited for his decree.

Despite being a former spy, Gideon had never had to decide a person's fate before. He had been a soldier in a way, one who carried out the orders and directives of his superiors—even when he'd been forced to kill.

As an earl, he would eventually make decisions that would profoundly affect the lives of hundreds of people, but this was the first and most direct application of the power of his title.

He made eye contact with Clarke, who seemed to understand his dilemma.

"You can't stay in England," he said finally.

Mrs. Spencer paled. "You're having me transported?"

His nod was short and sharp. "A woman of your abilities will survive well enough on her own in the colonies or Australia. I will even provide you with a small sum to get started—but you can't stay here. And don't even think about trying to evade the authorities. Through your actions, you caused the death of at least one innocent man, perhaps more if we investigate what you and Clarence got up to together."

She opened her mouth, her gaze shifting between him and Amelia as if to remind him that he had her now because Martin was gone, but she wisely chose not to speak.

"I want to leave immediately."

Naturally. So long as the wild golem was at large, she'd be safer putting an ocean between her and it.

"As you wish," he said before signaling to the others that it was time to depart.

He had a trap to bait.

CHAPTER 29

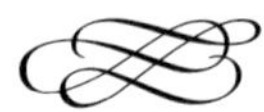

"This will never work," Amelia said, lacing up her loosest corset on Gideon's tiger.

"You're supposing this creature has good eyesight," Gideon pointed out. "We don't know it does. And it only needs to be convincing for a few moments."

He patted John on the arm. "Don't worry. You'll not be in any real danger."

Young John nodded stoically, putting up a brave front that Amelia saw through. The poor boy was trembling.

They were at Lilywood Cottage, Gideon's small property in Devon. It lay a few miles away from the ruins of the Abbey, where Gideon had laid his trap.

"Now, tell me again your role so I know you've understood."

John's arms hung awkwardly at his sides. He looked so ill at ease in her gown Amelia wanted to tell him she would be the lure in their scheme, but she knew better than to try. Gideon refused to allow her to take part, and she was tired of arguing with him.

The entire ordeal had been so draining that Amelia had spent most of the time since arriving in Dorset sleeping.

John recited his instructions as if they were a school lesson. "I keep my wig and cloak on at all times and don't show too much of my face at any of the windows. The men outside will light torches all around. At your signal, they're going to fall back and pretend they've seen it somewhere off the grounds. If *it* comes the men hidden in the house will run out with their long hammers, forcing the creature to one of the weak spots in the floor. I must stay on the other side of one of these so it will try to cross and fall through."

Gideon nodded approvingly. "The fall is long enough that it will most definitely shatter when it hits the ground underneath."

"And if *it* doesn't come to the house for my facsimile?" Amelia asked with folded arms, frowning at the soreness of her breasts.

Was it her imagination or were they more ample than she remembered?

Gideon adjusted the wig and sent John out of the room with a little push. "Then we try again tomorrow night and every night hereafter until it comes."

He put his hands on her shoulders. "It *will* work. I'm certain of it."

Amelia suspected he was not being entirely truthful but decided not to take issue with it. It wasn't as if she had a better plan.

Rubbing her arms, she went to the window. It was safe, so long as she didn't open the curtains. In life, Sir Clarence had not been aware of this property, or that it belonged to Gideon. They had arrived via an anonymous hired carriage, using her more distinctive conveyance as a decoy. Gideon would take that one up the main drive before guiding his faux-countess inside.

Mr. Clarke had disguised himself as a clergyman, one summoned to the Abbey on the pretext of blessing the grounds before they rebuilt the house. In the meantime, their superfluous male staff were making themselves visible on the house's grounds.

Crispin, along with half a dozen of Gideon's best men, would stay behind at the cottage to watch over her. That suited Crispin just fine. He wasn't eager to set foot in the ruin again. "I'm about as graceful as a sow with this leg. I'll end up falling through the floor myself."

Gideon assured him such a thing wasn't likely. The men who would face the creature were secured to the stairs and the beams undamaged by fire with strong rope. The rest would be tied to each other. If one fell, the strength of the others would keep them from plunging into the abyss.

The earl was sure he had thought of everything. Amelia hoped he was right.

In a few minutes, Crispin came up to inform Gideon that everything was in readiness. Then he went back down to check the state of his pistols again.

"He's loaded and reloaded those guns at least three times now," she said.

"It makes him feel better to be armed. And bullets do damage it, just not as easily as I would like." Gideon took her in his arms. "Please don't worry. We have everything ready."

His big, warm hands moved to cover her stomach. Self-conscious because her middle had expanded a trifle the last few weeks—the richness of the food again—she tried to shift his hands.

"Rest," he ordered. "Growing an entire person is exhausting."

Amelia's mouth dropped open as her mind wrapped itself around what he was saying. She couldn't be increasing! She would have known.

As if on cue, a sudden wave of dizziness rose to overwhelm her. Gideon caught her up and set her on the wide double bed. "As I said, growing an entire person is exhausting for any woman, but bearing my heir is enough to tax even a goddess like you."

Amelia slapped his hand. "How long have you known?"

His grin was smug. "Not long."

"And you didn't think to tell me?"

He kissed her forehead and drew back. "You had enough on your mind."

But he conveniently tells me now so I won't worry. Amelia's arms tightened around his neck, pulling him close for a fierce hug.

"Come back to me in one piece or suffer the consequences," she said, fighting tears.

"You have my word," he vowed, holding her tight.

CHAPTER 30

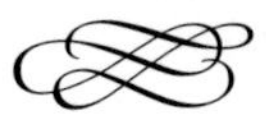

"It's midnight," Clarke whispered, squinting at his fob watch in the weak moonlight.

Gideon didn't need the reminder. He'd been checking his own watch often enough in the last few hours. "I don't think tonight is the night," he muttered.

"Poor John is probably exhausted. I don't think he stays up this late as a rule and traipsing around in that heavy winter gown is probably not helping."

Gideon was sympathetic, but the wool gown was a necessity. If they had dressed his tiger in one of Amelia's lighter gowns, the boy's distinctive shape would have been more noticeable.

"Call him back and have him set himself up in the caretaker's cottage. He's to sleep in the wig."

Clarke snorted but hurried off to pass his order along.

The air was frigid here at the ocean's edge. Taking a quick look at the cliff line, Gideon wrapped his greatcoat around himself, making sure nothing of his white shirt was revealed.

Mrs. Spencer had told them that seeing through the golem's eyes distorted the image from a distance, but it was clear enough to make out details and colors when up close.

So Sir Clarence would have seen Amelia clearly when she lay in bed next to him, nude. The brief surge of anger was sufficient to warm him, but he waited impatiently for Clarke to return before heading back. Once he did they slipped away along the cliff's edge, sticking to the shadows whenever they could.

He knew something was wrong when they reached Lilywood cottage. The house and grounds were dark, with no lamp in either the coach house or outside the stable.

"Where are the men?" Clarke asked.

Gideon didn't answer. He broke out into a run, rounding the corner. He faltered when he saw the open door and then began shouting. "Amelia!"

Clarke was right behind him when he barreled through the front door.

They found the first man just inside. He was groaning. Another was coming down the stairs, helping Crispin make his way down.

"Crispin!" Clarke rushed to the other man, taking him into his arms, making it down the final few steps with a little jump.

"It got her," Lord Worthing cried, touching his head gingerly. It came away stained with blood. "The other men, the ones who could still walk, went after them. They're trying to track it."

Clarke held Crispin's hand tightly. "We'll find her, don't worry."

Lord Worthing's eyes were shattered, but he didn't respond as if he was afraid to share his fears in front of him.

Gideon held his hands to his stomach, pressing hard, physically holding himself together.

"If something of Sir Clarence is in there, it won't kill her," he said slowly, trying to make himself believe his own words.

It had to be true. If it was, then it would keep her alive...He crushed the next thought, refusing to think about what horrors might befall his wife.

Gideon had badly miscalculated. He didn't know how the creature had seen through their ruse. All he knew was Amelia was in the hands of a monster, one made flesh by one man's obsession with her.

CHAPTER 31

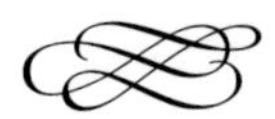

Amelia groaned and came to on a rough stone floor. Her skull throbbed. Slowly, she dragged herself into a seated position and opened her eyes.

Her head ached viciously. Tentatively, she touched an egg-sized bump on the left side of her head. A jumble of images swept through her, thrills of terror chilling her blood to ice in the cold room.

Oh, my God, Crispin. He could be dead! The last thing she remembered was his body crumpling to the floor. He'd been in front of her, trying to protect her. After that, she could recall only fragments, a sense of movement with a view of trees up above, and then the rocky shore.

She couldn't see anything around her, but the roughly hewn floor didn't feel like a cave. Was she in one of the old Roman basements?

Good God, was she *under* her old home?

The Abbey was built over the natural cave formations native to the area. Crispin had almost fallen into one when the floor had given way underneath him. But according to her father, the network of tunnels extended for miles along the coast.

She shuddered. Where was the golem? It was nowhere in sight—but then, she couldn't see her hand in front of her face.

Had it brought her down here to die?

Amelia's hands flew to her waist. *No.* That wasn't going to happen. She had to protect her child—Gideon's child. She had lost too much already to give up now. She'd smash the golem to pieces with her own hands first.

Now she simply had to find it.

GIDEON COULD FEEL the cold sweat running down the back of his neck, but he didn't let his panic show. With hoarse instructions, he ordered the men who remained in a search.

"Where would it have taken her?" Clarke had calmed down enough to come to his side. It helped that Crispin had pleaded with him to help with the search.

Gideon spared a second to analyze that moment between the two men. It seemed so obvious now—their sudden close friendship. And he hadn't seen it.

Clarke had always been discreet about his relationships, and now Gideon knew why. He had always assumed his friend had a lover or two tucked away somewhere over the years. Before this, he would have guessed those lovers had been female.

Where was my head? Why didn't I see it?

"Later," he said aloud, giving himself a little shake.

"What?" Clarke stopped to look at him.

"I'll congratulate you later."

"*Oh.*" His friend's eyes were wide, and he might have flushed but it was hard to be sure in the lantern light. "Yes, we'll talk later."

Clarke's uncertainty was baseless, but the need to reassure his friend was distant and hard to reach.

Amelia. Gideon could feel himself growing colder as hope ebbed away.

The sudden punch in the shoulder snapped him to full consciousness. He stared at Clarke, who scowled at him. "You're losing faith. *Don't.*"

"But what if—"

Clarke held up a hand "I said don't! For God's sake, this is Amelia we are talking about—she brought you to your knees. A single monster doesn't stand a chance."

Gideon snorted and found the strength to take a deep breath. "Have the men who followed it come back?"

"Not yet, but they will soon. And then, we'll have them both."

He nodded, continuing to trudge through the scrub brush before turning to the cliff. "We need to get down to the beach."

How else would the monster move without being seen? It had to be walking along the deserted beach. If something of Sir Clarence was still in there, he wouldn't want to be seen.

Clarke understood his reasoning without explanation.

"Let's go."

CHAPTER 32

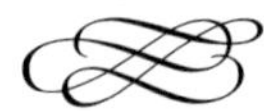

Amelia's knees ached. She tried to stand up and walk, only to bump her head on an unseen stone ceiling. So she crawled and crawled until she could feel the space around her opening.

By that time, her knees were scored and likely bloody, but she couldn't see them. The monster had attacked after she'd prepared for bed, and though the thick material of her sleeping gown had offered some protection, it hadn't been enough. Her hands had also suffered.

It could be worse. She could be trapped alone with the beast.

She had woken alone, no pair of glowing eyes staring down at her. Amelia tensed at every imagined sound, expecting the golem to jump out at her. Had it abandoned her here to die?

All Amelia knew was it wasn't here now—it might not even return. She had to find her own way out of the dark.

Fighting tears, she stiffened her spine. I've done it before, Amelia told herself sternly. She had made her way out of a stark and unhappy childhood, finding some measure of happiness with her best friend. It had been a pure but loving marriage. Then when she had lost Martin she had mourned him, finally reaching a place where she could live a life full of love and happiness with Gideon, the man she had adored almost her entire life.

Martin would have approved. In fact, he would have gloated and said, 'I told you so' a dozen or so times.

True, she had more or less fallen into the relationship of her dreams, but it took some courage to forget the scars of the past and accept love, didn't it?

No one, not even a monster, was going to take that from her.

Her brave words fell to dust a few minutes later when she made her way into a big cavern where part of the ceiling had collapsed, letting in the moonlight.

The golem was sitting against a stone wall on a big boulder. It looked right at her and hissed, the sound sending a bolt of fear through her.

Oh, God. Oh, God. What do I do?

Amelia clutched her hands together, afraid to breathe, let alone move.

It hissed again and she trembled.

Stop. Don't panic. She needed to think clearly or she would never get out of this—never see Gideon again.

Meeting the monster again was terrifying, but also revealing. Its massive size mocked her earlier resolve to destroy it. She didn't have the strength—and then there was her child to think of.

According to Mrs. Spencer, the golem had taken some of Sir Clarence's *anima,* so there should be enough of him in there to understand her.

"You should congratulate me, Sir Clarence. I'm carrying Gideon's child."

The banked hellfire of its eyes brightened to red glowing coals and the hissing grew so loud it hurt her ears.

Amelia clapped her hands over them and sobbed, immediately contrite. *"I'm sorry."*

The creature didn't respond, but the hissing abated. Sniffling, she racked her brain for what else the mistress had said.

Mrs. Spencer hadn't been able to get close enough to get the chem, the script with the sacred words, out of the golem's mouth. Would it let Amelia get close enough?

Sir Clarence had never been an affectionate or trusting man. Pretending it was him and trying to hug it wouldn't work.

Amelia's stomach roiled when she remembered the only time Sir Clarence had allowed—nay demanded—she be close to him.

After my lessons.

A pit opened in the bottom of her stomach, threatening to swallow her up. More than anything in her childhood, she had hated going to her guardian's study to recite what she had learned in her lessons that day.

Her hands shook as she brushed an errant curl out of her eye. *This is the only way to get close enough.*

She wiped away the moisture that was making it hard to see and stepped forward, her head down, hands clasped in front of her, the way she had every time she'd done this as a girl.

"I'm finished with my tutor, Sir Clarence."

She waited, and then inhaled sharply when it whistled and moved its hand to wave her over, exactly the way Sir Clarence always had.

Inch by inch, she stepped closer, her thrumming heartbeat deafening her. She couldn't even hear her own footsteps.

The clay hand reaching for her was an abomination. She knew that. But buried inside the earthen automaton were the memories of a man—Sir Clarence—whose consuming lust she had been trying to evade her whole adult life.

She had to use that now. Amelia nodded to herself, reaching deep inside for the detachment she had discovered those long-ago afternoons in Sir Clarence's study.

When she reached the golem, she curtsied. It leaned back, making room to let her sit.

Just like before. Sick with fear, she turned around and sat on the golem's lap.

Buried memories rose. In her mind's eye, she could see Sir Clarence's hands opening her bodice, stroking her fourteen-year-old breasts. She'd already had a womanly shape by then, but Sir Clarence had insisted she was still a child—even when he was touching and weighing their fullness while asking, almost to himself, what he was going to do with her.

All the details she had avoided recalling for so long came rushing back—the sickly sweet smell of tobacco and stale peppermint. To this day, she couldn't abide tobacco smoke. Then there was the way he would sit, positioning her so her backside would rub along his hard staff.

It had never progressed farther than that. Amelia had been so ignorant back then; she hadn't even known what she was being spared. All she had known was that she abhorred Sir Clarence's touch.

She had been too ashamed to tell anyone...even Martin. But he had found out anyway when he'd arrived home from school unexpectedly one afternoon. Martin had walked in on them. Sir Clarence had yelled at him and sent him away, but he'd come to her later and she'd burst into tears.

That was the afternoon he'd first promised to take her away.

Yes, that was it. It had been his idea at first. She had repeated the request so often in the following years, she'd forgotten that detail. For years, she believed it had been her plan from the start.

The golem hissed in her ear, and she started in fear. *Of course.* She had to recite her lessons. *"Decem, viginti, triginta..."*

As if on cue, the clay hands moved to her bodice, but the woolen gown didn't have lacings.

Amelia opened her eyes wide. *Now.* She had to do this now before she lost her nerve entirely.

Turning around slowly, she rose to her feet in a slow sensual movement.

If she was right, there was a twisted little fragment of Sir Clarence in there that had been waiting, longing, for this moment.

"Happy birthday, Sir Clarence."

The kisses she had been forced to give him once a year had been perfunctory—quick closed-mouthed pecks finished as quickly as possible.

This was not one of those. Amelia stared down at the golem, imagining she could see Sir Clarence's whiskered face between her hands.

Then she knelt with parted lips that it met with a slow heavy movement of its head.

Ignoring the sharp exhalation of air that accompanied the creature's hissing speech, she met its clay mouth with her own. It didn't have lips, just a slash of an opening. But it acted as she predicted—like a man aware of a woman.

A little more. Amelia gingerly parted her lips. Her tongue touched the edge of paper—the chem. Fortunately for her, it stuck, allowing her to withdraw it enough to grasp it with her teeth.

Snatching it back, she reared away before the golem—Sir Clarence—realized what she had done.

It seemed to know. It looked at the chem, crumpled in her hand, and hissed a final time before slumping over. The light in its eyes dimmed and died.

Amelia stared at the creature for a long moment. The hazy outline blurred, and she realized she was crying.

Whatever Sir Clarence had been in life, he hadn't deserved becoming this.

And I didn't deserve what he did to me. That was something she had never admitted to herself before.

She shed a few final tears and resolved that the golem would stay here. She wouldn't let Gideon take it out. If he insisted on destroying it, he could send men here to do it, but this place—this would be Sir Clarence's final tomb.

Picking up the hem of her woolen gown, she turned around and walked away, leaving her most terrible memories behind.

CHAPTER 33

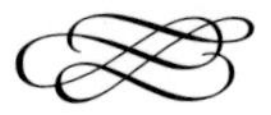

"My lord, we heard her!"

Manning and John came running up to him.

"Where?" Gideon asked, his heart in this throat.

"Back up at the house. Simmons was standing near the hole in the Abbey floor, and he heard her. We yelled, and she answered. Just *her*."

Oh, thank the good Lord. Gideon staggered, accepting Clarke's bracing hand before he fell out of sheer relief. Together, they struggled up the narrow cliff path. Heedless of how he looked to the other men, he ran across the grounds and into the house like a madman.

"Amelia?" he called down into the pit.

"Gideon!" Her voice was a little hollow as it echoed through the vast space below their feet.

Tears blurred his vision as he got down on his hands and knees. "Are you all right? Where is the golem?"

"It's dead, Gideon. I destroyed the chem."

Stunned, he stared down at the dark. Was it his imagination or was the touch of white her face?

"My lord, we have ropes, but they're too short," Manning said. "We are tying them together, and thought we would secure a lantern to the end so we can see her better."

"Yes, do it. But make sure those knots are secure," he ordered, glad someone had kept their head.

Good lord, Amelia had destroyed the chem. She had single-handedly slain the monster—without his help!

"We're lowering a lamp," he called down, pushing his astonishment and misgivings to the back of his mind.

The lamp in question was thrust into his hand, and he lowered it down himself. It bobbed at the end of his tether, lighting the rough brick walls that formed the basement of the old ruin beneath them.

A flurry of white moved toward the glow, growing brighter the closer it came to the source of illumination.

"Amelia!" She really was all right. In fact, she might have been smiling up at him as she took the lamp and grasped the handle in her hand.

"Get more rope," he called out, eyeing the jagged edges of the floor. What if they frayed the rope? "And blankets," he yelled behind him.

Feet pounded away to obey his orders, but Amelia called out to him before they got too far.

"Gideon, I think there's a way out to the beach from down here. I can see a bit of it through a gap in a cavern adjoining this one. I can even feel the wind!"

If they could break through the wall, it would be much safer than hauling her through the hole in the Abbey floor. He didn't even know if she could tie a proper knot to secure around herself. "We'll go down there," he decided. "Which direction is it in?"

Amelia held the lantern up to illuminate her arms better and pointed.

"Go. Wait at the gap. I'll be right there," he promised.

"Hurry!"

Calling all the men to him, Gideon and Clarke searched the shoreline for a break in the stone walls that would lead them to the cavern where Amelia was.

Worried when he couldn't hear her, Gideon was about to send someone to rouse the local magistrate. He would insist on having every able-bodied man join the search.

A shout went up, and he and Clarke rushed forward.

"Gideon!" Amelia's white fingers almost glowed against the unrelenting darkness of the stone around them. They were poking out of a small gap the width of his hand.

He grabbed them and swore. "Tell me you're all right!" he barked, his voice sharpening in his distress.

"I'm fine. My head hurts a bit and I'm cold, but I'm fine."

Gideon put his mouth to the gap. "Is it really dead?" he asked.

He could see some movement on the other side and realized she was nodding.

Gideon didn't want to know anymore. Explanations could come later. Picking up the axe himself, he ordered her back and got to work.

Breaking down the wall was the work of a few minutes. They had been prepared with picks and mallets to use on the golem. Instead, he and his men used them to break down the rock face—alternately using their hands to expand the narrow opening of the cavern when necessary. The space must have been part of the network the Abbey had been built over.

As soon as the opening was wide enough, Amelia squeezed through, practically leaping into his arms.

Gideon didn't care if everyone was watching them or that they were cheering, or like young John, crying in relief. He held Amelia tightly to him, his grip a little too hard.

"Take me away, Gideon," she whispered into his neck.

"Anything you want," he promised.

Confirming that the golem was really gone—and cracking it to pieces—could wait.

His wife wanted to go home.

EPILOGUE

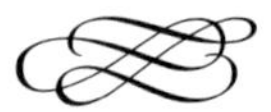

"Martin Wells, you come out from behind there *immediately*."

Gideon paused to admire his wife's rounded backside as she knelt on the floor in front of one of her office's many cupboards.

A boyish giggle emerged from inside the cupboard, and Gideon smiled. He found his son's new habit of hiding and jumping out to scare him priceless. It reminded him of Martin. His cousin had done the same thing as a child.

Gideon could never admit to being amused aloud of course. The game of hide and screech was driving Amelia daft. She was always worried baby Martin would be lost forever in the vast interior of Tarryhall.

He had learned a trick that helped, however. A few berry-flavored biscuits would lure his son out of wherever he had secreted himself. Gideon had taken up the habit of carrying them in his pocket and leaving them out in whichever room he suspected his son of hiding in. Inevitably, the treat would get Martin's chubby little legs moving. He might take the cookies straight back to his hidey-hole, but a telltale trail of crumbs would usually point the way.

The housekeeper did not agree with his method, nor did Amelia, who chided him for it outright.

"You may as well hang out a sign welcoming vermin, Gideon," she would scold every time she caught him putting the biscuits out.

Instead of arguing with her, he'd distract her with a kiss. If he remembered right, it would be a few years before they'd be able to break Martin of this new habit.

Today, he was able to take advantage of his wife's current position to kneel behind her, running his hands against her lush curves.

"Do you need a biscuit?"

He laughed and ducked when Amelia turned to swat him.

"You only encourage him to hide so he can wheedle more sweets out of you."

He acknowledged her words with a hum. "Perhaps, but we've already lost the war, love. It's time for concessions. Or—"

Gideon reached into the cupboard suddenly and pried his son's fingers away from the interior, pulling him out with gentle force. "Or it's time for outright trickery. And possibly a nap."

Martin laughed in his face and yelled. "No nap!"

"I understand your reluctance, my son, but I must insist. Naps are a necessary evil." He walked to the door and called for the nurse. She took his son away before Gideon added "bath" in a whisper before nap.

He waited for the resulting howls to die away before turning back to Amelia with a wicked grin.

She rolled her eyes and went to her desk.

"The invitation came today," she said, waving a cream-colored envelope at him.

He groaned aloud. "We just came back from town."

"The wedding won't be in London. Mrs. Chisholm finally gave up the idea of having the ceremony in St. Georges."

"Good for Crispin," Gideon murmured. "I didn't think he would prevail on that score."

Lord Worthing's future mother-in-law was a termagant. He worried for Crispin's future wedded bliss, but also worried for Clarke, his closest friend. It couldn't be easy to watch the man one loved marry another, even if it was destined to be a typical polite and bloodless ton union.

"Cecily is a far more reasonable creature."

"But equally determined," he pointed out. "It's been at least two seasons since she started chasing Crispin. One must admire her persistence."

"Yes, well, I can't really blame her for setting her cap at him," Amelia said loyally. "He is a wonderful friend and will make a doting husband. Her finances aside, theirs will prove an advantageous match on both sides. She gets the security her family needs, and Crispin gets the understanding wife he always wanted."

Gideon sniffed, aware Lord Worthing had once wanted Amelia to fulfill that role. But it had worked out as well as was possible given the circumstances.

Cecily Chisholm was in fact, an imminently practical young woman. Her family had spent the last of their dwindling fortune on her two seasons. They needed her to marry well or the whole lot would be ruined. Cecily had taken stock of the ton's eligible bachelors with a startlingly discerning eye. She had chosen Lord Worthing, apparently aware that his inclinations lay elsewhere—and not for Amelia as the ton had assumed.

Yes, Cecily had been very perceptive. Her next move proved it. Giving up on gaining ground with Worthing himself, she had spoken to Amelia. After their private conversation, the details of which neither would disclose, his wife had agreed to champion Cecily's cause. After all, Crispin still needed to marry and produce an heir. He also had sufficient wealth to be able to overlook a lack of dowry and some family debt in his prospective bride.

The ploy had worked. Shortly after, Crispin had made it official with an announcement in the times. Now the day was nearly upon them.

"I don't care where the wedding is as long as it's not in London. In fact, if it weren't for my business at the Lords and your meetings with your attorney Callaghan, I would say let's never go back."

Amelia reached up to put her arms around him. "You know, I could attempt to conduct most of my business with Callaghan via correspondence. The mails are fairly reliable between here and town."

His grin was wry. "If only the Lords would agree to take my vote by mail as well..." He narrowed his eyes at her cluttered desk and made a decision.

"Gideon. What are you doing?" she asked, laughter in her voice as he pulled at the bodice of her gown, undoing her laces.

"Well, whenever we make love on a desk, it's on the one in my office. It occurred to me just now we've never made love on yours." He squinted at the delicate wooden legs. "It should bear your weight; otherwise, it wasn't worth the blunt I paid for it."

He pulled her forward and tugged her gown over her head before adding "If it collapses, we'll never order from that carpenter again."

Amelia pursed her lips before leaning in and melting into his embrace. He set her down on the desk's surface, his hands on either side of her face.

"Don't you have more estate matters to attend to? I thought the miller was coming up to the house today to discuss the improvements he wanted to make."

"I spoke to him yesterday and delegated the rest to my estate manager. He's an astute man."

She laughed. "He better be, since I hired him."

Gideon gave her a wicked smile. "Yes, well, now that things are running smoothly here at Tarryhall and the other estates I thought it time I loosened the reins a bit and focused on us..."

He moved to stand between her legs, but his face was sober as he studied her beautiful face. He could spend a lifetime looking at her—several lifetimes if he had his way.

"I believe it's time we started working on a daughter. Little Martin should always be with little Amelia, don't you think?"

Tears shone in Amelia's crystalline blue eyes. "Yes, they should always be together," she agreed, a tear spilling over and running down her cheek.

He kissed it away and held her tight for a long moment.

He still thought about his cousin. The awareness that he owed his happiness to a great loss still weighed on him at times, but like Amelia, he believed Martin would have been happy for them.

In fact, he knew it for a fact. Shortly after returning from Devon, a solicitor sent him a letter written by his cousin. It was to be delivered only if a specific set of circumstances was fulfilled—his marriage to Amelia. His cousin had written others to fit different conditions, but the solicitor had been instructed to destroy the alternates.

He sometimes wondered what those other letters had said, but he was grateful for the one he'd received. Martin had known…so many things. Including that Gideon would need his blessing to be completely at peace with the happiness he'd found with his wife.

There was a poignancy to their lovemaking that afternoon. Amelia held him tight inside her body, her hands up around his back, their touch as desperate and possessive as his own.

Pulling her close, he came inside her, the lowering sun filtering through the window, lighting up his love for her in a warm glow.

No longer restless for adventure or thirsting for justice, Gideon had found his fate and succumbed headlong. In Amelia, he had found love, trust, and passion.

They held each other for a long time after, making promises and vows he knew would be kept, the way only soulmates could.

THE END.

AFTERWORD

Thank you for reading this novel! Reviews are an author's bread and butter. If you liked the story please consider leaving one.

Read the FREE short story The Hex, a Cursed Prequel

Available Now

Subscribe to the Lucy Leroux Newsletter for a *free* full-length novel!
www.authorlucyleroux.com/newsletter
or keep up with her L.B. Gilbert releases
www.elementalauthor.com/newsletter

ABOUT THE AUTHOR

Lucy Leroux is another name for USA Today Bestselling Author L.B. Gilbert.

Seven years ago Lucy moved to France for a one-year research contract. Six months later she was living with a handsome Frenchman and is now married with an adorable half-french daughter.

When her last contract ended Lucy turned to writing. Frustrated by the lack of quality romance erotica she created her own.

Cursed is the first of many regency novels. Additionally, she writes two bestselling contemporary series. The 'Singular Obsession' books are a combination of steamy romance and suspense that feature intertwining characters in their own stand-alone stories. Follow her on twitter or facebook, or check our her website for more news!

www.authorlucyleroux.com

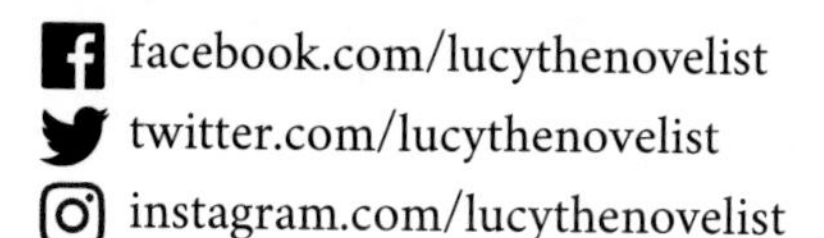

Manufactured by Amazon.ca
Acheson, AB